Kiss a Cowboy

KISS A COWBOY SERIES BOOK ONE

Deanna Lynn Sletten

Kiss A Cowboy

Copyright © 2014 Deanna Lynn Sletten

ISBN-10: 1941212182
ISBN-13: 9781941212189

Editor: Denise Vitola
Cover Designer: Deborah Bradseth of Tugboat Design

Novels by Deanna Lynn Sletten

Miss Etta

Night Music

One Wrong Turn

Finding Libbie

Maggie's Turn

As the Snow Fell

Walking Sam

Destination Wedding

Summer of the Loon

Sara's Promise

Memories

Widow, Virgin, Whore

A Kiss for Colt

Kissing Carly

Outlaw Heroes

Chapter One

Andi Stevens drove along highway I-90 East in Montana on a warm, July afternoon, marveling at the lush, mountain scenery all around her. She'd left her hometown of Seattle, Washington, that morning with a small portion of her life packed into her 2001 Ford Escape and the rest of her things waiting to be shipped to her destination, Buffalo, NY, where her fiancé awaited her arrival.

The first few hours of driving, Andi had seen mostly fields of dry grass in the eastern part of Washington, but since driving through the beautiful town of Couer d'Alene, Idaho, the terrain had changed to mountain roads and pine trees for as far as the eye could see. Even now, miles from Couer d'Alene, the road continued to rise and fall and the landscape was filled with greenery so beautiful, it took her breath away. Andi wished she could stop by the side of the road and sketch the beauty all around her, but she knew that wasn't a smart idea since she was traveling alone. Her fiancé, Derek Hensley, would have been horrified if he'd known she'd even thought of it. So, Andi had to satisfy herself with a few quick photos taken from safe, populated, roadside stops instead.

Andi sighed as she thought about leaving her younger

sister, Carly, behind this morning. True, Carly was twenty-four years old, was a college graduate, and had a good job managing the art gallery where Andi sold her paintings and sketches. She was capable of taking care of herself now. But after years of caring for Carly, it was hard for Andi to say goodbye. The two girls had been inseparable since the day Carly was born and four-year-old Andi had claimed her baby sister as her own. They'd become even closer after the tragic death of their parents in a car accident when Andi was eighteen and Carly was only fourteen. From that time on, Andi had become Carly's main guardian and caretaker, and although they'd had their ups and downs, their relationship was steadfast.

Andi knew Carly had tried being brave when she said goodbye that morning. "Your future is with Derek now," Carly had said. "It's your time to be happy. I'll be fine." Carly had been putting up a front to make her feel better about leaving. Yet, Carly was right. Andi's future lay ahead of her in Buffalo, where Derek had been sent by the national bank chain he worked for to become a manager and to eventually work his way to a Manhattan, New York, branch. At thirty years old, he was a rising star in his company, and he had the ambition and ability to go as far as he wanted. Andi marveled every day at the fact that this intelligent, hard-working man wanted her, a simple artist, by his side as he rose to the top of the banking industry. Derek and she had been dating seriously for almost three years when he announced to her that not only was he getting a promotion, but he wanted her to share his life with him. Andi had been dumbstruck. She'd always thought of herself as a Seattle girl, so she was uneasy about moving to New York. But Derek was a good man and she would have been crazy to say no to his proposal. So, here she was, in the mountains of Montana, driving toward her future.

Of course, Derek hadn't been thrilled by her form of transportation to Buffalo. In fact, he'd told her she was crazy to want to drive across country in her old Ford when she could just ship her things and fly out with him. Andi had insisted, though. She wanted to keep her car. She wanted her most cherished possessions with her on her journey, and most of all, she wanted to see the country between the two cities. While she'd traveled up and down the west coast from Seattle to San Diego over her lifetime, she'd never been east, and that was something she wanted to experience. Derek did not believe in car travel. He was always in too much of a hurry and flew everywhere he went. Andi knew this would be her only chance to see this part of the country before she became immersed in Derek's up-and-coming lifestyle.

As Andi's car began climbing yet another incline on the mountain road, it felt like the vehicle was struggling. Andi held her breath until she reached the top and began the descent. Driving across country in an old car probably wasn't such a smart idea, but Andi loved her car and she hadn't wanted to give it up just yet. Derek told her that as soon as she came to Buffalo, he wanted her to trade it in for a new car. Andi knew that eventually she would have to give up her old beater, just not yet. After all she'd been through since the death of her parents, she'd had very few things to depend upon. One was Carly, the other was her car. And now, of course, steadfast, reliable Derek.

Andi glanced at the dashboard clock as she entered the town of Superior. It was a little after seven o'clock in the evening. For a moment, she wondered if she should stop for the night, then decided against it. The larger town of Missoula was only another hour away and she felt she could easily make it there and find a nice motel before sunset. With that in mind, she breezed through the small town and continued on, looking forward to a good meal and a nice warm bed once she reached her destination.

* * *

Luke Brennan pulled his pick-up truck beside his log cabin home, parked, and stepped out. He stood a moment, gazing out to the west, watching the sun slowly drop behind the mountain. He lifted his dusty, black cowboy hat off his head and ran his hand through his wavy, dark hair. He both loved and hated this time of day. Work was done and his belly was full from a warm supper served at the main house. He was tired and should be looking forward to falling into his bed for a good night's sleep, but instead, he always hesitated for a moment before entering his home. Alone.

With a sigh, Luke turned on the heel of his boot and walked up the steps of the front porch. He thought for a moment about starting up the generator for lights, but then decided against it. He'd only be awake for a short time and maybe read a book. He preferred the light of the old oil lamp to the brightness of electric lights. The soft glow of the oil lamp made him feel less alone in the empty cabin.

At only thirty-two years old, Luke was an old soul who preferred the past to the present.

The cabin was growing dark inside as Luke entered. He slipped off his boots and set them beside the bench by the door and then hung his hat by the others on one of the hooks. Slipping off his flannel shirt, he shook it out and hung it beside his hat before walking into the living room and lighting an oil lamp.

The lamp came to life, leaving a soft glow on the walls and furniture in the room. Walking through the living room, past the island, and into the kitchen, Luke opened the refrigerator and pulled out a bottle of beer. It was still cold, even though he hadn't run the generator since this morning. Cold enough for him. He opened the bottle, took a swig, and then set it on the counter before walking to the back of the house where the two bedrooms and bathroom were located.

It had been a hot July day, even in this mountain terrain. He'd worked all day cleaning out the horse barn and laying clean straw on the floor, so he knew he smelled of sweat and manure. He went into the bathroom and stripped off his T-shirt, ran what was left of the water into the sink, and cleaned off as best he could. Tomorrow, he'd turn on the generator and take a hot shower. Tonight, he was too tired, and there was no one around who'd know the difference anyway.

Luke dried off and went into his bedroom to retrieve a clean T-shirt, then walked back out into the living room. He reclaimed his bottle of beer, picked up the mystery book he was reading from the oversized, walnut coffee table, and stretched out on the soft, leather sofa next to where the lamp was lit. He figured he'd drink his beer, read a few pages of his book, and relax before heading off to bed.

* * *

The sun was fading as Andi drove up yet another incline on the mountain road when suddenly her car started acting strange. No matter how far down she pushed on the gas pedal, the car lost power. Andi's heart raced. She looked at the column to make sure the car hadn't somehow fallen out of drive, but it was right there, set on the big D. The car continued to slow, and when Andi hit the gas, all it did was rev the engine, but not go faster. As the car started to crawl up to the top of the incline, Andi pulled it over to the side of the four-lane highway. Finally, it came to a complete stop.

"Oh, my God. Now what?" Andi said aloud. She put the car in park and turned it off. Then she turned it on again and the engine came to life. Hopeful, she shoved the gear into drive and pressed on the gas pedal. Nothing. The engine just revved noisily, but the car didn't move.

Andi picked up her cell phone and turned it on. There was only one bar for reception. She pulled her wallet from her purse for her roadside assistance card and tried calling with that one bar. The call wouldn't go through.

"Crap."

Andi locked her doors, turned on the hazard lights, and sat there, assessing her situation. Even though I-90 was a main interstate, she had seen few cars pass her over the last hour. She'd driven by a gas station/bar/restaurant about a mile or two back, but that was all she'd seen for miles. There was no way she was going to walk down the highway alone, back to the gas station.

Andi sat another moment, thinking that maybe a local sheriff or highway patrol might drive by and find her. But daylight was fading fast and if none came soon, she'd have to spend the night in the car. That thought didn't settle well with her. What if a stranger came by and offered to help? Could she trust a stranger around here? Her big-city girl upbringing said no. What was she going to do?

Andi started scanning the land around her to see if there was any sign of life other than the cattle and horses grazing in the fields. Her eyes caught sight of a small light in the distance. She saw the outline of a house, or maybe it was a cabin, she couldn't tell. It wasn't lit up too brightly, but there was a light on in the window. She looked past that and saw an even bigger shadow in the distance that looked like a larger home with lights on in several windows. Andi took a deep breath, trying to decide what she should do. She needed to get to a phone, and she needed to do it before the sun went completely down. Her choices were limited. Trust a stranger driving by or a stranger in a house? Neither one sounded safe, but she had no choice.

Grabbing her keys, phone, fleece jacket, and purse, Andi stepped out of the car and locked it before walking over to the side of the road. The air was cooling fast and she felt chilled after being in the warm car, so she slipped on her jacket. Pushing her thick, dark red hair away from her face, she stood there, deciding how far to go. The cabin was the closest, so that was the obvious choice. As she began her trek down the side of the road toward the cabin's driveway, she prayed that the person inside the cabin was trustworthy and that he—or she—had a landline phone.

It took Andi longer to walk to the cabin than she'd first thought and the sun was almost down when she stepped up on to the wooden porch and knocked softly on the door. When no one answered, she knocked louder, hoping someone was home. There was a Dodge pick-up truck in the driveway and a soft light in the window, so someone must be there. Just as she raised her hand to pound on the door one last time, it swung open and a man filled the doorframe.

Andi took a step back in surprise. The man was tall, well over six feet, with long, jean-clad legs and a white T-shirt stretching over a muscular chest. His arms were bare, showing off sculptured biceps and forearms. He stared at her, looking confused, as if she'd awoken him from a deep sleep.

What stunned Andi the most was his square, chiseled face and deep blue eyes. His face, hair, and body were so perfect, he looked like a male model from a Calvin Klein underwear commercial. Andi felt the heat of a blush rise on her face at that thought as she stood there, mute, before him.

Mr. Tall, Dark, and Handsome ran his hand through his hair and shook his head, seemingly to clear it before those blue eyes zeroed in on Andi. "Who are you?" he asked, his voice deeply male.

Andi blinked. Never had she been so startled by a person before. He just seemed too perfect looking to be out here in a cabin in the middle of nowhere. She swallowed hard, then tried to stand as tall as her five foot, seven inch frame would allow. Her green eyes met his. "I'm sorry to bother you," she said. "My car broke down on the highway and your house was the closest. There's no cell service here, so I couldn't call for help. May I use your phone?"

The male model frowned at her, as if trying to understand what she was saying. Andi glanced around him and saw that the cabin was lit only by an oil lamp. She wondered if he even had electricity. *Crap. I picked a house with no power and probably no phone.*

"Where's your car?" the man asked her, looking past her toward the highway. It was too dark now to see the highway or the car.

Andi pointed in the direction of the road. "Out there. It just died. I didn't know what to do."

The man shook his head, turned, and started pulling on a pair of western boots. He slipped on a flannel shirt that had been hanging by the door and placed a hat on his head. Andi just stood there, watching him, wondering if he'd let her in to use the phone or not. Without a word, Mr. Perfect turned and walked to the back of the house. Andi's eyes followed him, wondering where he'd gone. She surveyed the room he'd just walked through. The floors were a light, shiny oak and there was a large, river rock fireplace on the wall in front of a leather sofa. Beyond that she saw a kitchen, but it was too dark to see it clearly. The cabin looked clean, though, and very cozy. She told herself that he couldn't be too bad of a person if he lived in a place like this. At least she hoped that was true.

He strode back into the living room and blew out the oil lamp. For a second, Andi stood in complete darkness, but then he turned on a flashlight he had in his hand.

"Come along," he said, walking out the door and closing it behind him. He strode right past her and down the porch steps, his boot heels clicking on the wood.

Andi was startled. "Where are we going?"

The cowboy stopped and turned to look at her, practically shining the flashlight in her eyes. "You need a phone, don't you? I don't have one. I'll take you to the main house." He turned and headed to the truck she'd seen in the driveway earlier.

Andi hesitated. She needed help, but should she get into a truck with a complete stranger? He hadn't been friendly, which didn't help to raise her opinion of him. He may be good looking, but that didn't mean he wasn't a serial killer.

"You coming?" the cowboy asked from the driver's side of the truck.

Andi closed her eyes. *Please let this be safe. Please let this be safe.* She finally made one foot step in front of the other, walked over to the pick-up, and climbed in.

Hot Cowboy turned over the engine and put the truck in drive. With the headlights on, Andi saw that his driveway snaked all the way up to the other house. She supposed he was a ranch hand and the ranch owners lived in the bigger house. As the truck crushed gravel under its tires, Andi sat there in silence, wondering if he'd ever speak. He didn't.

"I appreciate you taking me to a phone," Andi said, trying to sound normal despite her heart pounding in her chest. "My name is Andi, by the way."

The cowboy just kept driving, looking straight ahead.

Andi bit her lip. "I didn't catch your name," she said, trying hard to be friendly.

"That's because I didn't tell you it," the cowboy said, not even looking in her direction.

Andi's mouth dropped open. She couldn't believe how rude he was. A sharp retort about unfriendly cowboys came to mind, but she held her tongue. After all, she'd probably awoken him and now he was going out of his way to drive her to a phone. It was best if she just stayed quiet.

Chapter Two

A short time later, the truck pulled up to the back of a house and stopped. Andi peered at it in the dark. It looked like an old farm house, two stories high, but was quite large. There were lights on in three of the windows. Andi hoped they were actual electric lights, not oil lamps.

Without a word, the cowboy stepped out of the truck and walked with long strides up to the door. Andi quickly hopped out and followed. When a security motion light popped on, she sighed with relief. Real lights.

A brick porch with three steps led up to the door. Andi followed the cowboy up the steps and entered a mudroom. A row of boots stood beside a bench and jackets and cowboy hats lined the walls. The cowboy wiped his boots on the rug in the doorway and headed into the next room.

Andi followed Hot Cowboy as they walked into the kitchen. Immediately, the delicious aroma of freshly fried chicken and warm bread hit her nostrils and she suddenly remembered how hungry she was. There was another aroma as well, but she couldn't place it. It smelled sweet. Some kind of berry, she thought.

The cowboy didn't even turn to look at Andi. He pointed to an old, tan telephone hanging on the kitchen wall and said, "There's the phone." Then he walked through another doorway, hollering, "Ma! You have company."

Andi was taken aback. Ma? So, his mother lived in the main house. She looked around her. The kitchen was from another time, yet it looked cute and cozy. On her left, there was a long, oak table along one wall with a bench seat on one side and beautifully, carved oak chairs on the other and at each end. A round, lazy Susan sat in the middle holding salt and pepper shakers upon it. To her right were the stove, refrigerator, and a long, butcher block countertop with cabinet space underneath. Farther down on the wall past the doorway the cowboy had exited through was more counter space, cabinets, and a huge farm-style sink. The floors were polished oak and plush rugs sat in front of the sink and counters. A staircase rose up along the back wall of the kitchen with an oak handrail held up by spiral posts. Even though the appliances looked fairly new, the ambiance in the kitchen still made Andi think of days gone by.

Andi walked over to the phone that hung on the wall by the doorway and set her purse on the counter. She dug out her roadway assistance card and was about to call when she heard a female voice say, "Well, my, my. What a pretty thing you are."

Andi looked up into the face of a middle-aged woman. Her dark blond hair was pulled back with a butterfly clip, and her hazel blue eyes were bright and twinkling. She wore a dark blue T-shirt with a pair of worn jeans and had a pair of soft leather moccasins on her feet. She was almost as tall as Andi, and when she smiled, her face looked kind and welcoming. Behind her trailed a black and white dog that stopped and sat beside the woman, looking up quizzically at Andi.

"Luke said you showed up on his doorstep. How lucky was he?" the woman said, grinning.

Andi stared at her, not quite sure what to say. She was trying to process everything. Luke must be Hot Cowboy, and her son. Well, at least now he had a name.

"Oh, my goodness. Where are my manners?" the older woman said. "I'm Ginny. Virginia Brennan, but just call me Ginny. Luke says your name is Andi."

Andi nodded. So, the cowboy, er, Luke, had heard her name. Andi offered her hand in greeting. "I'm Andi Stevens," she said, shaking Ginny's hand.

"Well, it's sure nice to meet you, Andi," Ginny said.

Andi reached down to let the dog sniff her hand before petting it behind the ears. "Who's this?" she asked.

Ginny smiled. "This is Bree. She's our cattle dog, but much to Luke's annoyance, I baby her in the house. She's my nightly protector."

Andi squatted down to pet Bree. "She's beautiful. Is she a Border Collie?"

"Australian Shepherd. They're great for herding cattle."

Andi nodded and stood.

"Now, you go ahead and call whoever you need to and I'll get you something to drink," Ginny said. "Do you like iced tea? I just made up a fresh pitcher."

Before Andi could respond, Ginny was already at the refrigerator with Bree at her heels, pulling out the pitcher of tea. Andi smiled. Actually, a glass of iced tea sounded pretty good.

Andi set about calling roadside assistance. She answered all their questions, but when they asked her exactly where she was, she hesitated. "Do you have an address here?" she asked

Ginny, who'd set down a glass of tea for her on the counter.

"Just tell them you're in front of the Brennan Ranch. Carl will be the one they send to tow your car, and he knows exactly where we are," Ginny said.

Andi repeated what Ginny had said to the assistance operator, hoping it was enough information for them to find her car. The operator said to stay by the phone and they'd have the tow-truck driver call her before he headed her way.

Andi hung up and stood there a moment, wondering what she should do. She took a sip of her tea. It was delicious. Before she could say anything to Ginny, she heard footsteps on the staircase and a young man appeared and stared openly at her. He was almost as tall as Luke, but was more slender. His hair was sandy blond and a bit shaggy, but he had those amazing blue eyes like Luke's. He stood there in a white T-shirt and jeans, looking at her as if she was an oddity.

"Colt, don't just stand there staring at our guest. Come meet Andi. Her car broke down out on the highway and she's using our phone," Ginny said.

Colt quickly stopped staring and walked slowly to the bottom of the staircase with his eyes lowered. He just stood at the bottom and said shyly. "Hi, Andi."

Andi smiled at him. He was younger than she, probably more her sister's age, and he was adorable.

"Colt is my youngest son," Ginny said. "He works the ranch with Luke."

"Colt?" Andi asked, wondering if she'd really heard right. *How much more western could you get than that?*

Ginny laughed. "Goodness gracious. I can imagine how that sounds. Colt is his nickname, but that's not what I named my son. His name is Cole, but when he was just a little thing, Luke started calling him Colt, and it stuck."

Andi smiled, a bit relieved. She had almost felt like she'd stepped into an episode of *Bonanza*. "Nice to meet you, Colt," Andi said.

Colt nodded and looked like he was trying not to stare at her. The doorway between the kitchen and the living area filled with the tall, muscular Luke. He stood there, leaning against the doorframe with his arms crossed. "So, are they sending help?"

Andi just stared at him a moment. It was the first time he'd actually addressed her. Clearing her throat, she finally answered. "They said I'd get a call back from the tow-truck company, so I should stay by the phone."

"Well, then, come sit down and relax, Andi," Ginny told her, pointing to the kitchen table. "It may take a while. It's late, and we all know how slow Carl can be."

Andi picked up her glass of tea and set it on the table before pulling out a chair and sitting down. Ginny sat across from her. All the while, Andi felt Luke's eyes on her. She wasn't sure if it was his stare or just being in a stranger's home that made her feel uncomfortable.

Bree immediately came over and sat beside Andi, so she began stroking the dog's silky fur.

"Bree, go lie down," Luke commanded.

The dog stared at her owner, considering whether to obey or not.

"She's fine," Andi insisted. "I love dogs."

Luke narrowed his eyes for just a second, turned on his heel, and headed back into the other room.

Ginny shook her head. "Don't mind Luke. He can be a bit prickly at times. Colt, come on over and sit. You don't have to stand there all night staring at this pretty girl from across the room."

Colt's face reddened, but he made his way over to the other end of the table and sat down.

Ginny stood again and walked toward the refrigerator. "I bet you haven't eaten supper yet," she said to Andi. "We have plenty of leftovers. Let me heat some up for you."

"Oh, please don't bother," Andi told her. "I don't want to put you to any trouble."

"No trouble at all, dear. There's some delicious fried chicken left and I'll heat up some of my homemade bread. I made much more than I should have tonight. Randy usually eats with us, but he went into town tonight, so there's plenty left."

Andi watched as Ginny moved about the kitchen. She made up a plate of chicken, covered it, and set it in the microwave to heat. Then she sliced up some bread from a new loaf and heated that after the chicken was warm. She brought it all to the table and then went to get plates and silverware. Before Andi knew it, there was food in front of her and it smelled so delicious, she just couldn't resist.

"Is Randy your son, too?" Andi asked, wondering just how many cowboys lived here.

"No. He's our ranch hand, but he's been around our family for so long I think of him like a son." Ginny handed Colt a plate, too. "You might as well eat again too, dear."

Colt waited for Andi to select a piece of chicken and some bread before he put some on his plate. Andi figured that at his age, he could probably eat all the time and it would never show.

Andi buttered her slice of bread and took a bite. She sighed. "This is heavenly," she told Ginny, who smiled wide at the compliment. After that first bite, Andi forgot about being shy and dug right in. The chicken was perfect—crunchy on the outside and tender on the inside—and Andi couldn't eat enough of the bread and butter. Normally, she never touched bread at home, but this was like eating dessert, it was so delicious.

Ginny sat across from Andi again. "Now tell me, dear. Why is a pretty thing like you out driving alone in the middle of nowhere? Are you visiting family around here?"

Andi swallowed yet another bite of chicken and wiped her lips with a napkin. "I'm driving across country to Buffalo, New York. I'm from Seattle. I left there this morning. I figured I could make it to Missoula by nightfall, and that was when my car broke down."

Ginny's eyes grew wide. "You drove all that way alone today? And you're heading out to Buffalo? My goodness, dear. Well, it's a good thing you broke down here and not somewhere dangerous."

Andi grinned. Ginny did sound like a mother.

"What's waiting for you in Buffalo?" Ginny asked kindly. "A new job?"

Andi shook her head. "Actually, my fiancé is waiting for me there. He just transferred to Buffalo for his job at a bank and we're both moving there."

Andi saw Ginny glance down at her ring finger, which was bare. Derek hadn't gotten around to buying her an engagement ring yet. He'd said he'd buy one when she came out to Buffalo.

"He's not a very smart man, letting you drive across country all alone," Luke said from the doorway. He stood there again, this time with his hands in his pockets.

Andi noticed that every pose he made looked like a modeling shot, he was that handsome. Unfortunately, he didn't seem to be as pleasant as he was good looking.

"It wasn't his choice," Andi said defensively. "I decided I wanted to travel across country."

"Luke, be nice, will you?" Ginny told her son.

The phone rang, startling Andi, although no one else seemed disturbed by the screeching ring. Ginny walked over and answered it.

"Hi, Carl. Yep. It's out in front of our place on the highway. Oh, really? That's terrible. Hmmm. Let me tell her. Hold on a moment." Ginny put her hand over the receiver and addressed Andi. "Carl and the other tow-truck driver were just called out to an accident near Superior right before he got the call about you. They have to pick up two cars and the passengers and take them to Missoula. He won't be back here for another two to four hours, and then it's another hour drive again to Missoula."

Andi sat there, trying to figure out what to do. It was already past nine o'clock. "Is there another tow-truck driver I could call?"

"I'm sure one from Missoula could come out here and get it, but you still wouldn't get there until after midnight and you'd have to find a place to stay the night," Ginny said. "Carl said he could pick up your car early tomorrow morning if you'd be willing to stay the night here."

"I couldn't impose on you like that," Andi said. "Is there a hotel around here where I can stay?"

Ginny smiled. "Oh, honey, you don't want to stay at one of the old mom and pop motels around here when I have a nice room right here. You're more than welcome to stay the night."

Andi glanced over at the doorway and caught Luke's eye. His steady gaze didn't give anything away. She looked back at Ginny. She seemed like a nice person and Andi felt it would be safe to stay here. But still, she hesitated. "I don't know."

Ginny pulled her hand away from the receiver. "Carl, why don't you just go home after this haul and get some sleep. Tomorrow will be fine. We'll have the car in the driveway, waiting for you. Yep. Night, Carl."

After Ginny hung up, she walked over to Andi. "No sense in arguing. I'm happy to have you here and I'd feel better about it if you weren't out in some hotel without your car."

Andi nodded. She really didn't have a choice. "Thank you. That's very kind of you," she said softly.

"Don't think anything of it," Ginny said. She turned to Luke. "Hon, you and Colt go and pull Andi's car into the ' driveway so it's off that busy road and it's safe."

Luke stepped through the door and headed toward the back porch, not even glancing in Andi's direction. He didn't look happy. "Come on, Colt," he bellowed. Colt darted out of his seat and followed behind.

Andi jumped out of her seat and followed them to the mudroom where Colt was already pulling on a pair of boots. "I have my things in the back of the car," she said to Luke's back. "My suitcase and my painting supplies. Can I get those before they take my car tomorrow?"

Luke turned and looked down at her, his eyes focused deeply on hers. "I'll get it all out for you and bring it back up to the house."

Andi stood there, wringing her hands. "I don't want to be a bother, but my camera is in the back seat and there's a painting wrapped up in the back. Can you bring those, too? I don't want anything to happen to them."

"I'll get everything," Luke assured her. He put out his hand.

Andi frowned at his open palm. Was she supposed to shake it? Give him five?

"Your keys. I need your keys," Luke said.

"Oh." Andi ran back to her purse to retrieve her keys. She handed them over to him.

Without another word, Luke turned and walked out the door with Colt on his heels.

Andi returned to the kitchen, a worried frown on her face.

"Don't worry, hon. Luke will get everything," Ginny said. "So, you're an artist?"

Andi nodded.

"Well, that is exciting. Is there anyone else you want to call tonight? Family? Your fiancé? Let them know where you are and that you're safe."

Andi thought about it a moment. She would feel better if someone knew she was here. She didn't think it was a good idea to call Derek and tell him because he'd flip out. Plus, his time zone was two hours ahead, so it was after eleven in Buffalo and she knew how much he valued his sleep. No, she'd call him tomorrow after she found out what was wrong with her car. Hopefully, it could be fixed right away and she would already be on her way. She decided to call her sister to let her know where she was.

The phone rang three times before her sister finally answered. Andi heard loud music in the background and wondered where on earth her sister was on a Wednesday night.

"Hello?" Carly asked tentatively.

"Carly? It's Andi."

"Oh, Andi," Carly said, sounding relieved. "I didn't recognize the number. I tried calling you a few times, but you never called me back. Where are you?"

"My car broke down outside of Missoula," Andi told her.

"Missoula? Where the heck is that?"

"Montana," Andi answered. "I'm in the western part of Montana, in the mountains. My cell doesn't work here, so I'm calling from a ranch house near where the car broke down."

The music in the background grew quieter and Andi figured that Carly had walked farther away from it so she could hear her better. "You're what? You're at someone's ranch house somewhere in Montana?"

"Yeah. I'm at the Brennan Ranch, about forty miles from Missoula. I just wanted to let you know where I was and give you this number in case you needed to call me."

"Whoo-whee! An actual ranch? Are there any hot cowboys there?"

Andi sighed. Her sister was wild and man-crazy. Andi should have known she'd turn the conversation around to men. "Actually, yes, there are," she said wryly.

"Wow. Lucky you. Stuck at a ranch full of cowboys and here I am with a bunch of nerds in a Seattle bar. You have all the luck."

"Carly, breaking down isn't lucky. Hopefully, I can get it fixed tomorrow and be on my way. And by the way, why are you out at a bar on a Wednesday night? You mean to tell me that the very first day I leave, you go out partying with friends?"

"Oh, stop being such an old bore," Carly said. "It was two-for-one Margarita night and I came out with a couple of the girls from the gallery. But I'm glad you called to let me know where you are. Are you okay there?"

Andi smiled into the phone. Her sister did care about her, and that made her feel good. "Yes, I'm okay. The Brennans seem like nice people. Just keep this number close in case you need to call me or if I call you again, okay? I'll let you know what happens tomorrow."

"Okay, Big Sis. Enjoy the ranch, and be sure to kiss a cowboy for me," Carly said, giggling, before she hung up.

Andi rolled her eyes as she hung up the phone. Her sister was too wild for her own good. Uninvited, the chiseled face and steely blue eyes of Luke Brennan came to mind. Andi shook her head to remove the image. *Kiss a cowboy. Yeah, like that was going to happen.*

Chapter Three

Luke strode outside and across the way to the tool shed where he retrieved a tow chain and then headed back to his pick-up where Colt waited for him. He hopped in behind the wheel, turned the truck around, and headed out to the dark highway.

"That Andi, she sure is pretty, isn't she?" Colt said into the quiet truck cab.

"Hmmm hmmm," Luke replied.

"Did you see all that silky red hair of hers? Isn't it pretty?"

"Yep. Kind of hard to miss it, Colt," Luke said evenly.

"And her eyes," Colt said, dreamily. "They were green. Did you see how green her eyes were?"

"Can't say that I really noticed," Luke said. He stopped the truck at the end of the driveway and looked to the left. There was a shadow of a car down the way. Luke heaved a heavy sigh. He'd have to drive down the wrong side of the road to get to it, otherwise it meant driving a mile or so out of his way just to get to a turnaround. He slowly turned left on the edge of the highway and began driving toward the car.

"How can you say you didn't notice Andi's green eyes?" Colt asked. "You looked right at her."

"I wasn't paying much attention," Luke told him.

"You'd have to be dead not to notice her," Colt said, shaking his head. "She's the prettiest thing I've seen around here in a very long time. Do you think she's a real redhead? She has really pretty skin, a little tan, not pale with freckles like most redheads have."

Luke turned and frowned at Colt. "Why in the world does it matter?"

Colt shrugged. "I don't know. Just saying. She sure is pretty, though. And she seems really nice, too."

"She's also engaged and is only going to be at the house for a very short time, so don't get all tied into a knot over her, okay?"

Colt stared hard at his brother. "You know, Luke, you sure know how to squeeze the fun out of everything. Can't you just enjoy the fact that a pretty girl is at our ranch for even a short time?"

Luke had pulled up by the car by now and he did a quick U-turn in the road and backed the truck up to the front of the car. He put the truck in park, then turned and looked at his brother. "For all you know, Colt, she dyes her hair red, wears green contacts, and tans in a tanning booth. She could have mousy brown hair, dull blue eyes, and pasty skin when she doesn't get herself all fixed up."

"You are one sour pickle, you know that Luke?"

"Hmmm hmmm," Luke replied. He picked up a spotlight that was lying on the floor by Colt's feet and stepped out of the cab.

Colt hopped out and grabbed the tow chain out of the back of the truck.

"Let's hook it up first and pull it home. We'll unload everything in the driveway. I don't want to be out on this highway very long in the dark," Luke said.

While Luke and Colt hooked the chain to the two vehicles, Luke thought about the moment he'd opened his door to see Andi standing there, looking startled. He'd fallen asleep on the sofa while reading his book, and he hadn't been fully awake when he'd opened the door. In fact, he'd thought he was dreaming.

Luke had felt lonelier than he had in a long time that night as he'd watched the sun slowly sink behind the mountain. Usually, he didn't allow himself the luxury of feeling sad and lonely. Life was hard, and so was he. He could handle it. But every once in a while, he let the past envelope him and he'd remember how nice it was to have someone by his side, only to feel even more empty when he had to go to bed alone. Luke was a tough, proud man, but even the toughest man needed someone soft beside him at the end of a long day.

All those feelings had been bottled up inside him tonight when he'd fallen asleep, and then there stood Andi, with her tall, slender body, long, red hair, and big green eyes. In that one instant while he felt he was still between sleep and waking, he thought he was looking at a dream come alive.

"All hooked up on my end," Colt said. "Throw me the keys and I'll ride in Andi's car while you pull it."

Luke pulled the keys out of his pocket and looked at them a moment. There was a door fob, two car keys, and what looked like a house key on the ring. Also hanging from the ring was a gold heart with a photo in it of Andi and another girl making silly faces in one of those photo machines, and a small, stuffed frog hanging on a chain. Luke grinned at the photo, then at the frog. *Girls.* He tossed the keys to Colt.

"Boy, this sure is an old car," Colt said, getting in and turning on the engine. The car started just fine, but when he pushed down on the gas, it didn't move.

Luke came to stand beside the car a moment, listening to the engine rev. "Bet it's the transmission," he said. "What do you think?"

Colt nodded. "Probably. That won't be cheap."

Luke thought the same thing. "Well, let's get this pulled into the driveway so we can go home to bed. Sunrise will be here fast."

* * *

Andi awoke the next morning to the aroma of fresh coffee, pancakes, and bacon making its way up the stairs and into her bedroom. She looked at her phone. It was only six o'clock a.m. Andi sighed. They started work early on a ranch.

Last night after her phone conversation with Carly, Ginny had taken her up to the guest bedroom and had shown her where the towels were stored and where the bathroom was. Soon afterwards, Ginny had brought up Andi's suitcase and had told her that the boys had brought in all her other things and left them downstairs. Andi had thanked Ginny profusely for being so nice and letting her stay, but the older woman had only waved her appreciation aside.

"If I had a daughter like you, I'd hope that someone would be just as nice to her," Ginny had said kindly.

Andi knew in that very instant that she really liked Ginny.

It was past midnight by the time Andi had settled into the cozy, country room. The house had been silent by then and she knew Colt and Ginny were already asleep. To her surprise, she was more exhausted than she'd thought and she'd fallen into a deep sleep almost immediately.

Now, with daylight streaming through the small window,

Andi took a good look around. The room was painted a creamy white and the window was trimmed in oak and decorated with blue, calico curtains. On the bed was a soft quilt made up of a blue and white star pattern, and an antique, oak dresser stood on the other wall with a lace doily runner sitting upon it. The gleaming oak floor was covered in part by a large, cotton rag rug, also in blue and white. The room was as country as could be and even though Andi was a city girl, she loved it.

The aroma coming up from the kitchen beckoned as Andi's stomach growled. She couldn't resist it any longer. She slipped out of bed and rummaged through her suitcase for necessities and clean clothes, and then she stepped out into the hallway and walked the short distance to the small bathroom. Hurriedly, Andi showered and dressed, pulling her thick hair back into a ponytail. After putting her things back in her room, Andi went downstairs.

"Good morning, Andi," Ginny said with a big smile. "I hope we didn't wake you. I didn't expect you'd be up this early."

Andi saw Bree lying on her dog pillow by the staircase. She bent down and scratched the dog behind the ears before turning to Ginny. "Good morning. Breakfast smelled wonderful. I couldn't resist."

"Aren't you a sweetie?" Ginny said. "All these boys here ever do is grunt a hello in the morning and stuff their faces before running back out. I'll take your compliments any day of the week."

Andi looked up and saw Colt sitting at the table with a full plate in front of him and another man sitting across from him who she assumed must be Randy. Luke wasn't there.

"Mrs. B, you know I always love your cooking, even though

I don't always say so," the man across from Colt said. He smiled up at Andi and nodded.

"Oh, Randy, I know you do," Ginny said. "I'm just teasing. An empty plate is a compliment as well." Ginny turned to Andi. "This is Randy Olson. He's our full-time ranch hand. He just lives a ways up the road from here. He and Luke were in the same grade in school and have known each other forever. He's just like one of my boys."

"Nice to meet you, Randy," Andi said.

Randy stood, wiped his hand on his jeans, and offered it to Andi. "Nice meeting you, too," he said. "Sorry about your car."

"Thanks," Andi said as she watched Randy sit down and finish eating. He seemed like a nice guy. He wasn't quite as tall as Luke, but he was slender and muscular. He had brown hair and eyes and was tan from working outdoors. Rugged was the word that came to mind. Luke was rugged, too, but he was also so damned perfect looking, it was hard not thinking of him as Hot Cowboy.

"Go ahead and sit and dig right in, Andi," Ginny said. "I'm coming to eat in a minute."

Andi sat down on the bench seat near Colt and smiled over at him. "Morning, Colt," she said. He grinned up at her and said a shy "Morning, Andi," before turning back to concentrate on his food. Andi thought his shyness was cute.

Ginny came over and set a cup of hot coffee in front of Andi, then sat down across from her. Andi started filling her plate.

Randy stood with his plate in hand and walked over to the sink. "Thank you, Mrs. B," he said. He nodded to Andi and headed out of the kitchen.

"Do you want syrup or strawberry jam on your pancakes,

Andi?" Ginny asked, moving both the syrup bottle and a Ball jar of preserves over in front of her.

Andi looked at both. "You sure make this hard to choose," she said.

"Mom makes the best strawberry jam in the county," Colt piped up. "Probably the whole state. She's won blue ribbons at the fair every year for it. And for her raspberry jam and peach preserves, too."

Andi smiled over at Colt. "Then that decides it. I have to try the jam." She spooned out some strawberry jam and spread it over the pancake on her plate. The sweet smell wafted up to her, and her eyes lit up with recognition. "That's what I smelled last night," Andi said. "When I came in, I smelled something sweet. It must have been your jam."

Ginny nodded. "Oh, yes, I'm sure it was. I was canning fresh jam all day yesterday. I did both raspberry and strawberry. I'm sure the kitchen air was filled with it."

Andi took a bite of her pancake and jam. She sighed with delight. Not too sweet, yet rich and delicious. "Oh, Ginny, this is wonderful. I can see why you win blue ribbons."

"Told ya," Colt said with a grin. He got up and put his plate away. "I'm heading out to the horse barn. Give me a holler if you need a ride to town later," he said, glancing at Andi.

"Thanks, Colt," Andi said as she watched him walk out the door.

Ginny shook her head and chuckled. "That boy sure has a crush on you."

"He's a cutie. But I think he's more my sister's age," Andi told her. She picked up a slice of bacon and took a bite. It was crispy and just melted in her mouth.

"What's your sister like?" Ginny asked.

"Her name is Carly. She and I are total opposites, but

she's a sweet girl. She's four years younger than me and has long, straight blond hair and blue eyes. She's smart and a hard worker, but she also likes to party a lot, too, and she's man-crazy. But she has a good heart."

"What about your parents? They must be worried about you driving so far from home," Ginny said.

Andi stopped eating. "Our parents died in a car accident about ten years ago," she said softly. "It's just Carly and me."

Ginny's face creased with concern. "Oh, I'm so sorry, dear. Why, you must have been quite young when they died. Did you live with other relatives?"

Andi shook her head. "No, there was no one else. I had just turned eighteen before they died, and Carly was fourteen. It was up to me to take care of Carly after that. We did okay, though. I got through college and then put Carly through. She has a good job now, and we own a nice townhouse. We did the best we could, considering." Andi thought back through the past ten years. It had been difficult at first, but they'd made it. Now she hoped Carly would someday find a dependable person to spend the rest of her life with, like Andi had found with Derek. Of course, that was if Carly ever got over her wild ways.

"Where's Luke?" Andi asked, changing the subject. "Did he already eat breakfast?"

Ginny's face softened and she nodded. "Yep. He's always the first one up and ready to eat. Oh, I should have told you right away. Carl came to pick up your car this morning and Luke went down to talk to him. He's taking it to the Ford dealership garage for you. He said that they would call you as soon as they find out what's wrong with it, or you can call to check on it later today."

"Wow. He sure got here early to pick it up," Andi said in amazement.

"Well, Carl figured you'd be anxious to have it looked at and he felt bad he couldn't pick it up last night. I told the boys to stay close to the house today in case you need a ride into Missoula."

"Thank you, Ginny," Andi said warmly. "How in the world will I ever be able to repay you for all you've done for me?"

Ginny reached over and patted her hand. "Don't even think twice about it. I'm happy to help you." Ginny stood and started taking plates to the sink. "By the way, Luke brought in your stuff from the car. It's in the sitting room." She pointed through the doorway Luke had stood in last night.

"Sitting room?" Andi asked as she stood and helped clear the table.

Ginny laughed. "Sorry. I must sound like someone from another century. This house was built way back when the Brennans homesteaded this land in the mid-1860s and in those days, the main room was called a sitting room. The name has just stuck, I guess. Of course, it's a lot larger now than it was in those days, but that's what we still call it."

"That's nice, actually," Andi said. Even though Seattle was filled with history, she'd always lived a more modern lifestyle. It was nice to hear that some people stayed in their family home for years, even centuries. Actually, it was pretty amazing.

Andi helped Ginny clean up the breakfast dishes, and then she went into the sitting room to find her things. The room was much larger than she'd originally expected. It was built on the front of the house and had a tall ceiling with exposed beams. On one side was a huge river rock fireplace, a bigger version of the one she'd seen in Luke's cabin, and there were large windows on either side of it. The room was wide open and there was a main staircase against the far wall. There was a large entry door, and outside of that was a screened-in porch that ran the length of the front part of the house. Over by the staircase was a door that led to yet another room.

The sitting room was outfitted with two big, brown leather sofas facing each other, a heavy, square walnut table in-between them, and a big, fluffy rug underneath on the polished oak floors. A large, brown leather chair and ottoman and a smaller oak rocker sat by the fireplace. A little oak table and chairs sat in front of one of the big windows. Andi thought it made a cute breakfast nook.

Luke had set her things on the table and leaned her wrapped painting against one of the wooden chairs. She walked over to the table. Her cases with her oil paints and drawing pencils were stacked on the table and her camera sat beside them. Her laptop computer bag was also on the table. Everything looked to be in good shape.

Ginny came into the sitting room. "You have to excuse a nosy old lady, but is that one of your paintings?" she asked, pointing to the large, rectangular object.

Andi smiled. "Yes, it is. It's my favorite and I didn't trust having it shipped to Buffalo." She glanced over at Ginny. "Do you want to see it?"

Ginny nodded. "But only if it's easy to unwrap and rewrap. I don't want anything happening to it here."

"It's no problem," Andi assured her. She began untying the string around it. "I've wrapped so many paintings over the years that it's pretty easy." She slipped the string from around it and then carefully began unwrapping the heavy, brown paper so as not to tear it. Finally, it was completely exposed.

Ginny gasped with delight when she saw it. The painting was large, twenty-four by thirty-six in size, and had a heavy, oak frame. It looked so real that the colors seemed to jump off the canvas.

Before Andi could say a word, a voice came hollering from the kitchen.

"Hey, where is everyone?"

Ginny and Andi turned to see Luke fill the doorway. He wore a white T-shirt tucked into his form-fitting Levi's jeans and had a short-sleeved, blue plaid cotton shirt over it, but it was left unbuttoned. His hat was in his hand and his boots clicked on the wood floor. Andi noticed that his shirt brought out the intensity of his blue eyes.

"What's going on in here?" Luke asked, coming to stand between his mother and Andi.

"Andi was showing me her painting," Ginny said. "Look, isn't it beautiful?"

Luke glanced down at the painting propped up against a chair.

"It's the Lone Cypress near Monterey, California," Andi explained.

"I know what it is," Luke shot back at her.

Andi was taken aback. She hadn't meant anything by it. She'd just wanted to explain what it was.

"Oh, be nice, Luke," Ginny said. "I've never seen the Lone Cypress in person, but I've seen plenty of photos," she told Andi. "And you sure did capture the beauty of it."

"Thank you," Andi said. "Most people think of this tree as being lonely, but I see it more as a part of its entire surroundings. The tan and white rock against the blue Pacific Ocean makes the perfect backdrop for the deep green of the tree. I also love the white foam below as the ocean hits the boulders near the shore. There's so much going on around the tree that I just love it."

Luke stood there, silent, examining the painting. Andi stole a quick glance at him. His face seemed to be in turmoil. She wondered what he was thinking.

"You sure are a talented young lady," Ginny said in awe. "Do you sell your paintings?"

"Yes, I do, but not this one. I have prints made up in various sizes for each of my paintings and I sell those. I also have a deal with a greeting card company. They use two of my images for items like blank cards, coffee mugs, coasters, placemats, and other novelties sold in gift shops. Since I generally paint seascapes and landscapes along the coast, my images work well for tourist shops. I have done a couple of paintings of downtown Seattle and San Francisco, too, but I prefer the open countryside."

"Luke went to college in Sacramento," Ginny said. "I suppose you got a chance to see this in person, huh Luke?"

His mother's words seemed to pull Luke out of his trance. "Yeah, I saw it once," he said brusquely. He turned to Andi. "So, what's going on today? Am I driving you into Missoula, or what?"

Andi frowned. Why was Luke being such a jerk to her? "I haven't heard from the Ford garage yet," she told him.

Ginny spoke up. "There's no sense in Andi going anywhere until she hears about her car. Just go on back to work, Luke. We'll call you if we need you."

"I can't hang around here all day waiting," Luke said. "I have work to do."

"Colt offered nicely to drive me into town," Andi said, staring hard at Luke. "I'll ask him so I won't be a bother to you."

Luke stared at Andi a moment, then turned on his heel and headed to the kitchen doorway. He stopped there and turned around again. "If anyone drives you into town, it'll be me, not Colt. I'll be back behind the barn, chopping wood. Holler when you're ready to go." He turned again and disappeared through the door.

Andi sighed. He was just so damned obstinate.

Ginny patted Andi's arm. "Don't let Luke get your goat," she said. "He's actually a very nice man, he just gets ornery. The past hasn't been very kind to him. Here, let me help you wrap up your painting again."

As Andi and Ginny carefully wrapped up the Lone Cypress, Andi wondered what in Luke's past had turned him into such a beast.

Chapter Four

Luke stormed out of the house and walked with long strides to the back of the horse barn where he'd been chopping wood earlier. He pulled off his shirt, slipped off his T-shirt, and laid them over the nearby fence. Then, with all the energy he could muster, he began methodically splitting each piece of wood from the large pile and placing it in the stack of firewood between two tree trunks.

It was a warm July day, and after a few minutes of chopping wood, sweat began to trickle down his back and sides. Luke didn't mind. Each swing of the ax helped to ease the tension inside of him. Tension that seemed to build up when he was around Andi.

"The Lone Cypress," he muttered aloud. "Telling me what it is as if I was just some dumb cowpoke who'd never left the ranch in his life."

He had to admit, though, that she'd said it nicely, and he supposed she hadn't meant to insult him. But for some reason, it had irked him. And worse than that, the painting had been so breathtaking, it had taken him by surprise. The colors were so rich and vivid. He'd felt like he'd actually been standing there, feeling the ocean wind blowing across his face and hearing the waves beat against the rocks below. It had reminded him of the day he'd actually visited the site. He hadn't been alone that day. He'd been with Ashley.

Angrily, Luke grasped a thick chunk of wood with one hand and placed it on the chopping block, then drew the ax back and split the chunk in half.

Luke knew how it felt to be the Lone Cypress. Like the tree, he'd been alone for too long now. The painting had drawn out such raw emotion from him, it scared him. It was as if Andi had seen his loneliness and pain and painted it right there on the canvas. And when she looked at him with those big, green eyes, he almost felt as if she was looking at his heart. A heart that he'd kept well hidden for years now.

Luke chopped another piece of wood. He could do this all day, and probably would. The main house and his cabin used a lot of wood in the winter for heat, so he had to cut and chop several cords of wood before the end of summer. Maybe if he chopped enough wood, his muscles would burn and hurt so much that he'd forget the pain he felt every time he was alone. Every time he was reminded of Ashely.

Unfortunately, Andi had been the catalyst of reminders of Ashley. Usually, Luke pushed thoughts of her aside, but having Andi here made him think of nothing else but how lonely he was. It was time she left. Andi had no right being on the ranch. City girls belonged in the city. They didn't like ranches and they grew tired of cowboys. His life would be better the minute Andi was off the ranch.

* * *

By noon, Andi still hadn't heard from the garage. She called them and found out that they hadn't even had a chance to tear into her car and that they'd call her as soon as they did. With a sigh, Andi hung up. She couldn't put off calling Derek much longer. By the looks of it, she'd be at the ranch at least another night, if not longer, and she had to let him know where she was. Since the men were coming in for sandwiches for lunch, she decided to wait until later in the afternoon when she'd have a little privacy to call Derek.

So far, the grouchy cowboy, alias Luke, hadn't appeared for lunch. Andi sat with Colt and Randy and ate a turkey sandwich and drank iced tea. Colt was getting more comfortable with Andi and talked a little more this afternoon than he had this morning. He said he'd been helping the neighbor haul hay bales all morning. He explained that they had a deal with the neighbor—he cut and rolled the bales and they split the hay fifty-fifty. That way the Brennans wouldn't have to maintain the expensive equipment for cutting and baling hay. They had completed their first cutting already and by fall they'd have a second, Colt told her. After both men took off again, Andi had to smile. She'd learned more about ranching in one day than she had in her entire life.

After lunch, Ginny excused herself to go off to her office and do some paperwork and told Andi to make herself at home and wander the ranch if she wanted to. Ginny also told Andi that the ranch house had wireless internet, because she needed it to do business, so Andi could use it if she wanted to. Andi quickly emailed her sister to tell her she was still there and to let her know she could be contacted by email. After that, Andi ran up to her room where she'd put her drawing supplies, picked up a large pad of drawing paper and two charcoal pencils, and went back downstairs and stepped outside.

The day was warm with the sun shining brightly and a soft breeze coming through the hills. This was the first time Andi had seen the house and land by daylight, and she gasped in delight as she walked away from the house and looked up behind it. It was set up against a backdrop of tall hills covered in pine trees, with lush green for as far as the eye could see. As she turned in a circle, she saw open fields by the big, red barn, another long building with a tin roof, and yet another smaller building. Fencing ran around at intervals near the horse barn, creating a small corral and opening up to larger fields that Andi figured were for grazing. The gravel driveway forked off with one path going over to Luke's cabin in the distance and the other heading to the highway, also far away. In front of the house was a green lawn, and on the other side sat a huge vegetable garden. Farther from the house was a small building that looked like a miniature barn with wire fencing all around it. Chickens scratched around outside the little barn. There were trails that led off in different directions away from the house and up into the hills. Andi wondered where they led, and if it was possible to horseback ride up them for an even better view.

Over by the barn, a brown horse with a white streak running down its nose stuck his head through the corral's fence, trying to reach the green grass on the other side. Andi laughed. *The grass is always greener.* She walked over closer to the barn and found a big boulder to sit on that gave her a side view of the front of the barn and the horse. She wanted to sketch it as it stretched its neck out toward the fresh grass.

Opening her sketchpad, Andi began preparing the page by running her charcoal pencil over it to give it a gray background. It was always easier to draw on a gray surface than on a clean, white page. That way, if she made any errors, she could smudge them right into the background.

Once the page was ready, she began sketching the scene before her. She started with the bare bones of the rail fence and the horse, then the front of the barn. As she sketched, she filled in areas with light and dark, smudging with her finger where necessary to create shadows and contrast. She drew quickly, and soon the drawing came to life in front of her eyes.

A noise caught her attention from behind the barn. It was a constant, rhythmic sound of something hard hitting a surface and then a swift cracking noise. Time and time again this sound echoed across the yard, until Andi's curiosity got the better of her. She stood from her boulder and stepped back a little, over to another fence that ran along the front side of the property. That's when she saw Luke. He faced the back of the barn, allowing her to view him at a side angle. His shirt was off, and a sheen of sweat covered his back and chest. She watched as he easily picked up a full log with one hand, placed it on a flattened stump, then gracefully lifted the ax and slammed it down to split the log in two. Andi stood there, mesmerized by the sheer power of Luke's swing, yet how smoothly he did this, time and time again, like a steady dance between man and ax. His arm and back muscles rippled and bulged with each swing. This was the most virile display of manhood Andi had seen in a very long time.

Andi leaned back against the rail fence and tried focusing on her horse and barn drawing again. She began shading the horse, showing the contrast between its dark mane and the lighter brown of its neck. But time and time again, with each chop of the ax, Andi's gaze returned to Luke's powerful body at work.

Andi turned a page in her sketchpad, quickly prepared the page, and fervently started sketching. She watched how

Luke's body moved and observed the flex of his arm and back muscles. She noted his slim waist as it narrowed down into his jeans. His long sturdy legs were planted on the ground, slightly apart. And that six pack. This guy had a serious set of muscles across his abdomen. Andi had sketched a variety of good-looking men in her art classes in college, but Luke's body put them to shame. Plus that chiseled face of his. She knew that she just had to sketch his face while she was here.

She didn't sketch Luke chopping wood. Instead, she sketched him standing beside the barn, facing her, his cowboy hat slung low over his eyes, his thumbs in his pockets, and his arms out at each side. Almost the same stance he'd had last night in the doorway, except shirtless. She knew she shouldn't, and she'd have died if Luke saw it, but she couldn't help herself. He was the epitome of the hunky cowboy that all girls dreamed of, and it would have been a sin not to sketch him.

As Andi concentrated on the light and shadows of her sketch, she suddenly realized it was completely silent around her. The chopping had stopped. She looked up in Luke's direction. He stood there, staring directly at her, the ax hanging by his side.

Andi's face grew hot. Had he noticed her staring at him? She hoped not. Trying to act calm, she slowly closed her sketchpad and stood up straight, stepping away from the fence. She looked up at Luke again, and he still stood there, staring. She smiled, gave a little wave, and then walked as calmly as she could back to the house.

After putting her drawing supplies away in her room, Andi decided it was time to call Derek and let him know where she was. It was three in the afternoon here, so it was five in Buffalo, and he'd be off of work and heading back to the townhouse he was renting. Andi went down to the quiet kitchen and dialed his cell phone. It took four rings before he answered.

"This is Derek Hensley," he said briskly.

"Hi, Derek. It's Andi."

"Andi? It's about time you called. I've been trying to reach you. I didn't recognize the number. Where are you?"

Andi bit her lip. Derek sounded worried, and she felt bad for not calling sooner. "I'm sorry I didn't call you right away, but there's no cell service where I am and I didn't want to wake you up last night. My car broke down last night outside of Missoula, Montana. It's at the garage right now, but they haven't told me yet what's wrong. It looks like I'll be staying here another night."

"Oh, my God, Andi. I knew something like this would happen with that old beater. Are you okay? Where are you calling from? Are you staying in Missoula?"

Andi winced. The first thing Derek had said was he knew this would happen. Although, he had also sounded worried about her being safe. Derek liked taking care of Andi. That was one of the things about Derek that Andi appreciated. He felt it was his job to do everything for her, and after years of taking care of Carly and herself, it was a welcomed relief to let someone else be in charge. Sometimes, though, his concern could be overwhelming.

"I'm fine," she finally answered. "I'm staying with some very nice people who own a ranch just outside of Missoula. They were the closest place to where I broke down, and they have been very hospitable."

"You're what? You're staying with strangers? Andi, that's crazy. You need to get into Missoula and to a safe hotel right away," Derek said, sounding incensed.

Andi's shoulders drooped. "Derek, it's okay," she said meekly. "They were very kind to let me stay here. The woman who owns the ranch, Ginny, is very sweet, and I'm actually safer here than in a hotel alone. As soon as my car is fixed, I can be on my way to Buffalo."

"This is ridiculous. I told you not to drive across country for this very reason. Your car is just too old and unreliable for you to be traversing around alone in the middle of nowhere."

"But Derek," Andi said, but was interrupted.

"Is there an airport in Missoula? I want you to leave your car there and hop the next plane you can get on to Buffalo. I don't want you staying there with strangers, and I certainly don't want you driving any farther in that wreck of a car."

Andi took a deep, calming breath. "Derek, I can't just leave my car and fly there. I know you're worried, but I'm fine. As soon as the car is fixed, I'll be on my way again."

Derek let out a heavy sigh. "I just don't understand what it is with you and that old car. I offered to buy you a new one. And driving out here instead of flying with me. It's just crazy. I almost feel as if you don't want to come here at all."

Andi blinked. How had the conversation turned from her breaking down to her not wanting to be with him? "Honey," Andi said soothingly. "Of course, I want to come out there and be with you. I just wanted to see some of the country, that's all. And you know how much you hate driving trips. I promise, as soon as the car is fixed, I'll be there in only a few days. Okay?"

There was a long pause on the other end before Derek finally answered. "Fine. But keep me informed as to where you are and what's going on. I have to go. I'm having dinner with a client and I'm at the restaurant now. Please be safe, okay?"

Andi nodded even though he couldn't see her. "I will. I'll call you as soon as I know anything. Love you, honey."

"Goodbye, Andi." The phone clicked off.

Andi stood there a moment, frowning at the handset before hanging it up. The phone call had left her feeling hollow inside. She knew Derek cared about her, but it was as if he hadn't even listened to her. Sighing, she walked into the sitting room and sat down on the soft, leather sofa. She didn't hear the sound of the kitchen door gently opening and Luke walking outside again.

* * *

Ginny came through the door by the stairs in the sitting room and caught sight of Andi sitting on the sofa. "Hi, dear. Is everything okay?"

Andi stood and nodded. "I just called my fiancé, Derek. He was upset about the car breaking down."

"Well, honey, he should be. He's probably just worried about you, out here all alone and staying with strangers, no less. He has no idea who we are or what we're like."

Andi nodded. "I guess." She followed Ginny into the kitchen. Ginny began pulling food out of the fridge to start cooking supper. "Is there anything I can do to help you? I feel useless with everyone else working around me."

"Oh, dear, you've been a big help. And if we're lucky enough to have you stay another day, I'll be happy to put you to work tomorrow. You can help me can more strawberry and raspberry preserves."

"I'm afraid I don't know anything about canning," Andi said.

Ginny waved her hand through the air, dismissing Andi's

concerns. "You don't need to know anything. I know how. I can teach you. It will be fun."

Andi laughed. She just loved how easy it was to be with Ginny.

"You know, there is something you can do to help me," Ginny said. "Have you ever picked strawberries before?"

"Sure. We used to go to a berry farm and pick our own when I was younger. It was fun."

"Great." Ginny went to a closet in the kitchen and pulled out three one-gallon plastic pails stacked inside of each other. "Did you see the garden when you were outside?"

Andi nodded.

"If you can pick as many ripe strawberries as there is left on the vines for me, I'd really appreciate it. I picked a huge batch of them the other day, but there were still a lot that weren't ready. Some should be ready now."

"I'd be happy to do that," Andi said, taking the pails.

From her spot in the kitchen, Bree's ears sprang up with interest as Andi walked to the door.

"Go along then, Bree," Ginny said. Bree stood up and followed Andi outside, staying right on her heels.

Once outside, Andi stopped for a moment, listening. She didn't hear the sound of the ax chopping wood anymore. She looked around, wondering where Luke was, and then told herself it didn't matter. She was becoming too obsessed with the obstinate cowboy.

Andi looked down at the attentive dog. "Come on, Bree. This way." Bree followed happily.

Andi walked around to the other side of the house and into the garden, leaving Bree to lie in the green grass beside it. It was a large plot of land. She looked around. She wasn't an expert on gardens, but she spotted the string beans, carrots, and squash growing there. Other plants she couldn't identify. Walking carefully through the garden, she found the rows of strawberries. She started on one end of the first row and searched through each plant, picking only the bigger berries and leaving the smaller ones to grow larger. The ripe strawberries were plump and deep red. They looked delicious.

Meticulously, she made her way to the end of one row, then turned and headed down another. She'd worn jeans and a short-sleeved T-shirt today, along with her sneakers, and she felt the heat of the late afternoon sun on her back and arms. It felt good, as she made her way from plant to plant.

Andi's hands were getting dirty, but she didn't care. She just rubbed them on her jeans from time to time. She'd never been a girly girl, like her sister, and she didn't mind a little dirt. Her hair was pulled away from her face in a ponytail, but it was so wavy and thick, strands of it pulled out from the band and fell down around her face, getting in her way. Several times, Andi pushed a loose strand of hair behind her ear as she concentrated on her berry picking. By the time she was almost through all the rows, she had two-and-a-half pails filled to the brim with strawberries.

"What on earth are you doing?" a deep voice said from behind her.

Startled, Andi stood and turned to look up into Luke's steely blue eyes. She'd been concentrating so hard on picking berries that she hadn't heard him walk up behind her.

"Geez, do you have to scare me like that?" she asked. "What does it look like I'm doing? I'm picking strawberries for your mom."

Luke stood there, staring down at her. He was wearing both of his shirts again, but his arms were an even deeper brown than they'd been earlier this morning.

"Did the Ford garage call yet?" he asked.

Andi shook her head. "Not yet."

"Hmmm."

He just stood there, staring at her with that intense gaze. Andi wondered what he was thinking behind that hard-set jaw and level stare. To her amazement, he raised his hand and placed it along the side of her face, cupping her jaw. Her heart pounded and she was sure her knees would give out at his touch. Slowly, he rubbed his thumb across her cheek twice, and then let his arm drop back to his side.

Her eyes were wide as she stood there and stared at him, astonished.

"There was a dirt smudge on your face," he said. Then he turned and strode away, back toward the horse barn, with Bree at his heels.

Andi watched him walk away, her heart still pounding in her chest. She wasn't sure if there had been a dirt smudge on her face or not, but his touch had sent shockwaves through her entire body like nothing she'd ever felt before.

Chapter Five

Luke walked away from the garden and into the coolness of the barn to get as far away from Andi as he could. *Damn. What in tarnation did I just do?* He leaned up against a horse stall and looked down into Bree's golden eyes. The dog cocked her head and stared back at him.

"Did you see that?" Luke asked Bree. "What was I thinking?"

Bree only stared back. She panted from the heat of the day, but to Luke, it looked like she was grinning at him.

Luke turned and walked over to an empty horse stall. He picked up the pitchfork and began pushing the loose straw around in the stall. There was nothing wrong with the straw or the stall, but he had to keep his hands busy or he'd go crazy.

What had possessed him to touch Andi? Damn. What had possessed him to go into the garden in the first place? He knew damned well what she was doing, so why go and give her heck about it?

Because as he stood there looking at her, he couldn't resist the urge to see if her skin felt as smooth and soft as it looked. And it had.

Luke stabbed furiously at the straw as that thought spun around in his head.

Earlier, when he'd been chopping wood, he'd been surprised to see Andi leaning against the fence, sketching. He'd wondered what she was drawing, and why she was constantly looking over at him. He'd been chopping wood to ease the tension in his body that she caused him by just being there. But instead, he was still wound up tighter than a spring. There wasn't enough wood to chop in the entire world to get that red-headed woman out of his mind. No matter how hard he'd swung that ax, his mind had kept coming back to her and those damned green eyes.

And then he saw her there in the garden and he was like a moth to a flame. Cripes. He was acting no better than Colt.

"Think you have that straw shuffled around enough?" a male voice asked from behind Luke.

Luke turned abruptly to find Randy standing there, grinning.

"I was just loosening it up a bit," Luke said.

"I see that."

Luke frowned at Randy. They'd known each other since Kindergarten. Randy knew Luke as well as his own brother did. Maybe even better. But there was no way Luke was going to confide what he felt for the red-headed vixen.

Luke stepped out of the stall and leaned the pitchfork against the wall. "Is there something you wanted?" Luke asked brusquely.

Randy chuckled, which only infuriated Luke more.

"Do you want me to go out to the summer pasture next week to check the cattle and fences, or are you going?" Randy asked. "I mean, since you have company and all."

Luke narrowed his eyes at Randy. "I don't have company.

Andi's just some girl whose car broke down in front of our ranch. Besides, she should be on her way by next week."

Randy shrugged. "Colt thinks it's her transmission that went out. If that's true, she'll be here a lot longer than a couple of days."

"Well, what does that matter? She's my ma's guest, not mine."

"Just saying, that's all," Randy said. He slid his hands in his jean's pockets and leaned against the stall. "She sure is pretty, though. Don't you think? All that shiny red hair and those green eyes. Or, haven't you noticed?"

"Now you're sounding just like Colt," Luke said. "She's engaged to some guy in Buffalo, so everyone needs to leave her alone, okay?"

"Oh, sure thing," Randy said, his eyes twinkling. "Does that include you, too?"

"What are you getting at?" Luke asked, his tone menacing.

Randy laughed. He slapped Luke good-naturedly on the back. "Luke, old buddy, you need to loosen up. You're as tight as a corkscrew. I'm just kidding you. Listen, it's my turn to go out to check on the cattle, so I'll go next week and stay a couple of nights at the summer cabin."

Luke thought about it a moment. Randy was right. If Andi's transmission was out, she'd be here at least a week while the garage replaced it. Maybe going for a few days to the summer grazing pasture was a good idea. It would keep him away from Andi.

"No, I'll go this time," Luke told Randy. "It will be nice to go there and spend a few peaceful days away from here."

Randy nodded. "You're the boss," he said as he turned to leave.

"Oh, and Randy?" Luke said.

Randy turned and looked at Luke. "Yeah?"

"I meant it when I said Andi is off limits. She's engaged. We need to respect that."

Randy nodded. "I understand. I'll be nothing but brotherly to her." He grinned, and then left.

Luke sighed. Now if he could just get himself to think that way about Andi, everything would be fine.

* * *

After Andi finished picking strawberries, she brought them into the kitchen and rinsed them off before putting them away for the next day. Then she helped Ginny with supper. It was past six o'clock, and she still hadn't heard back from the garage, so she gratefully accepted Ginny's offer of staying at the ranch another night.

"Stay as long as it takes," Ginny told her. "I'm in no hurry to see you go. It's nice having another woman around here for a change."

Andi peeled potatoes and helped cut up carrots to boil. Ginny had a roast in the oven and was busy making homemade cornbread. Together, they served up the mashed potatoes, carrots, roast beef, and cornbread when the men came in for supper.

Randy and Colt were already sitting at the table when Luke sauntered in. He sat in a chair next to Randy, and across from where Andi sat beside Colt. Ginny sat in the chair at the end of the table. Andi noted that Luke had changed his shirt, and the ends of his hair were damp. *Had he showered before supper?* She wondered if he did every night or if he had because of her.

The men ate with as little conversation as possible. Andi

was amazed at how much food they could shovel in and yet look so fit and trim. Derek watched what he ate and spent a lot of time in the gym just to stay in shape. But not these guys. They ate as much meat, gravy, potatoes, and cornbread as they wanted. And lots of butter. Real butter. Of course, these cowboys didn't have to work out in a gym to stay fit. Their job was a workout.

Andi thought about Luke wielding the ax for hours today, splitting wood. That took a lot of stamina. She didn't know anyone at home who had that kind of strength and endurance. The men she'd known throughout her life were lightweights compared to Luke.

"Pass the butter, please?"

Andi looked up at Luke, startled. "What?"

Luke frowned. "You daydreaming over there? Butter, please?"

Andi gazed around her, feeling her face turn hot. She eyed the butter, picked it up, and handed it to Luke. Everyone at the table stared at her.

"Sorry," she stammered. "I was just enjoying all this delicious food and I didn't hear you."

"Uh, huh," Luke said. He slathered butter liberally on his third piece of cornbread.

Andi glared at him.

"Andi, I saw you had your sketchpad out," Ginny said. "Did you get any drawing done?"

Andi's eyes opened wide as she thought about the sketch of Luke. *Please don't let her ask to see it.* "Yes, a little. There was a horse stretching its neck through the fence rails by the barn, trying to eat the grass on the other side. I was sketching her and the barn."

"Hmmm. The grass is always greener, right?" Luke said.

"That's what I thought," Andi replied, smiling up at him.

"So, did you sketch anything else?" Luke asked.

All eyes turned to Andi.

"No. Why?" She hoped she didn't look as guilty as she felt.

Luke stared at her a moment. "Just wondering," he said, and then returned his attention to his food.

His stare felt almost like an accusation. Andi glared at him, but he wasn't looking her way any longer. *Geez, that guy is irritating.*

After supper, everyone went their separate ways. Luke disappeared outside and Randy left for home. Colt, having no excuses left to hang out in the kitchen, went up to his room. Andi helped Ginny clean up the supper dishes, and then went outside to sit on the stoop while Ginny organized her jars and supplies for canning the next day. Bree followed Andi outside.

The sun was slowly making its way down behind the hills and the air was cooling fast. Ginny had told Andi to wear a jacket from the hooks in the back porch, so she'd grabbed a women's blue fleece jacket and slipped it on. Andi pulled out her phone and emailed Carly to tell her that her car wasn't fixed yet and she was still at the Brennan Ranch. She then emailed Derek to tell him she did have Internet, so he could email her if he needed to contact her.

In the stillness of the evening, Andi heard a horse neigh over by the barn. She looked up and saw it was the brown horse she'd been sketching earlier that day. She smiled. "Should we go visit the horse?" Andi asked Bree, who'd been sitting on the grass, sniffing the air. Andi patted Bree on the head and walked over to the fence with the dog at her heels.

The horse neighed again as Andi drew closer. It stretched its neck over the rail fence as if asking to be petted. Andi walked over and raised her hand to the horse's nose, letting it smell her scent, before slowly rubbing her hand up the side of the horse's face. The horse drew even closer, so Andi pet it down the front of its face.

"Hey there, sweetie," Andi cooed. "Are you a girl or a boy, huh?"

"She's a mare," Luke said, coming up behind Andi.

Andi tried not to jump at his voice. *Why is he always sneaking up and startling me?*

Taking a breath, Andi said calmly, "Ah, a girl."

Luke came to stand beside her by the fence. "Yeah. She's five. She startles easily, though, so be careful. She may nip at you."

Andi continued rubbing her hand down the horse's nose. It felt warm and soft.

"She seems fine to me. Maybe it's you who startles her, like you always seem to try to do to me."

Luke cocked his head and stared at her, but Andi continued giving her attention to the horse. He was so close, she smelled his aftershave. It was light and spicy, very male. So, he had showered before supper.

"I guess I have come up behind you a time or two today," Luke said softly. "I didn't mean to scare you. You just always seem so immersed in whatever you're doing that you don't hear me walking up."

Andi turned and looked directly at Luke. This was the first time he'd ever talked to her in a nice tone. She laughed. "I guess you're right about that. When I'm working on something, I usually give it my full attention. My sister, Carly, says that when I'm painting, a siren could go off in the room and I'd never hear it."

"That's dedication," Luke said.

"I suppose."

Luke looked directly in her eyes. "That's a good thing. It means you're giving it everything you have. Not many people do that these days. Most people are easily distracted by everything around them."

"Are you easily distracted, Luke Brennan?"

Luke stared at her a moment, a crease between his brows, and then suddenly his face broke into a smile and he let out a laugh. The powerful sound startled the mare, and she backed up and ran off to the other side of the corral.

Andi grinned up at Luke. "Well, look at that. You do know how to smile. I have to say, you are much better looking when you smile than when you scowl."

The sun had disappeared and darkness surrounded them. A security light by the house was all that shone in the night. But neither of them had noticed the growing darkness as they stood there by the fence, close to each other.

"I guess I haven't been the nicest person to you since you came here last night," Luke said. "I'm sorry."

"You have been rather rude, and I accept your apology," Andi said. "But I also can't blame you. I mean, I showed up on your doorstep uninvited and now I'm staying with your mother, and you don't know me from Adam. I'm sorry about that, but I can't say I'm sorry I'm staying here. Your mom is the sweetest person I've ever met. If nothing else comes of me staying here, at least I got a chance to know her."

"She is pretty amazing. I have to agree with that," Luke said.

"I don't know if I can stand this. Now we're even agreeing on something. It's a miracle."

"Smartass," Luke said, grinning.

Andi laughed. It felt nice to finally ease the tension between them and have a normal conversation.

"I take it your fiancé isn't too happy about you staying here, though," Luke said.

Andi's brows rose. "How do you know that?"

Luke looked down sheepishly. "Sorry. I had come in just as you started talking with him and I overheard the conversation. I didn't mean to, it just happened."

Andi dropped her eyes. "Yeah, he wasn't very happy. If he had his way, I'd trash the car and be on a plane to Buffalo right now. But I don't want to do that. This will probably be the only time I have a chance to see any of the country between here and Buffalo, and I'm not giving that up. Not that or my car."

"I'm sure he's just worried about you," Luke told her.

Andi sighed. "I know."

Silence filled the night air. Luke turned toward the corral, gazing at the three horses that stood nearby. "So, do you ride?" he asked.

Andi looked up at him and smiled. She was happy to change the subject. "Yes, I do. My parents were firm believers in a person trying everything at least once. Carly and I both took lessons when we were younger."

Luke wrinkled his nose. "Lessons?"

"Oh now, don't mock me. I'm sure you've been on a horse since you were two years old and riding comes naturally for you. But for those of us who live in the city, we have to take lessons."

Luke stared at her, his expression serious. "Western saddle or English?"

Andi returned his stare. "Is there anything but Western?" she asked with mock indignation.

Luke chuckled. "Well, maybe we can go riding sometime while you're here."

"I'd like that."

They stood out there a while longer and then finally Luke walked Andi back to the house with Bree following behind.

"Well, guess I'll see you tomorrow," Luke said as Andi stood on the back steps.

"Guess so," Andi said. "I can't go anywhere."

"Goodnight."

"Goodnight."

Andi watched Luke drive off in his pick-up, back to his cabin. She couldn't believe how in less than a day, the obstinate cowboy had managed to get under her skin.

Chapter Six

Andi walked into the quiet kitchen with Bree right behind her. The room was dark, except for the light on over the stove. It was only ten o'clock, but considering how early everyone got up around here, she supposed that Colt and Ginny had already gone off to bed.

Restlessly, Andi wandered into the sitting room. She turned on a light by the sofa. Her painting was still leaning against the chair by the table. Andi thought she should move it out of the way so it wasn't blocking the table, so she glanced around and found a spot against the wall to set it. That done, she walked over to the fireplace mantel and looked at the row of photos displayed there. Several generations of Brennans stared back at her. Some of the photos looked very old, some newer. One showed a big, burly man standing beside a sturdy looking woman in front of a small house. Andi figured it must be this house, only generations before when it was smaller. Even in black and white, she noticed the man had a distinctive square jawline and piercing eyes, but he looked kind. He definitely had to be a grandfather or great-grandfather to Luke.

Looking down the row, Andi smiled when she recognized

a photo of a much younger Ginny and a good-looking man. She knew instantly that this was Luke and Colt's father because he looked so much like them. With his wavy dark hair and chiseled face, he was indeed a hunk in his time. And Ginny was very pretty, too. It was no wonder that Luke looked as good as he did. The Brennan gene pool was filled with handsome men.

As Andi gazed at the generations of Brennans, she thought about Derek and how he compared to Luke. Derek was a handsome man, no doubt, with his dark hair, chocolaty brown eyes, square face, and prominent cheekbones. Derek wasn't as tall as Luke, but he was taller than her. Women always looked twice at Derek when he was out, Andi had witnessed it often. But Derek's good looks were more of the uptown, upward mobile style than the ruggedly handsome kind. Derek spent a lot of time on his looks, styling his hair just right in the morning, wearing tailored suits, and going to the tanning salon since he rarely had time to be outside. But Luke's good looks came naturally. She doubted Luke spent much time on his hair since he was just going to plop a hat on it for the day, yet it always fell into place perfectly when the hat came off. He definitely didn't spend hours in a gym, and tanning came with his job. He didn't even have tan lines as was so obvious when he'd had his shirt off today.

Suddenly, guilt crept over Andi for comparing the two men. It wasn't fair. Derek was a good man who worked hard at his job and was successful, and he wanted to share that success, and his life, with her. She should be proud that such a man loved her, yet here she was, comparing him to Luke. It was apples and oranges. There was no comparison. They were two different types of men living two very different lifestyles.

Andi turned out the light in the sitting room and walked

quietly through the kitchen. Bree lay on her pillow by the staircase. Andi knelt down and petted her a moment before heading upstairs to her room. It had been a long day and she was tired. Luke had been near her at every turn today, so it was no wonder she'd thought of him so much. Tomorrow would be different. She'd help Ginny, find out more about her car, and possibly be on her way to Buffalo by Saturday. Luke would be a distant memory in a few days. As Andi lay down in bed and pulled the covers over her, she couldn't help feeling a bit sad at the idea of never seeing Luke Brennan again.

* * *

Luke lay in his bed, replaying the day in his mind. The window was open, letting in the fresh country air as well as the sounds of crickets chirping in the fields. Night sounds. They were always comforting to him. But tonight, he found it hard to fall asleep.

For the first time in years, Luke hadn't come home as the sun was setting and watch it fall behind the hills with a heavy heart. Instead, he'd hung around the ranch after supper, pretending he had a few more chores to do that could have easily waited until morning. He hated to admit it, but he'd been waiting to see if Andi came outside, and to his surprise, she had. He'd watched her from the barn as she walked along with Bree and then headed over to the horse by the fence. He should have just left her alone and gone home, but again, he was drawn to her as she talked softly to the horse.

Thinking back, he was glad he'd approached her. He knew he'd been acting like a jerk to her all day, so at least tonight he hoped he'd made up for it. But she'd caught him off guard when she'd asked, "Are you easily distracted, Luke Brennan?"

That loaded question had more than one meaning at that moment, and he had been taken aback by it. The first answer to come to mind was *I am most definitely distracted by you.* And that was why he'd let out a laugh. Just imagining Andi's reaction to that answer had caused his laughter. Surely, she hadn't meant the question in the flirty, teasing way she'd asked it. Had she? She was engaged to another man, a man who was on the path of becoming very successful by the sounds of it. She certainly wasn't flirting with a plain old cowboy like him.

Luke ran a hand through his hair and sighed. Colt and Randy were right. Andi was a pretty woman. No, she was beautiful. She was everything a man could want with her long legs and slender body, curvy in all the right places. Her long, dark red hair was thick and wavy and made a man want to run his hands through it. And those green eyes. They were large and expressive, and kind. Even when she was glaring at him, those eyes drove him crazy.

"Well," he said into the dark room. "She won't be here long, so stop driving yourself crazy over her." As soon as the garage figured out that her transmission was shot, Andi was sure to leave her car behind and fly to Buffalo. Even if she didn't want to, by the sound of it, her boyfriend would insist on it. She'd be out of there by Saturday, maybe Sunday at the latest. Then he could forget about those long legs and lovely green eyes and get back to life as usual.

* * *

The next morning, Andi was up as soon as the sun shone through her window. She showered and washed her hair, then pulled it up in a ponytail to keep it off her face. Looking into the mirror over the dresser in her room, she considered whether or not she should bother with makeup. A little mascara won out, just to emphasize her eyes, she told herself, and she swiped on a light coat of foundation as well to protect her fair skin from the sun. She dressed in a simple green T-shirt and jeans, then headed downstairs to join the others for breakfast.

Just like the morning before, Randy and Colt were still eating, but Luke had long since eaten and headed out to work. Disappointment at missing Luke washed over Andi, and then she quickly admonished herself. *I'm engaged. Stop thinking about Luke.*

As soon as the men left and Andi had eaten, she and Ginny went right to work. They cleaned up the breakfast dishes and then Ginny pulled out two large pans and put them on the stove.

"First, let's cut up the strawberries, and then I'll show you what we mix together with them to make them sweet and delicious," Ginny told her.

Andi and Ginny worked side-by-side at the sink, hulling and cutting up the strawberries. Ginny explained that they were going to make three separate batches today because strawberry jam turned out better if done in smaller batches.

Andi looked at the dozens of pint and half-pint jars sitting in boxes on the table. "Do you really use that much jam in a year?" she asked.

Ginny laughed. "No, we'd never go through that much just here at the ranch. I make dozens of jars of each type of jam to sell at the Missoula State Fair each year. Two of my friends and I always rent a small booth there for the week and sell our jams and preserves. It makes a nice extra income."

"Don't most people around here can their own?" Andi asked.

Ginny shook her head. "Over the past twenty years, we've had a huge influx of people buying up property along the Clark Fork and Bitterroot Rivers and building vacation homes. Tourists come to the fair as well. People like buying homemade items."

Andi was surprised. She hadn't realized how busy the area was.

Once they'd cut up the strawberries, they mashed them with a hand tool before measuring them out into three batches of six cups each. Ginny filled the one tall pan half-full with water and turned the flame on under it to bring it to a boil. She dumped one bowl of mashed strawberries into the other pan and started the flame under it. "Here," she said to Andi. "You stir these so they don't burn while I mix the sugar." Andi began slowly stirring the strawberries over the heat. It was warm outside, so Andi was happy that the ranch house was modern enough to have air conditioning, otherwise the kitchen would feel like a sauna.

Ginny poured cups of sugar into a bowl. Then she mixed a portion of sugar with something from a box.

"What's that?" Andi asked as she stirred. This whole process was really interesting to her.

"Pectin. It helps to give the jam texture so it isn't too runny."

Ginny poured the pectin-sugar mixture into the strawberries while Andi stirred. Once it was mixed well, Ginny poured in the remaining sugar.

Andi continued stirring the strawberry mixture until it came to a boil, and then stirred some more. Ginny readied the jars and lids on the counter. She'd also placed a large-mouth funnel next to the jars.

Finally, Ginny took over the stirring so she could determine if the jam was ready to pour. After a while, she declared it was, so she removed the pan from the heat. She spooned some foamy liquid off the top of the jam and then began ladling the jam into the jars. It was Andi's job to put on the flat lid, before twisting the ring lid over that.

"Careful," Ginny warned. "The jars are hot."

Once they'd accomplished filling and closing up the jars, Ginny checked the boiling water on the stove. "Okay, let's get these in the pan," she said.

Andi looked at her like she was crazy. "Really? You're going to put the full jars in there?"

Ginny nodded. "It seals and preserves the jam." She grabbed what looked like oversized tongs to Andi and picked up one of the jars with it. Then Ginny carefully placed the jar in the boiling water. She did this with all the jars. Ten minutes later, she pulled them out and set them on a rack to cool.

"One batch done, two to go," Ginny said happily. She began washing the pan they'd boiled the strawberries in.

"That's it?" Andi asked. "I didn't expect it to be so easy."

"Yep. Tomorrow, when they're cool, we'll put stickers on the lids telling what they are and tie some cute ribbon around the neck for decoration. People like that. They make good gifts that way."

The two women began the process again, and about halfway through the third batch, the phone on the wall rang.

"Can you get that, dear?" Ginny asked.

Andi went over to the phone and answered, "Brennan Ranch."

"May I speak with Andi Stevens please?" the caller asked.

"This is she."

"Hi, Andi. This is Jeff Jorgeson at the Ford garage. We've taken your car apart and I'm afraid I have bad news for you. Your transmission is completely gone."

Andi stood there, confused. "What do you mean, gone? You can't fix it?"

"Well," the man said, hesitating a moment. "A rebuilt transmission could be put back in, but it's costly."

Andi frowned. "How much would that cost?"

"Between the transmission and labor, it could cost you around twenty-five hundred, maybe three thousand. And that's depending upon us finding a rebuilt transmission for this year and model. Quite frankly, ma'am, that's almost more than your car is worth."

Andi stood there, stunned. She wasn't sure how to respond.

Jeff continued speaking. "If you really want it done, we can start searching for a rebuilt. It might take some time to find one for this car. Then it would have to be shipped here."

"What other option do I have?" Andi asked. She was still shocked by the price of everything.

"Well, we do have quite a few used vehicles on the lot that might interest you. I'm sure they'd give you a little something in trade-in for your car. Personally, I wouldn't put that much money into it, but that's your choice, not mine."

Andi wasn't sure what to do. She didn't want to buy another vehicle, but she also wasn't sure if it was smart to put so much money into this one. Plus, it would eat up the money that she was going to use for the rest of her trip. She wished she had someone who could help her make this decision. Suddenly, Luke came to mind. She wanted to know what his advice would be. She already knew what Derek would tell her. He'd say to leave it behind and grab a flight out east, so she didn't want to call and ask him.

"Can I call you back?" she finally asked Jeff. "I need to think about this."

"Sure. I'll give you my direct line and you can call me as

soon as you decide." He told Andi the phone number and she hung up.

Ginny came to stand beside Andi. "By the look on your face, it must not have been good news."

Andi sighed. "It wasn't. The transmission is out and needs to be replaced. It's going to cost a lot of money."

"Oh, dear, I'm so sorry. What are you going to do?"

Andi shrugged. "I don't know. I have to figure something out."

"Well, let's have some lunch while you're thinking about it. The men will be in soon. Maybe one of them will have a suggestion."

Ginny had finished with the last batch of jam, so Andi washed up the pans and utensils while Ginny made a few cold roast beef sandwiches for the men. She set the plate out on the table along with leftover apple pie from the night before as Colt and Randy came in. Luke came in last. When he saw the worried frown on Andi's face, he bypassed the table and walked directly over to her.

"Something the matter?"

"I heard back from the garage. The transmission is shot," Andi told him.

Colt piped up from the table. "Just what we thought," he said. "Sorry, Andi."

"Thanks, Colt." Andi looked up at Luke. "Can we talk a minute?"

Luke nodded. "Let's go outside." He let Andi walk past him and he followed her out the back door.

Andi walked halfway to the barn, then turned and faced Luke. "I'm not sure what to do. I thought you'd have a better idea of what would be best."

"Okay. Tell me what they said."

Andi relayed what Jeff had said about the transmission. "He said that replacing it was going to cost me almost what the car is worth and suggested I come in and buy another car instead. I'm sure he's right. My car is a 2001 and it's old, but I also don't want to buy a car right now. Either way, it's a lot of money."

Luke looked thoughtful. "Shouldn't this be a conversation between you and your fiancé?"

Andi looked up at him, her expression serious. "I want to know what you think."

"Okay. Maybe the guy at the garage is right. It doesn't make much sense to put more money into a car that's not worth it. Maybe you should cut your losses and do what your boyfriend wants you to do. Just be done with it and fly to Buffalo."

Andi frowned. "That means giving up my car, and I can't afford a new one right now."

Luke put his hands in his pockets and shrugged. "I'm sure your fiancé will buy you a new car when you get out there."

Andi's eyes flashed with anger. "But that's the point. I don't want him to buy me a new car. I like my old one. Geez, first a guy buys you a ring, then a car, and before you know it, he owns you."

Luke frowned. "You're just marrying this guy, Andi. He's not buying you."

Andi's anger abated as quickly as it had risen. "I know. It's just that my car is the last thing that I have that is all mine. I'm giving up my life in Seattle for him, I'm leaving my sister behind, and I'm not even sure what will happen to my art career. I just wanted to keep one thing that belonged to me."

Luke walked up closer to Andi and placed his hand under her chin. He gently lifted her face so their eyes met. "If you feel that strongly about your car, then you have your answer. Keep it. Who cares if the transmission costs more than it's worth. Apparently, this car is worth more to you than just its Blue Book value. So, keep it."

Andi gazed into Luke's blue eyes. Yesterday, she'd called them intense. Today, they looked warm and kind. She'd heard what he'd said, but more than that, she'd seen the truthfulness of his words in his eyes. Slowly, she smiled up at him.

"You're right. It does mean enough to me to fix it. I knew you'd have the right answer," she said softly.

Luke dropped his hand to his side, but their eyes still held.

"You know, if I wait for it to be fixed, I'll be here a while. Maybe a long while," Andi said, a grin tugging at her lips.

"Your boyfriend isn't going to be happy about that, you know," Luke told her.

Andi nodded. "Nope. What about you? Can you stand me here for a week or two?"

Luke chuckled. "We'll see."

They turned and walked back to the house. Andi had made up her mind. She was going to tell the garage to find a transmission and fix her old car. She wasn't ready to let it go yet. She just had to figure out how she was going to make some extra money to replenish her savings after she paid for this repair. Now that she'd made a decision, she felt better. But one thing was for certain. She wasn't looking forward to telling Derek her plans.

Chapter Seven

"You're going to what? Are you crazy?" Derek's voice came over the phone line loud and clear. Andi was relieved that there was no one else in the kitchen, because they would have heard him clear across the room.

Andi spoke softly. "I decided it was best to have the transmission replaced so I can continue my drive there. I really don't want to buy another car right now, and I was looking forward to seeing more of the country."

"How long is it going to take?" Derek asked.

Andi bit her lip. "I'm not sure. The guy at the garage said he'd start searching for a rebuilt transmission right away. Then it will have to be shipped here, and then the mechanic can put it in. It may be a week, maybe two. It all depends upon how long it takes to find one."

There was silence on the other end of the line. Andi almost preferred Derek's loud voice to silence. At least she knew what he was thinking when he was talking.

Finally, in a controlled voice, Derek said, "Andi, if this is about money, you know that I offered to buy you a new car when you came out here. I'll be more than happy to. If you'd just forget this silly idea about driving and fly here instead, we can get you a new car by next week."

Andi sighed. Derek just didn't understand. "It's not about money or a new car, Derek. It's about keeping *my* car. I love my car. It's the first one I ever bought and the only thing I was ever able to pay off on my own. You know how hard things were for Carly and me after our parents died. Dealing with all their bills. Having to sell the art gallery and the house. My car is the only thing I've been able to keep all these years. I know it's not much, but it means a lot to me." It surprised her that she had to explain this to Derek over and over again. He'd known her for almost three years, but he still didn't understand. Luke had known her for only two days, and he got it.

"Okay. Fine," Derek said. "But where are you going to stay? At that ranch with strangers? I don't feel comfortable about you staying there."

Derek's tone really irked Andi. Sure, she'd only known the Brennan family for a short time, but she trusted them completely. How dare he question her safety when these wonderful people took her in and have treated her like family? "I feel safe here, Derek, and that's all that counts. Ginny said she'd love to have me stay, so this is where I'm staying."

"Andi, so much has happened to you in the past couple of days, I'm wondering if you're thinking straight," Derek said soothingly. "Maybe I should fly out there this weekend and we can talk face to face. It might be fun. We can get a hotel room and spend some time together. Maybe you'll change your mind then."

Andi's mouth dropped open. Really? He actually believed that if he came here and romanced her then she'd just want to leave her car behind and fly away with him. Hadn't he heard a single word she'd said?

"I know what I'm doing," Andi told him. "I want to keep my car. I promise, I'll be back on the road as soon as it's fixed."

Derek's tone changed from soothing to snide. "Fine. Be stubborn about it. Is it so wrong of me to want you here with me? I miss you, Andi. I was looking forward to you being here. Plus, the bank is giving a welcome reception for me next Friday night, and I had hoped you'd be by my side. We are engaged, after all. Or have you forgotten that?" Derek asked.

Andi looked down at her bare ring finger. Were they engaged? He'd asked her, but hadn't bought her a ring to seal the deal. "No, I haven't forgotten. I'm sorry that I'll miss the reception, but I'll be there for other big moments, okay?"

From the ensuing silence, Andi knew it wasn't okay, but Derek did keep his cool as he finally said goodbye and hung up. She replaced the phone on the handset and sat down on a kitchen chair with a sigh. She and Derek had never really had any reason to fight before this. When they'd met, he'd always been courteous and attentive to her needs. He'd taken her to nice places and wined and dined her like no other man ever had. He hadn't pushed himself on her, and their relationship had grown over time. Sure, he'd never really approved of her sister, but he'd also never said an unkind word about her to Andi. She could tell he didn't like Carly by his reaction to some of the things she said and did. He'd also not been too keen on where they lived, even though their townhouse was very nice and in a good neighborhood. Instead, he'd always sway Andi to stay at his apartment in a more upper class neighborhood. Andi had never fought with him on anything. There had been no need. But now she realized that the reason they'd always gotten along so well was because she'd been so agreeable. Until she'd decided to drive across county. Derek had fought hard against it, but to no avail. At one point, even

Andi had wondered why she'd fought him on it. After all, it would have been much easier to just fly there with him and have her stuff shipped. But she'd been stubborn about this one thing.

Maybe because I didn't want to move to Buffalo in the first place. The thought hit Andi hard. True, she wasn't keen on the idea of moving so far away from her home and her sister. But she loved Derek and wanted to spend the rest of her life with him. Or, at least she thought she did. Wasn't that what all women wanted, eventually? A steady man who would be their partner in life? Someone to share everything with? When Derek proposed, she'd thought she'd wanted all that. Did she still?

Andi heard the back door open and Ginny came in from the mudroom with a basket full of fresh eggs.

"The chickens sure are laying nicely this year," Ginny said as she headed for the sink to rinse off the eggs. "Is everything okay? You look a bit down."

"Derek wasn't happy that I decided to stay and have the car fixed," Andi said.

"I'm sorry, dear. If it makes you feel any better, though, I'm sure happy you're staying. It's nice having you around."

Andi smiled. Ginny was so sweet and kind. It had been a long time since Andi had a mother figure around. She appreciated spending time with Ginny.

"I'm happy to stay, too," Andi told her. "I made the right decision to get my car fixed whether Derek likes it or not."

"I noticed you asked Luke's advice on what you should do. I'm glad you and he are getting along better. I know how prickly he can be sometimes."

Andi stood and walked over to the refrigerator to pour a glass of iced tea. She poured one for Ginny, too, who accepted it with a smile. "I trust Luke's judgment. Maybe even more so, because he can be disagreeable. I knew he'd be honest."

Ginny laughed as both women sat down at the table. "I actually saw him smiling today. It must be because of you. It's rare for Luke to smile."

A serious expression crossed Andi's face. "Why is that? I know it's not my business, but I'm curious. You mentioned before that he's had a hard time of things. What happened?"

Ginny looked thoughtful. "Well, I guess it's really no secret, so it wouldn't hurt to tell you. Luke left home for college right after high school. He's very smart, and he likes working with his hands, so he went to an engineering college in Sacramento. His father, my Jack, thought it was a good idea for Luke to get out into the world a bit and try something new. He didn't want Luke to stay on the ranch unless he really wanted to. So, off Luke went. He really enjoyed college, and he was good at what he did. While he was still in school, he met a beautiful young woman who was also going to college at the time, although it was a different one. Her name was Ashley. She was tall, slender, and had beautiful, long blond hair and blue eyes. And she was very talented. She played the violin and the piano and was a music major in college. Well, Luke fell head over heels in love with her. And she loved him, too, I'm sure." Ginny stopped a moment and sighed.

"Anyway, they were married the minute they both graduated college and moved down to southern California where Luke got a job with Boeing and Ashley taught music at a school for the arts. I know that at that time, Luke would have been happy to return home to work with his dad on the ranch, but Ashley loved California and wanted to stay there. I think she had her hopes set on being in a big symphony orchestra there. They lived there about two years, and that was when we found out that Jack had cancer. It was the swift kind, where you find out one day that you have it, and you have very little time left."

"I'm so sorry," Andi said, remembering the photo of the good-looking man on the mantel. "That must have been devastating."

Ginny patted Andi's arm. "Thank you, dear. It was. Jack was a good man. Anyway, Luke decided it was time to come home. He talked Ashley into moving here and he built her that cute little cabin that Luke lives in now. At first, he thought it would work. She could teach music in the schools here, maybe even private lessons, but after a while, he realized he couldn't hold her here. She missed the big city and all the people. And she was giving up her career to be on the ranch. She only lasted here a year, and then left."

"That's so sad," Andi said, feeling bad for Luke. "Why didn't he follow her?"

"I think Luke felt he belonged here. He loves this ranch, and he's so good at running it. He also loves the quiet of the mountains and the open range. He tried the city, and wasn't happy there. They just weren't meant to be together."

"So, that's why he's angry? Because he lost Ashley?"

"I don't think he's angry as much as he's sad, even lonely. But of course, *real men*," Ginny rolled her eyes, "don't show their emotions, so he hides behind his grouchiness. After Ashley left, Luke didn't even finish up the house. He just put in a generator instead of having electricity hooked up, and he has no phone. I think he just gave up on it. It's a cute little cabin, though. It would make a wonderful place for a family. I keep hoping that someday he'll meet the right girl and he'll be happy again."

He'll have to be a lot friendlier if he wants to find a woman. The thought popped into Andi's head, and then she felt bad.

She hadn't known Luke long enough to pass judgment on him. "I'm surprised someone around here hasn't snatched him up. Or Colt, for that matter. You have some very handsome sons, Ginny. They both belong on the cover of GQ."

Ginny laughed. "Yeah, the Brennan men are a good looking bunch, I'll give you that. But Luke doesn't want just any woman. He needs the right woman. One who'll stand up to him, but also accept him for who he is. And one who'll want to live out here, on a ranch. That's a rare find."

Andi supposed it was, although no one would have had to twist her arm to live here. She was already falling in love with the ranch.

* * *

A while later, armed with her pencils, sketchpad, and camera, Andi went outside to take photos and do some more sketching. The day was beautiful, warm with blue sky and white puffy clouds drifting overhead. Andi walked a short distance from the house and stood a moment, listening. She didn't hear the sound of wood being chopped, so she knew Luke wasn't behind the barn at the woodpile. The biggest horse from the corral was missing, so she thought he might be out riding, checking the property. Bree was also nowhere to be seen. Maybe Bree was with him.

Andi walked up to the corral fence and looked out into the field. Five horses grazed in the outer field. Andi walked along the corral fence to the fence farther away from the barn. She set down her pad and pencils, then climbed up on the rail fence, threw one leg over it, and sat down. From here, she had an amazing view of the field of horses with the hills covered in pines as a backdrop. She lifted the camera from around her neck and began snapping photos, both close ups and distance photos. She thought this view would make a beautiful painting, with the horses lazily grazing and the green hills in the background.

After taking several photos, Andi stepped down off the fence. She walked back to the other side of the barn and down the road that led to Luke's cabin. The cabin looked so cute, set on a hill with a green pasture behind it. The covered porch had a bench swing hanging on one side and a single chair on the other. Andi stood there, trying to imagine Luke sitting in that single chair, alone, staring out into the distance. It made her sad just thinking about it. A man as handsome as Luke shouldn't be alone. If he lived in a big city, he'd be fighting off women with a stick. This thought made her laugh. No, Luke didn't belong in a city. He belonged right here, riding the fences and rounding up cattle like a good cowboy did.

Andi found a grassy spot on a hill that overlooked Luke's cabin and began sketching it. There were patches of yellow and purple wildflowers growing in the grass that surrounded the cabin, adding color to the mostly green surroundings. Andi thought that if it were her home, she'd put flowerpots on the porch with a mixture of brightly colored flowers in them, and maybe even plant some flowering bushes around the edges of the house. And she'd have a little table on the porch with two chairs where she could sit and enjoy her morning coffee as day broke. She could see herself sitting there with her husband, smiling at each other, sharing a private moment before the busy day began. The only problem was that no matter how hard she tried, she couldn't imagine Derek sitting in the other chair. She only saw Luke.

A strong urge to paint a picture of the cabin with its peaceful surroundings hit Andi. It would remind her of her stay at the ranch. Once she left, she might never get a chance to see this place again, so she wanted to remember it exactly as it was.

After Andi had finished her sketch, she took a few photos of the house and the area around it. As she zoomed in her lens on a trail far off in the distance, she recognized the dark brown horse from the corral trotting toward the barn. Luke sat on it, his hat on his head, his strong hands holding the reins. Beside him ran Bree, keeping pace with the horse. As Andi took photos of Luke riding, he turned and looked right at her. Andi pulled the camera away from her face, startled. Even though Luke was far away, it was as if he'd looked her right in the eye. *Geez, he managed to startle me from a distance this time.* Her heart pounding in her chest, Andi picked up her pad and pencils and headed back to the house.

Chapter Eight

Luke was hot, dusty, and thirsty and was looking forward to riding home, cleaning up, and having supper. Now that he knew Andi's car wouldn't be finished for a while and he didn't have to drive her into town, he spent the day riding the fences around the front grazing fields to check for spots that needed repairs. He'd mapped out a few areas that were bad, and in the next few weeks, he, Colt, and Randy would take turns fixing them. Next week, when he was in the summer pasture at the back of the property, he'd do the same. He'd also check on the cattle to make sure they were fine and the new calves were doing well.

As Luke rode toward the barn with Bree running beside him, he looked up toward his cabin and was surprised to see a small figure standing on a hill not far from his house. Even at this distance, he knew instantly by the shape of the figure and the way it moved that it was Andi. *How can I know her so well after only a couple of days?* He wondered why she'd been near the cabin. Then, he wondered if she'd been sketching it. If she had, he surely wanted to see it.

A small smile played on his lips as he thought about this

afternoon. Andi had asked his opinion about her car. That had surprised, and truthfully, delighted him. She trusted his opinion. Although, she'd known all along what she wanted to do, just talking to him helped her make up her mind. He liked that. She could have asked anyone on the ranch, but she'd asked him.

Andi had disappeared by the time he'd ridden his horse, Chance, to the barn. He supposed she was in the house, helping his mom make supper. In just two days, Andi had already made a place for herself in his mother's home and in her heart. She certainly wasn't a slouch or a diva city girl. She pitched right in and helped where she was needed. Luke admired her for that. The only problem was the more she ingrained herself into their lives, the more she'd be missed when she left. Luke didn't like that thought at all.

Luke put the horse's saddle and bridle away and brushed him down before leading him into the corral. He decided he needed a little cleaning up himself before supper. He didn't want to smell like dirt and horse sweat. He hopped into his truck and headed to his cabin for a quick shower and change of clothes.

* * *

Andi was helping Ginny finish washing the last of the supper dishes when Luke walked into the kitchen. Colt had left with Randy to go to a local bar to shoot pool. Normally, Luke joined them on a Friday night, but tonight he'd declined. Both women looked up as Luke entered the room.

Luke cleared his throat. "We have a couple of hours of sunlight left if you're still interested in riding," he said, looking at Andi.

"Sure," Andi replied. "Let me go grab a sweatshirt from my room and I'll be right down." She looked at her sneakers. "I'm afraid I don't have riding boots, though. It's kind of tough riding in these."

Ginny spoke up. "I'll bet there's a pair in the back porch that will fit you. I'll get them for you while you get your sweatshirt."

"I'll go saddle up two horses," Luke said, turning to leave.

"Wait," Andi said, making Luke turn back and stare at her. "I can saddle my own horse if you just give me a moment."

Luke shrugged. "Okay."

Andi ran upstairs and rifled through her things to find a sweatshirt. She knew it cooled down in the evenings here, and she didn't want to get chilled. She tied it around her waist then took a quick glance in the mirror. Her ponytail was coming undone and looked terrible. She quickly took a brush to her hair to smooth it down as best she could and pulled it back with a band. It wasn't great, but it would have to do. After all, she was just going riding, not on a date.

Ginny had a new pair of riding boots sitting on the floor by the table when Andi came downstairs. "Try these on," she told Andi. "Hopefully, they'll fit."

Luke leaned against the doorframe between the mudroom and the kitchen with his arms crossed. He looked like a hunky cowboy in an advertisement for blue jeans. He glared at the boots. "I'll wait outside," he announced, and then walked out the door.

Andi looked up at Ginny. "Were these Ashley's?"

Ginny nodded. "He'll get over it. No sense in these going to waste when someone can actually use them."

Andi slipped off her sneakers and pulled on one of the brown riding boots. It fit fairly well. She pulled on the other one.

"How's the fit?" Ginny asked.

"Fine."

"Good. They'll be better once you break them in," Ginny said.

Andi laughed. "That would take a lot of wearing."

Ginny winked. "Hopefully, you'll do a lot of riding while you're here."

Andi looked at her and smiled. "Yeah. Hopefully, I will."

"You go and have a nice ride. I'll see you later, Andi," Ginny told her.

Andi walked out the door and joined up with Luke at the bottom of the steps. He turned and walked down to the barn. Andi followed.

"So, you think you can saddle your own horse, huh?" Luke asked as they entered the barn. "You know these saddles weigh up to forty pounds."

"I can manage. I've saddled a horse many times before."

"Okay," Luke said. "I had Randy bring up a couple of horses from the pasture. What are you used to riding?"

"Anything that isn't short, slow, and fat," Andi said. "I like mine tall, fast, and spunky."

Luke turned and stared at Andi with one eyebrow raised. "Are we still talking about horses?"

Andi felt her face heat up. "You have a dirty mind, Luke Brennan," she said.

Luke chuckled. "I was just making sure. How about the mare you were sketching the other day? Is she tall enough for you?"

Andi nodded and Luke headed out to the corral and led in both the mare and his stallion, Chance. He tied the horses up a few feet apart so they'd have room to saddle them.

"There are your blanket, saddle, and bridle," Luke said,

pointing to where they hung over a rail near a stall. "Have at it."

Andi walked up to the horse and rubbed her hand down her face, then down her neck so the mare knew who was touching her and wouldn't startle. "What's her name?"

"Abby."

"Abby," Andi repeated. "Cute. Did you name her?"

Luke was busy saddling his own horse. "Nope. Colt did. He broke her, too."

"Hi, Abby," Andi said softly as she rubbed her hands along the top of the horse's back and its side where the saddle would sit.

"What are you doing?" Luke asked, staring at her.

"Checking to make sure there are no burrs or rough spots where the saddle sits that might get irritated. I don't want to sit on her and get thrown."

"Hmmm," Luke said. "Smart."

Andi grinned. "Learned that during my riding lessons."

Luke rolled his eyes. "Riding lessons," he said sarcastically. "But it's a smart idea."

Andi chuckled. She picked up the folded blanket and laid it across the horse's back, smoothing it out. The horse's back was at chin level for Andi. "How tall is Abby?"

"Sixteen hands. You said you wanted tall. Want me to toss up the saddle for you?"

"Nope. I'm fine," Andi said. She walked over to the leather saddle and picked up the stirrup and cinch strap on the right side, laying them up over the top of the saddle. Grasping the back and front of the saddle, Andi lifted it. It was heavy, but she could manage it. She walked over to Abby, swung the saddle back a little for momentum, then smoothly swung it up and onto the horse's back.

"Good job," Luke said.

Andi smiled. "Told you I could do it."

Luke shook his head and went back to working on his own horse.

Andi smoothed out the blanket under the saddle, then made sure no part of the saddle was turned under. Then she reached underneath the horse and grasped the strap, pulled in up under the horse's belly and through the cinch ring.

"You might have to…" Luke began to say, but stopped as he watched Andi.

She pulled the strap tight, and then nudged her knee into the horse's stomach to make her suck in so Andi could pull the strap just a little tighter.

"Oh, I guess you know that, too," Luke said.

"Yep. I don't want the saddle loosening up as we ride so I fall off," Andi said. She threaded the cinch strap up and around the ring, and then through the strap again to create a smooth knot. She wiggled the saddle to test it. It was firmly in place.

Next, Andi picked up the bridle and walked up to Abby's head. She held the bit with her left hand and the top straps that went around the ears with her right. Carefully, she placed the bit to Abby's mouth and pulled it up and around her ears before the horse could clamp down her teeth to stop the bit from going in. Andi strapped the bridle on, checked to make sure it fit okay, then took the reins and wrapped them around the saddle horn until she was ready to use them.

Luke was finished saddling his horse and had been watching Andi. "You're right. You know what you're doing. Now, let's see if you can ride."

"Don't worry, I can ride," Andi said. With Abby still tied to the fence, Andi put her left foot in the stirrup and pulled herself up into the saddle. She tried the other stirrup, but they both were set too high.

"I think I need to make these a little longer," she said, and was just about to slide off the horse when Luke came over and touched her right leg.

"Just stay there," he told her. "I'll fix them."

Andi pulled her right foot from the stirrup and moved her leg back so Luke could unbuckle the strap and lower it down to the next set of holes. When he was done, he put his hand on Andi's leg and guided it into the stirrup. He walked over to the left side and did the same. His hand was warm on her leg as he moved her foot back into place, adjusting her boot to fit perfectly in the stirrup.

"How does that feel?" he asked, taking a step away.

Andi's thoughts were still on how nice his hand had felt on her leg when he spoke. "What? Huh?"

"The stirrups. How do they feel?"

She stretched her legs and moved around in the saddle a moment to get a feel for them. "Perfect. Thanks."

Luke unhooked the lead rope from Abby, and then did the same for his horse. He pulled himself up into the saddle. "Let me lead out of the barn," he told Andi. "Abby hasn't been ridden in a while, so she might be a bit anxious. She'll follow Chance, though."

Luke took the lead and Andi followed. The horses walked slowly out of the barn. Once outside, Luke pointed to a well-worn trail that led up the hill to a grove of trees, far into the distance. "We'll head up there. By the time we make it to the trees, we'll have to turn around and come back. It's a pretty view from up there, though."

Andi nodded and soon they were riding side-by-side up the trail.

Andi inhaled deeply, enjoying the fresh, mountain air. It felt good to be riding again. She hadn't ridden for a couple of years because she rarely had the extra money to spend on trail rides. It was different here, though. Better. She wasn't riding with a group of people and she was free to walk, trot, or gallop if she so desired. Abby kept shaking her head from time to time, and Andi knew it meant she wanted free rein, but Andi held the reins firmly so Abby wouldn't take off in a sprint. Andi had asked for a horse with spunk, and she could tell that Abby was exactly the type of horse she enjoyed riding.

After a time, Andi asked, "Tell me the story behind Colt's name. Your mom said it's Cole, but you've always called him Colt. Why?"

Luke smiled and looked over at Andi. "Colt is eight years younger than me. When he was just learning to walk, he had these long, spindly legs and kept falling down. I said he looked like a newborn colt trying to learn to walk. From that moment on, we just started calling him Colt. My mom hated it at first, but my dad really liked it. I think if it had been up to him, they would have changed Colt's name on his birth certificate."

"Aw, so that's it. Well, now it makes sense. Colt seems to fit him, though, since he's tall and shy," Andi said.

"What about you?" Luke asked. "Andi must be short for another name."

Andi nodded. "You'd never guess what it's short for."

Luke looked thoughtful. "Andrea?"

"Nope."

"Adrianne?"

Andi shook her head. "No, but you're close. My full name is Adrianna. My dad's name was Adrian and my mom had a flare for the dramatic, so she named me Adrianna. Luckily, when Carly started talking she couldn't say my name so she called me Andi and that stuck."

"Adrianna. I like that. It's pretty. It suits you," Luke said.

Andi rolled her eyes. "Thanks. But I prefer Andi."

"So, if you're named after your dad, then who is Carly named after?"

Andi gave a little laugh. "My mom named her after her favorite singer growing up. Carly Simon. You know, the woman who sang "You're So Vain.""

Luke smiled. "I guess your mom did have a flair for the dramatic. So, can Carly sing?"

"Not my Carly. She can't hold a tune to save her life."

Luke sobered. "My mom says your parents died a while back. Do you mind if I ask what happened?"

Andi's smile faded. "They were in a car accident, driving one night on a curvy coastal road. No one knows how it happened. It could have been a wet patch on the road, or another car may have made them swerve. They just lost control and rolled the car. It happened when I was eighteen, right after I'd graduated from high school. Carly was fourteen. It was devastating."

"I'm sorry. I shouldn't have asked."

Andi shook her head. "No, it's okay. It was over ten years ago. We just had it rough for a long time after that."

"How'd you manage? Did they leave you some money? An insurance policy or something?"

"No, unfortunately, they didn't. What they left behind was a lot of debt." Andi sighed. She hadn't told anyone her story in a long time. "My parents liked living the high life. Growing up, I just figured they made enough money to live that way. We lived in a big house in an expensive neighborhood. They drove expensive cars. And they owned the art gallery where I sell my paintings now. My parents encouraged us to try everything that we wanted to. They both felt that experiences were the best way to learn. We took dance lessons, tennis lessons, and of course, riding lessons, whatever we wanted. When I started showing a talent for drawing, my parents made sure I took drawing and painting lessons at a local art studio. I was actually supposed to go to an art school in Paris, France, after high school, but all that ended the day my parents died. I soon found out that they owed money on everything, so much money that I had to sell the house, the cars, and even the art gallery just to pay everything off."

Luke frowned. "That's awful. I'm so sorry, Andi."

"Thanks. It was tough at first, but it worked out in the end. I had enough money to buy a small townhouse for Carly and I to live in, and I was able to pay for my college, and then Carly's college. Since our name had always been attached to the art gallery, the person who bought it let me work there while I went to school and also sells my paintings, too. Carly worked there while she went to college and now she manages it for them. She has a degree in business management, and art just runs in the blood, so she's very good at selling artwork. We did okay, but it was a lot of work."

Luke nodded. "And then your boyfriend came along and swept you off your feet?"

Andi stared at Luke a moment. She couldn't tell if he was teasing or being sarcastic. "Not exactly. But we started dating and slowly grew close. Derek's a hard worker. He's very ambitious. He put himself through Stanford and earned his MBA. At thirty, he's already on the fast track at the bank. He's sure to be head of a large bank in the next few years. That's why they sent him to Buffalo. It's just a stopping point before sending him off to an even bigger branch."

"Well, that sounds nice," Luke said softly.

Andi glanced at him. "You say that, but it doesn't sound like you mean it."

Luke shrugged. "It sounds perfect for him, but what about you? You're an artist. I would assume you like to be surrounded by beauty and peacefulness. Like the ocean and the countryside around Seattle, or the mountains here at the ranch. How are you going to like living the big city lifestyle in a few years?"

Andi thought about Luke's words a moment. Even though she'd wondered the very same thing, it somehow irked her that he'd said it out loud. *He barely knows me. How can he judge how I feel about it?*

"Derek's a good man. He'll make a good life for us. I'm sure I'll adapt just fine," Andi said sharply.

Luke continued staring straight ahead. "I'm sure you will," he said.

Andi glared at him, but didn't say another word.

By this point, they'd almost made it to the hilltop. "We should turn around and head back," Luke said. "It'll be dark soon."

They turned their horses around and stopped a moment. Andi let out a small gasp at the view before her. It was beautiful. No, more than beautiful. It was breathtaking. The hills and valleys below them were a colorful array of greens and tans sprinkled with a rainbow of wildflowers. The Clark Fork River that followed the highway sparkled like glitter as it snaked its way through the valley. Above, the sky was a brilliant blue with streaks of red and orange running through it as the sun made its way down to the top of the hills. Andi was used to beautiful landscapes, because Seattle was surrounded by beauty, but this was different. This view told the tale of wide-open spaces and untamed wilderness. It was magnificent.

"I told you it was a pretty view," Luke said, grinning.

Andi forgot all about being mad at Luke and turned to him with wide eyes. "This is more than pretty. This is breathtaking. I wish I'd brought my camera along. I'd love to paint this view. No, I *have* to paint this view."

"We can come here as often as you like," Luke said. "Every night, if you want."

Andi gave Luke a brilliant smile. "That sounds wonderful."

After absorbing the beauty of the landscape for a little longer, they finally walked their horses down the trail to flatter ground. Abby kept shaking her head, still not tired from the long walk.

Luke pointed to Abby and laughed. "I think she's anxious to let loose. Are you ready for a little run?"

Andi nodded. "I'll follow you," she said. "Let her loose."

Luke clicked his tongue and Chance sprinted off. Abby didn't wait to be told to run, she took off after Chance in a gallop. It only took Andi a minute to acclimate to Abby's stride and soon she was riding easily as the powerful horse stretched its legs and ran like the wind.

After a time, Luke pulled Chance to a trot, and Andi did the same with Abby. The horses were breathing heavily from their run. By the time they drew close to the barn, both horses were walking again. It was a little after nine o'clock and the sun was almost down. Luke pulled Chance up to the corral fence and slipped off, then held Abby's bridle while Andi stepped down, too.

"Thank you, Luke," Andi said, looking up at him. He was standing close, holding the bridles of both horses. "It was an amazing ride and such a beautiful view."

"Like I said, we can do this every evening if you like. Next time you can bring your camera along. And I'll try not to make you angry. I seem to do that a lot."

"Don't worry about it," Andi said. They stood there a moment as the night sky began to encircle them. Luke stood so close, Andi could smell his aftershave. She smiled a small smile. He had actually cleaned up before supper again even though he knew he'd be out riding.

"Here," she said, lifting her hand to grasp Abby's bridle. "I'll help you with the horses." Their hands grazed and their eyes met once more. There was only one word to describe Luke's blue eyes tonight. Intense. *Goodness, he's a gorgeous man.* Andi couldn't get over how incredibly hot he was.

"No. It's getting late. You go ahead in the house and I'll take care of them," Luke said huskily.

"Are you sure?"

Luke nodded. "Go on inside. I'll see you tomorrow."

Andi reluctantly released her hand from the bridle and took a step back. "Okay. Thanks, Luke. Goodnight." She turned and walked slowly back to the house. She was tempted to turn around and glance at Luke once more, standing there between those two powerful horses. But she knew if she did, he'd still be staring at her with that intense gaze. She wasn't sure if she was strong enough to not run back to him if she looked into those eyes for another second.

Chapter Nine

Luke watched Andi walk into the house, and then led the horses into the barn. He tied up each horse and began unsaddling Abby first. As he worked, he thought of Andi. He'd told her to go inside, because he hadn't trusted himself to stand beside her for one more second. She was everything he'd ever thought a woman should be. Beautiful, strong, opinionated, funny, and stubborn. Yes, even stubborn. Because any woman who was going to deal with a Brennan man had to know how to hold her ground, and Andi did that well.

Luke sighed as he finished with Abby and then began taking off Chance's saddle. Andi was a born and raised city girl, yet she didn't mind getting her hands dirty or letting her hair fall out of place as she rode like the wind across a field. She was just so damned sexy, it drove Luke crazy. Even when only moments before he'd practically insulted her, she'd turned to him with those beautiful, green eyes, wide with admiration over the beauty of the view from the hill and made his heart melt. She said the view was breathtaking, but all he saw was the way her lovely eyes sparkled and her face glowed with excitement. She was breathtaking. So much so, he'd nearly reached over to pull her to him and kiss her passionately on those luscious full lips. *Dear God, now he was thinking words like luscious.*

Luke went to the tack room in the barn and grabbed a horse brush, then walked over to Abby and quickly brushed her down. He had to stop thinking about Andi. Geez, he'd only known her for less than three days and yet it felt as if he'd known her forever. How could that be? He'd told Randy and Colt to leave her be because she was engaged to another man, and he had better follow his own advice. He was glad he'd decided to leave for the summer pasture on Monday, that way he'd have a few days to cool off and clear his head. Because thinking like he was about Andi wasn't going to get him anything but a broken heart. He'd already had one of those. He didn't want to go through that again.

* * *

The next morning, Andi had breakfast as usual with Ginny, Randy, and Colt. Luke had already eaten earlier, as he usually did. Even though it was Saturday, the ranch still ran like clockwork. The animals still needed caring for no matter what day of the week it was, so there were no days off for a rancher.

All through breakfast, Andi had a hard time concentrating on the conversation around her. Last night, she'd lay in bed for a long time thinking about her ride with Luke, and especially how he'd looked right before she'd come inside. She could have sworn he was on the verge of kissing her as they stood there between the horses. The worst part was that she'd kind of hoped he would. She knew it was terrible of her. After all, she was engaged to Derek. But standing there, staring up into those amazing blue eyes set in that chiseled face, his hat cocked to one side, he'd been the epitome of the hot cowboy. Handsome and hard to resist.

Andi remembered what she'd said about the type of horse she'd wanted, and mentally rolled her eyes at herself. *I like mine tall, fast, and spunky.* When Luke had asked if she was still talking about horses with that sly grin on his face, she could have died of embarrassment. Tall, fast, and spunky could have described him to a tee. Add in powerful and irresistible, too. Thinking that way, it was no wonder she'd had a hard time falling asleep.

Sure, Luke had questioned her relationship with Derek, and that had ticked her off. But all was forgiven as he'd looked over at her with those gorgeous eyes when they were at the top of the hill and she'd seen the amazing view for the first time. How could she be angry with him for saying out loud what she'd been thinking herself? She had no idea if she was going to be able to acclimate to city living in a place like Manhattan, if Derek was sent there as promised after Buffalo. The fact that Luke seemed to have already guessed that about her, after such a short time, unnerved her.

After breakfast, Andi and Ginny sat at the kitchen table and began labeling the jars of jam and tying ribbons made up from strips of red, blue, and yellow calico fabric around the lids.

"You have to make them look countrified," Ginny said with a laugh. "That's what people expect, so that's what we give them."

They labeled and tied ribbons on dozens of jars. Ginny had made strawberry, strawberry-rhubarb, raspberry, and blackberry jam. Andi was amazed at how many jars there were.

"Do you really sell this many jars?" she asked.

Ginny nodded. "I do. And I haven't even made my canned peaches yet. I have a shipment of peaches coming in on Monday at the co-op in Alberton. Next week we'll be canning quarts of peaches to keep and to sell."

Andi wondered if Ginny really needed the money her preserves brought in or if she just did it every year because she'd always done it. She wasn't going to insult Ginny by asking, though.

When they'd finally finished decorating the jars, Ginny went off to her office to do some paperwork so Andi decided to go outside with her sketchpad and camera.

It was another beautiful summer day on the ranch. Andi was used to rain in Seattle, and she wondered how often it rained here. She had thought that being up in such high elevation, it would be damper, but it wasn't. The weather was pleasant and warm.

She walked away from the house toward the trail that she and Luke had ridden on last night. Her leg muscles were sore, especially her thighs. Her body wasn't used to riding, and it told her so today. But she didn't care. She knew that the more she rode, the more used to it she'd become and soon the soreness would subside.

Andi had no idea where the men were today. Colt and Randy had been talking about mending fences in the lower pastures, but she didn't know exactly where that was. Andi stopped a moment and looked out into the horse pasture to see if Luke's horse was there. It wasn't. She supposed he was off riding somewhere, doing whatever it was cowboys did.

After walking a short distance, Andi turned and looked down at the ranch house. From here, she saw the cute little barn that held the chickens and the house not far from there. Beyond the house, in the distance, were the hilltops covered in pines. Andi raised her camera from the strap around her neck and snapped a few pictures from different angles. She thought it might be fun to paint the house and landscape around it. Once she settled in Buffalo, she'd have plenty of time to paint, and she knew she wanted to paint several scenes from the ranch. She had no idea if there was a market for such artwork, since she was used to painting pictures of the ocean and seaside areas, but she didn't think it would hurt to try. And she didn't care. If for no other reason, she wanted the paintings for herself to remind her of her time spent here.

After taking a few snapshots, Andi found a place to sit down in the soft grass and opened her sketchpad. She looked first at her sketch of Abby stretching her neck through the fence. She turned the page and there was the sketch of Luke. She thought maybe she should pull this one out of her pad and put it away. God forbid if Luke should accidently see it. Or Derek, for that matter. Either way it would embarrass the heck out of her. But holy cow, did he ever look like a hunk in this drawing.

Andi quickly turned the page and there was the sketch of Luke's cabin. It was so cute, sitting there with the wild flowers blooming around it. She wondered what it looked like inside, in the light of day. She'd only seen a little of it, and now she was curious about it. Maybe she'd ask Luke for a tour. Maybe not. She'd have to think about that first.

Finally, Andi got to a blank page and began softly running the charcoal pencil over the entire page to prepare it. Once the page was completely filled, she began outlining the house, chicken coop, and the hilltops. Drawing came naturally to Andi and she drew quickly, adding a line here, smudging a shadow there. She used an eraser like a pencil, creating lighter shading with it by erasing areas. It wasn't long before the house came to life on the page and the chickens were pecking in their caged yard around their tiny barn. Andi was concentrating so hard on her work, she didn't hear the footsteps coming up behind her.

"What'cha drawing today?" Luke asked, looking over her shoulder.

Andi jumped at the sound of his voice. She turned and looked up at Luke grinning down at her.

"Must you always sneak up behind me?" she asked sharply.

"I wasn't sneaking. I walked right up to you, crunching gravel and everything. You were just so involved with your sketching, you didn't hear me."

"Where did you come from?" Andi asked, looking around. "I didn't see Chance in the field, so I thought you were out riding fences or something."

Luke raised one inquisitive eyebrow. "So, you were keeping tabs on where I was?"

"No. I just figured if Chance was gone, then you were on him."

"Mmmm hmmm," Luke said.

"Don't mmmm hmmm me. I don't give a damn where you are all day. I just noticed your horse was gone, that's all," Andi said, irritated.

Luke smiled wide, showing perfectly straight, white teeth. Andi hadn't noticed how perfect they were before. She wondered if he'd had braces as a kid. Had he always been this cute? Maybe he'd been an ugly child who'd grown into a handsome prince. If the universe was fair, he had to have something wrong with him, because standing there right now in his blue jeans and white T-shirt, he looked too good to be true.

"Colt is riding Chance today. He's out with Randy, working on fences. Randy drove the truck with all the equipment.

I was just at the tool barn putting a few things away." Luke pointed over behind a copse of oak and maple trees.

"Oh, well that explains your sneaking around then," Andi said.

Luke crouched down beside Andi and looked at her drawing. "Can I see it?" he asked, holding his hand out.

Andi hesitated. It always unnerved her when someone looked at one of her unfinished drawings or paintings. "Well, okay. But don't get it dirty," she said.

Luke glanced at her charcoal smudged hand. "I don't think I could be any dirtier than you are," he said with a chuckle.

Andi looked down at her dirty hand and grimaced. She hoped she hadn't rubbed her face accidently or else he'd be trying to clean off the smudges like the other day. "Here." She handed him the sketchpad.

Luke looked at the sketch for a minute. "This is really good. I don't know how you get so much detail with just a pencil, but you manage to make the picture come alive."

"Thank you," Andi said softly. "It's not finished yet, though."

"It still looks good to me." Luke held the pad with one hand and used his other hand to pull the last page over and look at the sketch from the other day. "You drew my cabin," he said, sounding surprised. "So that's what you were doing the other day. I saw you when I was riding home on the trail."

Andi nodded. "It's such a cute house, I couldn't resist. Hope you don't mind."

Luke shook his head. "No. Not at all. It looks wonderful."

"I was hoping that someday you would show me the inside. I didn't see much of it that night I knocked on your door and I'm curious about what it looks like."

"Sure," Luke said. "Any time."

He reached for the next sheet of paper to turn it over and that's when Andi realized she had to get the pad out of his hands, fast.

"Here, give me that," she said, reaching for the pad, but just like a little kid not willing to give up his new toy, Luke pulled it out of her reach.

"I want to see the others," he said, teasing, and flipped the sheet of paper over. He stared at the drawing a moment before realization of who it was crossed over his face.

Andi covered her eyes with her hand. *Oh, God. This is so embarrassing.*

Luke looked over at Andi. "Is this me?"

Andi bit her lip. "Well, yeah, kind of."

"Is this how you see me?" Luke asked, staring at the half naked drawing.

Andi's face felt flushed. She knew it must look as red as it felt. "No. That's how you look," she said.

Luke continued to stare at the picture. "So, you were staring at me while I was chopping wood the other day?"

"Well, yeah. So?"

"When did I lean against the barn shirtless, looking like this? Like some kind of male stripper."

Andi reached out and snatched the sketchpad away from Luke. "It's just a sketch. I just used you as the model, okay? And you don't look like a male stripper in this. It's art."

Luke stared at her a moment, a deep crease between his brows. Slowly, his expression turned from serious to sly. A deep chuckle vibrated from his chest as he stood. "Okay. Whatever you say." He winked at her then turned and headed toward the barn.

Anger rose inside Andi. She stood and yelled at his retreating back. "Don't get so full of yourself, Luke Brennan.

You're not so special. I sketched dozens of male bodies in art class. Some were even nude." The moment the words left her mouth, Andi realized how ridiculous she sounded. Luke had stopped a moment and turned to flash a grin at her. Andi heard another loud chuckle come from him before he entered the barn.

Angrily, Andi picked up her things and headed toward the house. *Damn that Luke Brennan. What the hell does he know about art?*

Ginny had come outside with a basket and was heading toward the chicken coop to collect eggs. When Andi passed her, she asked, "What did I hear about nudes?"

Andi stopped walking and closed her eyes. *Could this get any more embarrassing?* She turned and looked at Ginny. "That son of yours can be so infuriating."

Ginny shrugged and grinned.

Andi stormed off into the house.

Chapter Ten

That evening it was only the four of them sitting around the kitchen table at supper eating grilled steak, fried potatoes, and home canned string beans. Randy hadn't joined them for supper, which made it even harder for Andi to ignore Luke as they ate. He just kept looking at her with that wicked grin of his that she wanted to slap off his face. Instead, she dived into her food with a vengeance. It wasn't hard to do. The steak was delicious. Living on a cattle ranch had its perks and fresh beef was one of them. Andi had never been much of a meat eater before, but here, she was slowly becoming a meat lover.

"Are you boys heading over to The Depot tonight like you usually do on Saturday?" Ginny asked as she served home-made apple pie for dessert.

Luke looked up and began to shake his head no, but Colt stopped him when he blurted out. "Yeah, we should. We can take Andi." Colt looked at Andi, his baby blues wide and sparkling. "Want to go dancing, Andi?"

Andi sat there, not knowing how to respond. Luke watched her with a serious look on his face. She ignored him. "What's The Depot?"

"It's a restaurant, bar, dance hall all rolled into one down the road about two miles from here," Colt piped up. They always have a band on Saturday nights, so we go there to dance. Randy is usually there, too."

"Ah, so that's where you meet all the pretty ladies and dance with them," Andi said teasingly, looking over at Luke. He glared back at her.

"You'd be the prettiest girl there, Andi," Colt said. "If you come along, I'll teach you how to line dance."

Andi smiled at Colt. She didn't want to dampen his excitement, but the last thing she wanted to do was go dancing, especially if Luke was going. "I don't know..." she began to say, but Luke interrupted her.

"Colt, stop bothering Andi. A city girl like her wouldn't enjoy a silly old country bar like The Depot."

Andi watched as Colt's excitement deflated. She glared back at Luke before turning to smile at Colt. "Sure, why not? It sounds like fun."

Colt's face lit up again.

Andi turned to stare at Luke and watched as he sat back in his chair and crossed his arms. *City girl, huh?*

"Are you coming along, Luke?" Colt asked. He finished the last bite of his pie.

Luke continued to stare at Andi. "Guess I'll come along for a while."

Andi and Luke just sat there having a stare off. Colt was so excited about bringing Andi to The Depot, he didn't notice. Ginny, however, watched them with interest.

"Well, isn't that nice," Ginny said. "You all will have such a fun time."

* * *

A little after eight o'clock, the three of them hopped into Luke's truck and headed down the highway. Andi sat in the middle of the truck's bench seat between Luke and Colt. She really hadn't wanted to come along, but after Luke's *city girl* comment, she'd been bound and determined to prove him wrong. Now, she sat there trying to keep her distance from both of them as the truck bounced down the highway.

Before leaving, Colt had told her that this was a cowboy hangout, so jeans and boots were a must. Andi wanted to blend in and not draw unnecessary attention to herself, so she'd worn her jeans, a white, cotton, button down shirt, and her riding boots. Colt looked adorable in his best Levi's, a blue plaid shirt that brought out the color of his eyes, and a brown felt cowboy hat that looked so new Andi guessed it was his dress hat. He'd showered, so his blond hair was shiny clean and he smelled lightly of fresh aftershave. She knew it was Colt's aftershave she smelled because Luke's had a distinctive spicy scent to it. Luke, of course, looked hunky no matter what he wore, and tonight he had on a black, button down shirt with his blue jeans. He also wore a new black hat instead of the usual dusty one he wore when he worked. Andi wasn't used to men wearing hats on a regular basis, but here, it just seemed to fit.

After a quick drive, Luke turned off on an exit and drove down a short hill. At the bottom was The Depot. Andi recognized it as the place she'd passed right before her car had broken down. A tall sign was lit up with the bar's name so it could be seen from the highway. There were trucks and cars parked everywhere, so Luke circled the parking lot before finding a spot to park a short walk from the entrance. Colt hopped out and then gave Andi his hand to help her down. Andi had to smile. Colt was a true cowboy gentleman.

The three of them walked up to the wooden steps to a narrow, outdoor porch with Colt leading the way. Standing on the porch, Andi heard the sounds of people talking and laughing inside and pool cues hitting balls. Colt opened the screen door and the interior door, and then stood aside to let Andi walk through ahead of him.

Andi entered the bar and looked around. From the outside, the place didn't look like much, but inside, it was actually very nice. The walls were a honey-colored wood decorated with western paraphernalia. She saw lariats, spurs, wagon wheels, and horseshoes, as well as western style paintings. Wooden tables and chairs sat to the right on the gleaming oak floor. Beyond that was a room with a dance floor in front of a stage where the four-piece band had set up. To her left was an antique bar that looked like it came from another century. It was long and curved at one end and made of polished oak with leather decorating the front. Wooden, padded stools stood in front of it and a large mirror hung behind it. Glasses of all styles sat on shelves in front of the mirror, and there were old, gold-trimmed hand pulls used to draw the many brands of beer they served. In the back of the room sat three pool tables.

The place was streaming with people already and most of the tables were occupied. There were a couple of open booths by the sidewall, so Luke led Andi there and the three of them sat down. Andi chose to sit next to Colt.

"I'll go get the drinks," Luke said. "What would you like, Andi?"

"Whatever you two are drinking," Andi said. She didn't drink alcohol often, but she didn't want to seem like a lightweight.

"Beer?" Luke asked.

Andi nodded.

"The band should start soon," Colt said. "I hope you like country music."

Andi smiled at him. "I'm not really familiar with country music, but it will be fun to listen to a live band," she told him.

Andi looked around the room. Luke was at the bar, waiting for the beer. There were plenty of women of all ages here, as well as men. Some younger women wore short jean skirts and clingy, low-cut T-shirts with cowboy boots and hats. The men wore their best jeans and shirts. Big belt buckles flashed everywhere. Andi noticed a few women staring at Luke, and a bleached blond in a tiny skirt strode up to him and started talking. She imagined that women flocked to him in a place like this. Probably to Colt, too. Maybe she was biased, but they were the cutest men in the bar.

Across the way, Andi saw Randy sitting with a young brunette whose jeans looked painted on. Andi smiled and waved, and he waved back. The brunette just frowned at her.

"Here we go," Luke said, bringing Andi's attention back to the table. He set down three big mugs of golden beer.

Andi took a sip. It tasted pretty good. Beside her, Colt guzzled down almost half. Andi stared at him with raised brows.

"Take it easy, Colt," Luke said. "Pace yourself, okay?"

Colt set his beer down and rolled his eyes at Luke. "Killjoy." He looked over at Andi. "Want to play pool?"

Andi glanced over to where the pool tables sat. There were several burly-looking cowboys playing on all three of them. "Maybe later," she said. "You go ahead, though."

Colt sat there a moment, looking like he wasn't sure if he should leave the table so soon. But the fun of a good game of pool won out. "I'll be back as soon as the band starts," he said.

He picked up his beer and was gone as fast as his long legs could carry him across the room.

"Well, that didn't last long," Luke said.

"What?"

"He's the one who invited you and off he goes right away," Luke said. "Good thing I came along."

"Oh, yeah. Lucky me," Andi said. "Please, don't feel you have to babysit me. If you want to go sit with that bleached blond by the bar, go right ahead. This *city girl* can take care of herself."

Luke glanced over at the bar, grimaced, and then looked back at Andi. "I'm not really into blonds, bleached or otherwise."

"Oh? So what are you into, Luke Brennan?" Andi asked, her eyes glinting with mischief.

Luke's blue eyes flashed wickedly as he leaned his elbows on the table and drew up closer to Andi. "I'm not sure, but definitely not redheads. They're too volatile."

Andi quickly sat back in her seat and frowned. "You are infuriating."

Luke chuckled, sat back, and took another drink of his beer.

The band started up with a slow country song to get the couples out on the dance floor. Luke did not ask Andi to dance. Occasionally, men passed by the table to say hello or nod to Luke. A few women did the same. Andi supposed since Luke came here often, he knew most of the people in the room, male and female alike.

The band played a livelier tune and then slowed it down again. Randy showed up beside their table. "Hey there, Andi. Would you like to dance?"

"No, she's sitting this one out," Luke answered for her.

Andi's mouth dropped open at the gall of him to answer for her. "Yes, Randy. I'd love to," she said, standing up and allowing him to lead her to the dance floor. She turned and glared at Luke who looked like he'd just sucked on a lemon.

Randy took her hand in his and placed his other hand on her back. They began dancing slowly to the music. Andi was used to seeing Randy in his work clothes, dusty and dirty, but tonight he'd cleaned up nicely. He wasn't as tall as Luke, but he was tall enough, and he had tiny lines creased around his warm brown eyes when he smiled. He was a nice looking man, not in the hot cowboy sense like Luke, but more in the ruggedly good looking category.

"I'd noticed Luke hadn't asked you to dance yet," Randy said. "I hope you don't mind me asking you to."

"Not at all," Andi told him. "Luke's just being his usual crabby self. I don't think he wanted me to come here in the first place. It was Colt's idea that I come."

"Ah. Well, that makes sense. Luke's probably afraid he won't be able to keep all the men away from you."

Andi laughed. "Oh, please. Men don't flock to me."

"I beg to differ," Randy said, twirling her around. "Are you enjoying your stay at the ranch?"

"Yes. More than I'd ever have imagined. Ginny is a sweetheart, and I love helping her. And being able to ride is fun, too. I've only been here a few days and I know I'm going to miss it when I leave."

"Well, you're surely going to be missed, too," Randy said. "And by someone in particular." He nodded his head in Luke's direction.

Andi looked up at him quizzically. "Luke? No, he'll definitely be glad to get me out of his hair."

Randy grinned. "I don't know. He's been wound up tighter

than a spring since you showed up at his door. I've never seen him so uptight."

Andi shook her head. "If he is, it's not because of me. Unless it's because I annoy him that much."

The song ended and Randy led Andi back to her table. He tipped his hat at her. "See you on Monday, Andi," he said, then turned and headed back to his table.

Andi watched him go before turning to look at Luke. She noticed his beer was already empty.

"What did he mean by that? See you on Monday?" Luke asked tightly.

"Nothing. He'll actually see me on Monday at the ranch. He works there, remember?"

"Humph."

Andi shook her head and rolled her eyes.

A lively song began playing and Andi noticed people were getting into position to line dance. Colt hurried over to the table and grabbed Andi's hand.

"Come on, let's join in," he said.

"But I don't know how to do this," Andi protested as he pulled her toward the dance floor.

"It's okay. You'll learn. Just follow along."

The music started up with a country tune Andi had never heard before and everyone began dancing. They stepped two steps to the right, and then one to the left, hooked their leg up, turned a quarter turn, then stomped their foot down and clapped twice before moving again. The next time they turned, it was a half turn. Hips swayed and boots stomped. Colt knew the steps by heart and kept to the beat. Andi was surprised at how easily he danced along. She could hardly keep up, but she was having fun just the same.

By the end of the dance, Andi was breathing hard and

laughed at how badly she'd danced. The band started playing a lively tune and before Andi knew it, Colt had taken her hand and put his other hand around her waist.

"Come on, Andi. Let's dance some more," he said with a big smile on his face. "Just follow me. We're doing a quick two-step."

Andi followed along as they two-stepped once around the floor. Just as she was getting the hang of it, Colt twirled her around once then pulled back before pulling her in towards him again with another twirl. Andi laughed out loud and Colt smiled down at her. They continued the same routine of the two-step, then the twirl, pull, twirl back. As the song ended abruptly, Colt held on tightly and dipped Andi before pulling her up again.

"Oh, my goodness, Colt," Andi exclaimed. "Where did you learn to dance so well?"

Colt grinned and shrugged. "I guess from spending so much time here."

Andi gave him a quick hug. "You've worn me out. I'd better sit for a while before I do any more dancing."

Colt looked disappointed, but he walked her back to the table. Luke wasn't there. Andi sat and took a sip of her beer. She noticed Colt looking longingly at the dance floor.

"You go and dance, Colt. I'll be fine here," she told him.

Colt's face lit up. "See you in a bit." He took off and grabbed the hand of a young, dark-haired girl who looked more than happy to join him on the dance floor.

Andi glanced around the room and noticed Luke was at the bar, buying another mug of beer. She hoped he didn't drink too much, because she didn't want to have to drive them home in his big truck.

A shadow fell across Andi and she looked up to see a man

standing beside her. He took off his hat and smiled. "Howdy, Miss," the stranger said. "Would you care to dance?"

Andi hesitated a moment, not sure how to politely say no. The man looked to be in his thirties, had jet black hair, was slightly overweight, and had dark, piercing eyes. Even though he smiled, it looked more creepy than kind.

"Sorry, Duane," Luke said, appearing suddenly. "But she promised this dance to me."

Duane narrowed his eyes at Luke, but didn't argue. He nodded to Andi, then turned and walked off.

Luke set down his fresh mug of beer and offered Andi his hand. "Guess we should dance since I said we were going to."

"Do I have a choice?" Andi asked, taking his hand and following him to the dance floor.

The band was playing an old *Eagles* tune and all the couples on the floor were slow dancing. Luke pulled Andi to him, his hand snug on the small of her back, and they began swaying to the music.

Andi listened to the lyrics a moment, then grinned. "'Desperado'. Really?"

"We cowboys like our cowboy songs," Luke answered, his face only inches from hers.

They slow danced quietly for a moment. Andi noticed Colt cozying up to the dark-haired girl and Duane had found a chubby cowgirl to dance with. "You know, I appreciate you saving me from that Duane guy, but I can take care of myself."

Luke pulled back a bit and frowned at Andi. "Believe me, you don't want to dance with Duane. And he wouldn't have taken no for an answer. He's not a nice person."

"Well, thanks," Andi said.

"You're welcome. I feel like I'm responsible for you since your boyfriend isn't here. These guys in the bar don't know you're taken, and if you're not careful, they'll be all over you."

Andi did a mental eye roll. She knew Luke was being serious, but he sounded ridiculous to her. "Oh, so in other words, every guy in this place is out to ravish me, except for you?"

"Well, maybe not every guy," Luke said. "But I saw a few looking at you like you were their favorite dessert. Just think of me like your big brother, protecting you."

The singer continued his sad song. They swayed to the music in perfect harmony. Luke was so close, his cheek gently touched hers and she felt his warm breath on her neck. He was a good dancer, keeping time with the music. It felt nice, dancing with him, but after what he'd said, she just had to tease him.

"You know," she whispered into this ear. "Having a big brother is new to me. Tell me, Luke. Would you really dance this close to your little sister?"

Luke pulled back as if he'd been slapped and looked at her with wide eyes.

Andi grinned. "I need some fresh air. I'm going outside for a minute." She turned to leave.

"I'll come with you," Luke said, following her.

Andi turned and put her hand on his chest. "No. Don't. Just give me a minute to myself, okay? I'll be fine." She turned and walked out of the bar.

Chapter Eleven

Andi stepped outside into the cool, dark night. She took a deep breath of the crisp air, clearing her head of the noisy bar and Luke's arrogance. She couldn't figure him out. One moment he was sweet and adorable, the next, infuriating.

Andi sat down on the long, narrow steps and pulled her phone out of her jeans' pocket. She was happy to see she had three bars for reception. Andi pulled up Derek's name and began texting him a message, hoping it would go through. They hadn't left on a good note when she'd last called him, and she felt guilty about it, even though he'd annoyed her with his tone. So, she texted him to say she was sorry she wouldn't be there for his reception and she'd make it up to him when she finally did get there. She would have preferred calling him, but it was almost midnight in Buffalo and she didn't want to wake him.

She sent the text and was relieved to see it went through. She decided to call Carly and see how she was doing. The phone rang twice before Carly answered in her usual excited voice.

"Hi, Andi. Your phone is working. Where are you?"

Andi smiled. Carly was always bubbly, even late at night.

Andi wished she had half her energy. "Hi, Carly. I'm just a short distance from the ranch and the towers are stronger here. I just wanted to call to see how you're doing."

"I'm fine. I'm out with friends right now. Can you hear the music?"

Andi didn't have to listen hard to hear music blasting in the background. "You're out again? Weren't you out the last time I called you?"

"Oh, don't be such an old lady. It's Saturday night. Of course, I'm out dancing. And there are some really cute guys here. I wish you were here with me. We'd have a fun time."

Yeah, right. She and Carly rarely went out together when Andi lived with her. Carly had a wild bunch of friends that Andi couldn't keep up with and frankly, hadn't even wanted to try. "I'm not looking for cute guys. I'm engaged, remember? That's why I got stuck here in the first place."

Carly sighed. "Oh, yeah. Derek. I almost forgot. Well, you aren't tied to him, yet. So, have you kissed a cowboy yet? Like that cutie, Luke?"

Andi rolled her eyes. In their emails back and forth, she'd mentioned Luke and Colt to Carly and how cute they were. Now, she wished she hadn't. "No, I haven't. I'm engaged. Sheesh, Carly."

"How much longer will you be staying at the ranch?" Carly asked.

"I'm not sure. It could be another week, maybe longer," Andi told her.

"Boy, I'll bet Derek was mad about that."

"He wasn't happy, that's for sure," Andi said.

The bar door swung open and two people came out and walked down the steps. Music spilled out into the quiet night until the door slammed shut.

"Hey, what's that I hear? Country music?" Carly asked. "Are you out with that hot cowboy?"

Andi winced. She hadn't meant for Carly to know where she was. "I'm out at a bar with Luke and Colt, but it's not what you think. I just came out because Colt invited me."

"Whoo whee!" Carly shouted into the phone. "You're out with the cowboys? And you were giving me a hard time about being out. At least I'm not *engaged*."

"Don't be silly. Nothing's going on," Andi insisted.

"Well, maybe something should be going on and then you can dump that workaholic and replace him with a hunky cowboy."

Andi's mouth dropped open. "Carly, that's terrible. How can you say that about Derek?"

"Oh, come on, Andi. You know I'm right. All Derek cares about is money and looking good. Having you on his arm makes him look even better. He's all show and no substance."

"Stop that. I'm going to ignore what you said, because you've been drinking and we both know you say stupid stuff when you drink."

"Fine. But you know I'm right."

"Change the subject. Did your friend agree to move into the townhouse and share the bills? What was her name? Beth?" Andi didn't want to pursue the topic of Derek any further. She couldn't believe that Carly would say such mean things about him.

"Yes. Beth is moving in next week. It won't be the same as having you there, but it will help with the bills. I guess it won't be so bad. She's an RN at the hospital and works all sorts of odd hours. I'll barely ever see her," Carly said.

"Good. I'll feel better knowing you have a roommate," Andi told her.

"Hey, I've got to go," Carly said. "We're heading off to another place. I'm glad you called. Take care. Call me again soon, okay?"

"Okay. Love you, Little Sis."

"Love you, too. Bye, Andi."

The line went silent. Andi sighed. She missed Carly, even if she partied too much and spoke her mind without a filter. She was, after all, her only sister.

The phone buzzed and startled Andi. She looked at the screen and was shocked to see it was Derek calling. "Hi, Derek. I didn't think you'd still be up."

"Hi, Andi. I got your text. I thought you didn't get reception at that ranch."

"I don't. I'm at a little restaurant down the road from the ranch and there's reception here."

"Oh. Are you alone?" Derek asked.

"I came with the family," she lied. Well, it wasn't an actual lie, but she didn't want to explain why she was at a bar with two cowboys on a Saturday night. "Anyway, I wanted to tell you how sorry I am that all this happened and I'm going to miss your welcome reception next Friday. I really never thought I'd break down like this and be stranded."

"I know," Derek said. "I'm sorry I was such a jerk on the phone, too. I was just disappointed. I had hoped you'd want to give up the idea of driving and just fly here to be with me. I miss you, Andi."

"I miss you, too," Andi said. "I promise, I'll be there as soon as I can." She heard music in the background over the phone. "Are you at home?" she asked

"Ah, no. The accounts manager invited me out to dinner so I could meet a couple of the bank's more prominent clients. They wanted to go listen to music afterwards, so we're at a club."

Andi frowned. A business meeting on a Saturday night? In the silence, she heard a woman's voice telling Derek to hurry up. "Who was that?" she asked.

"That was just one of the people in our party," Derek said smoothly. "Listen, Andi. I have to run. Call me as soon as you hear about your car, okay?"

"Okay," Andi said. She heard giggling in the background.

"Bye, Andi. Love you," Derek said. He hung up before Andi could say goodbye.

Andi glared at her phone a moment. Derek was out on a Saturday night at a "club" with "clients" that sounded like giggling women. Just what the heck was going on? Then she turned and looked at the bar where she was with two men she'd just met a few days ago. Andi sighed. She guessed it would be hypocritical to condemn Derek when she was doing the same thing.

The door to the bar opened again and Andi heard boots on the wood porch. She knew who it was before she even turned around. Luke came down a step and sat next to her.

"Have you been out here alone long enough?" he asked. "Or do you want me to leave?"

Andi sighed. "Sorry I was so rude. I just wanted a minute to myself."

Luke looked straight at Andi. "Is everything okay?"

Andi nodded. "Yeah. I just talked to my sister and to Derek. Neither one seemed to miss me all that much."

Luke grunted. "I highly doubt that."

"Why?"

"I'm sure your sister misses you plenty. And as for Derek, well, he'd be crazy not to miss you," Luke told her.

"Because I'm such wonderful company and I make a great little sister?" Andi teased.

"Smartass," Luke said with a grin.

Andi laughed. "Yeah, maybe. A little."

"Are you ready to go home?"

The question took Andi by surprise. Home? Funny, but the ranch did feel like home to her after only a few days. She smiled. "Yeah. I'm ready to go home."

"I'll go get Colt. He's had one too many beers already anyway." Luke stood and offered his hand to Andi. She accepted and he pulled her up. They stood there a moment, facing each other, hands still clasped as bugs buzzed around the light by the door and music drifted outside.

"You know what?" Luke asked, staring down into Andi's eyes.

"What?"

"You dance to country music pretty good, for a city girl."

Andi looked up into Luke's blue eyes. They were warm, inviting, and glinting mischievously. "Smartass," she said softly.

Luke chuckled deeply. Then he went inside to find Colt, leaving Andi on the porch, trying to sort out what in the heck was going on between her and Luke.

* * *

Andi spent most of the next morning after breakfast walking around the ranch property near the house taking pictures and sketching. It was Sunday, so Randy had the day off, but Luke and Colt still had chores to do. Ginny was cleaning out the chicken coop and had told Andi to relax and enjoy the sunny day. Andi took her advice and wandered the property with Bree at her heels.

Andi walked a little ways up the trail she and Luke had

ridden so she could get a view of the corral and barn with the river and hills in the distance. Three horses stood in the corral, lazily pulling up grass and chewing it. Abby was one of them, and there were two other mares with her. Andi saw Chance in the larger field behind the barn with several other horses. If Chance was close by that meant Luke was, too, because Andi had also noticed his truck was still in the driveway by the house.

"That means he'll sneak up and startle us at any moment," Andi said aloud to Bree. The dog cocked her head and stared at Andi, which made her laugh. "You won't let that happen, though, will you girl?" she asked, rubbing the dog behind the ears. "You'll warn me."

She sat in the grass beside Bree and began darkening a clean page of her sketchpad before beginning to sketch the corral, horses, and barn. A breeze caressed her face and bare arms as it made its way down the hill behind her and across the field. Taller grass in the corral that the horses hadn't yet devoured swayed gently. It was an idyllic scene and Andi's heart swelled with happiness at how attached she'd become to the ranch and its occupants. She'd always thought that the eclectic town of Seattle, the rocky cliffs of the coast, and the beauty of Puget Sound were home to her, but she could easily see herself living in a place as tranquil as this. It surprised her that she felt that way, much as the strange relationship between her and Luke surprised her.

The night before, Andi tried sorting out what was going on between them. He teased her mercilessly, and she gave it back as bad, if not worse, than he did. The worst part was, she had fun doing it. Andi had always been the serious sister. Her sister, Carly, was the flirt. But for some reason, Luke brought out the devil in her and she said things that she'd never have said to another man. Things that seemed to border on flirting. What was up with that?

Even now, as she sketched the landscape, all Andi thought about was Luke. That perfectly contoured face, those sultry blue eyes, and those full lips that grinned wickedly sometimes. *Sheesh. Now I'm thinking words like sultry. What is wrong with me?*

Andi could no longer concentrate on the barn and the horses. She turned the page of her sketchpad and quickly prepared it, and then she began sketching Luke's face from memory. She outlined his sturdy jaw line and chiseled cheekbones. His face was tilted down a little, in that way he looked at her from under those perfect brows. She added his deep-set eyes, glancing up, a glint of humor in them. His straight nose was next, then those delicious lips. She gave him a wicked grin, erased it, and then drew it into a soft smile. Liking what she'd done so far, Andi added his dusty black hat tilted up a bit so it didn't shade his eyes. She drew in wavy hair around the edge of the hat. She worked a long time, shading, erasing, darkening, and smudging to get it all perfect. Then, she added his neck and a shirt collar so she wouldn't be accused of drawing him shirtless again. When she was finally finished, Andi was surprised at how well she'd captured him.

Andi heard the crunch of gravel and looked up to see the real Luke walking towards her. He smiled when she caught his eye. Andi looked from her sketch to the real person and back again. She'd managed to capture the very essence of Luke without having him sit for her. His face was ingrained in her memory as if she'd known him her entire life. This thought surprised her the most.

She and Bree both stood as Luke drew near. Andi closed her pad. It would be too embarrassing if he saw she had sketched him again.

Luke stopped only a few feet away from Andi. He smiled at her, then down at Bree. "Looks like you've made a friend for life," he said, nodding toward Bree. "She seems to follow you everywhere."

Andi reached down and pet Bree gently. "She just has good taste, I guess."

Luke chuckled. "I guess so. I'm done working for the day. I thought you might like to go for a ride after lunch."

"I'd love to," Andi said. She stepped up beside Luke and the two of them walked side by side, with Bree following behind them, back to the house.

* * *

Luke just couldn't seem to help himself. When it came to Andi, he was like a moth to a flame.

After he'd finished his work in the barn, he'd glanced up and seen Andi up the hill, concentrating hard on whatever it was she was drawing. She looked so cute there on that patch of green grass with Bree lying beside her. Her hair was pulled back into a ponytail, but the breeze kept blowing tendrils of hair around her face. She'd swipe at them and push them behind her ears only to have them fall again.

All morning, Luke had told himself to stay away from Andi. Every time they were together, he either insulted her or flirted with her. He didn't mean to, it just happened. Like last night, when he'd told her redheads were volatile. What kind of a statement was that? Then the next thing he knew, he was dancing so close to her, his cheek rubbed against hers. His fault, not hers. And it had felt good. He'd enjoyed how she felt in his arms. Her sweet scent. The way they swayed together perfectly to the music. If she hadn't given him a hard time about his stupid big brother comment, who knows what he would have done.

Yet, here he was, walking up toward her like that damned moth to that damned flame. And he knew for certain that in the end, he'd be the one who got burned. Yet, he asked her to go riding anyway.

After lunch, he and Andi saddled up their horses and led them out of the barn. This time, Andi had brought her camera along. It was in its case and she wore it over her shoulder and across her body so it wouldn't be in her way when she rode. As they both pulled themselves up on their horses, Luke spoke. "Do you still want to see inside my cabin? We can ride there first, then take the trail that goes along behind it."

"Yes. I'd like that."

Luke nodded, leading the way to the cabin.

When they arrived there, they tied the horses to the porch railing. Andi stopped a moment and surveyed the front of the house. "You know what you need?" she asked in a soft tone.

He turned and looked at her with wide eyes. Yes, he knew what he needed, but he was almost certain it wasn't the same thing Andi was thinking. He thought it was best to keep his mouth shut and think pure thoughts. "What?"

"A few pots of flowers on the porch and maybe some flower beds lining the front and sides of the cabin, too. It would help to cheer the place up."

Luke nodded. Yep, that hadn't been what he'd thought he needed. Unwittingly, he grinned that wicked little grin of his.

Andi looked at him suspiciously. "What is that evil grin for?"

"Nothing. Not a thing," Luke said. He walked ahead of Andi and opened the door, then moved aside so she could walk in ahead of him.

The cabin had large windows that allowed sunlight in during the day, making the room bright and airy. The living room opened into the kitchen with a cathedral ceiling and exposed beams overhead. The river rock fireplace was on the right with the sofa and coffee table in front of it and behind that was a large space that held a big, walnut dining table with six chairs. Straight ahead was an island with bar stools on the living room side. The kitchen was very modern. There were dark marble countertops, stainless steel appliances, and the oak cabinets matched the shiny oak floors underfoot.

Andi looked once more at the fireplace. The rock was floor to ceiling, narrowing as it went up to the top. There was a rustic, wood mantel, with nothing on it. "A large painting on your mantel would be perfect," she pointed out. "Maybe one of the ranch, or the mountains."

"Or maybe one of the cabin, like you were sketching the other day," Luke said.

Andi looked over at him. "Yeah, something like that."

Luke walked across the living room and past the kitchen into a hallway. Andi followed. They stopped near a back door that led outside. "There's one bedroom back here," he said. "A small bathroom off the hallway, a closet here for the washer and dryer, and then the master bedroom straight ahead. There's a larger bathroom connected to it."

Andi followed Luke and peered into each room. The master bedroom had a king size bed with a large, masculine bed frame and matching dresser. There was a door to a bathroom across the room. She didn't walk in. The other bedroom was empty except for a few boxes.

"That's about it," Luke said.

"It's nice," Andi said as they returned to the living room. She looked down at the end table beside the sofa and saw a book lying there. She picked it up. "You like mysteries. He's a good author."

Luke nodded. It was the same book he'd been reading the night Andi had found her way to his door. Since that night, he hadn't had time to read any more of it. "Yeah, I like to read when I get a chance. Do you read mysteries?"

"Sometimes. Usually I read romance novels, though. You know, chick-lit." She grinned. "It probably sounds silly to you."

Luke grinned back. "Chick-lit, huh? So, have you read any good romances lately?"

Andi shook her head. "No, not really."

They stood there a moment in the quiet room, staring at each other. Luke thought he wouldn't mind a good romance. *Cripes! Pure thoughts, you idiot.*

"Let's go riding," Luke said quickly before his mind came up with any more stupid ideas.

Andi walked towards the door, but when she got close to Luke, she stopped. "Thanks for showing me the house. I really like it. It suits you."

Luke watched her as she walked ahead of him, out the door, trying hard not to think how well Andi suited him, too. Of course, his mind lost the battle and he thought it anyway.

They rode the trail behind Luke's cabin, around a fenced-in pasture, through a grove of tall evergreens, and across an open field before hitting the trail once again that came down the middle of the property and back to the ranch. Andi noticed the partially built building in the first pasture. "What's that?" she asked Luke, pointing to it.

"I'm building a small stable and pole barn," he said. "It's only framed in right now. I hope to finish it this summer."

"Why are you building it?" Andi asked, curious.

"I'd like to keep Chance down here. I ride him a lot during the day, so I might as well have him near my house."

Andi nodded as they rode on.

Several times, Andi stopped to pull her camera out of its case and take photos of the countryside. They spoke very little. Sometimes, they'd trot, and once they let the horses break loose into a full gallop, but mostly they just walked the horses and rode side by side. When they approached the view on the hill that had amazed Andi the first time they rode, they stopped so she could take photos.

"I really want to get this view at sunset," Andi said as she slipped her camera back into its case.

"No reason why you shouldn't be able to," Luke said. "I'm going to be gone for a few days this week, but you can certainly ride whenever you want. Although, I'd feel better about it if you took Colt along, just for safety reasons."

Andi looked at him quizzically. "Where are you going?"

"I'm going to spend some time at the summer pasture to check on the cattle. There's a small cabin there, so I'll stay a few nights."

"I was wondering where you were hiding all the cattle. I figured they must be somewhere. How far is it to the summer pasture?" Andi asked.

"About a three hour ride on horse if I don't ride too hard. Two hours if I rush it, but there's no need to. The pasture is at the back end of our property, and I'll be checking the fences and making sure the calves are doing fine."

"How many head of cattle do you have?" Andi asked.

"Close to eight hundred and fifty. Ma knows the exact number. She keeps all the records on the computer. We have them tagged so we can keep track of shots, illnesses, and which calf belongs to which cow."

"Wow. I never realized that raising cattle was so complicated. I just thought you bred them, fed them, and then sold them," Andi said.

Luke shook his head. "Nope. There's more to it than that. There are a lot of regulations to follow if you want to sell beef cattle."

"Hmmm. Interesting," Andi said.

They headed back to the barn, unsaddled the horses, and brushed them down before letting them go off to graze.

Just as Andi turned to head back to the house and help Ginny with supper, Luke reached out and touched her arm. She turned and looked up at him.

"I want to apologize to you for being rude last night," Luke said. "What I said about redheads was way out of line. I don't know why it is, but I seem to say all the wrong things around you. I'm sorry."

"It's okay," Andi said. "I've been rude to you, too. Maybe we can try being nicer to each other. Or, at least be more careful what we say to each other. It seems like everything I say to you comes out wrong."

"Really?" Luke asked. "I just thought you've been teasing me all this time. It's been kind of fun, actually."

Andi grinned up at him. "Yeah, it has. But maybe it isn't a very smart thing to do."

Luke nodded. "I suppose you're right. I'll try to be more careful."

"Me, too." Andi turned and walked the short distance to the house.

Luke watched her walk away. Maybe it wasn't the smartest thing to do, teasing each other that way, but if truth be told, he would miss it if they stopped.

Chapter Twelve

At supper that night there were just the four of them, so it was quiet throughout the meal. Colt had spent the afternoon with the little dark-haired girl from the bar the night before. No one asked him what they had done and he didn't offer the information. Andi had to laugh, though, when Luke kept teasing him about her. Colt just turned bright red and told Luke to shut up. Siblings! She knew exactly what it was like.

As they were eating apple cobbler with homemade ice cream for dessert, Luke announced he'd be gone for a few days to the summer pasture. "I probably won't be home until Thursday," he said. "I have miles of fencing to check, and the cattle, too."

"Are you going on horseback?" Ginny asked.

"Don't I always?"

"What about supplies?" Ginny wanted to know.

"All taken care of. I had Randy bring supplies up there last week with the truck. There's canned food, bottled water, and gas and oil for the generator. I'll have enough."

"Why don't you take the truck instead?" Andi asked. "Wouldn't it be easier?"

Colt laughed. "Because Luke likes doing everything the old-fashioned way. He can check the cattle and fences just fine in the truck, but he prefers riding."

Luke frowned at Colt. "Horses worked just fine for over one hundred and fifty years on this ranch. No need to change it now."

"I think it's nice," Andi piped up. "Keeping with the old traditions. Not many people do anymore."

Ginny looked over at Andi, and then at Luke. "You know, there are some really beautiful views out near the summer pasture. It's at a higher elevation, and there's one spot where you're on the top of a cliff and can see the entire valley below. It's just breathtaking. I'll bet Andi could get some wonderful photos there. And there'd be so many interesting landscapes to sketch."

Luke looked at his mother, a crease developing between his brows. "Maybe someone can drive her there while she's here," he said.

"Oh, we both know the best way to see that part of the land is on horseback," Ginny said. "Andi, you should go with Luke and stay a few days. You'd just love it there."

Andi sat there speechless. She glanced at Luke and could tell by the expression on his face that he didn't want her tagging along. Heck, she didn't even know if she wanted to tag along.

"Ma, you know how small that cabin is. And there's no indoor plumbing. Andi would hate it," Luke said.

"Don't be ridiculous, Luke. The cabin is fine. There's a generator for lights and a hand pump for well water on the sink. Andi wouldn't mind it, would you dear?"

"Well, I'm not sure," Andi started to say, but Luke interrupted her.

"See, she doesn't want to go. A city girl like Andi doesn't want to stay at a rustic place with an outhouse. It's best if she stays here."

Anger rose inside Andi. How dare he speak for her. "I didn't say I didn't want to go," she said, glaring at Luke. "Actually, it sounds like fun. It would be nice to see those views." She couldn't believe she'd said that. But he'd made her so mad by calling her a city girl again and assuming she couldn't rough it for a few days that her first reaction was to contradict him.

"The cabin is too small. There's no privacy," Luke insisted. "It wouldn't look right for me and Andi to be there alone for a few days."

Ginny laughed. "Don't be so proper, Luke. It's not the 1800s anymore. I'm sure you and Andi can share the cabin for a few days without anything indecent happening. You're just friends, after all. So, it's all settled. I'll pack up some food for you to bring along. You'll be so busy working, Luke, you won't even know Andi is there."

Andi saw that Luke wanted to protest some more, but he kept his mouth shut tight. Too tight. This time, he was really mad. *Well, that's what he gets for calling me a city girl.* Andi only hoped that she wasn't going to regret going along just to prove a point to him.

* * *

They left early the next morning, just after breakfast. Randy had saddled Chance and Abby for them and added saddlebags for their things. Luke had told her to pack light since it all had to be carried on her horse. Andi only packed one extra pair of jeans, her fleece jacket, a couple of T-shirts, and absolute necessities along with her sketchpad, pencils, and camera. She wore a sweatshirt over her T-shirt for the ride since it was chilly early in the morning.

Luke had glared at her as she put her few possessions into one of the saddlebags. "Is that all you're bringing?" he asked.

"You said not to bring too much, so I didn't."

"Hmmm," was his only response.

Andi looked over and noticed the rifle in its case strapped onto Chance's saddle. She also saw that Luke wore a pistol in a gun belt on his hip. "Are those necessary?" she asked, pointing to the rifle.

Luke nodded. "Anytime you go in the back woods around here they're necessary. You never know what is out there."

Andi didn't ask any more questions. She didn't want to know what was so dangerous that he needed two guns.

Before leaving, Andi had emailed Carly and told her she'd be out of touch for a few days. She hadn't told Derek, though. She could only imagine what he'd think if he knew she was going off to a cabin with Luke, alone. She just hoped he wouldn't try calling the house during that time.

They mounted their horses and headed up the trail in the middle of the property. Luke sat straight as a board in his saddle, his lips set in a tight line. Andi kept quiet as they rode along. She was tired. She'd hardly slept a wink all night worrying about sharing a small space with Luke, especially since it was clear he didn't want her along. Ginny's words kept echoing in her mind. *I'm sure you and Andi can share the cabin for a few days without anything indecent happening.* Maybe Ginny was sure, but Andi wasn't so sure about it. Of course, if Luke continued being angry with her the entire time, it would make it easier to resist anything *indecent*.

As they rode along, Andi found it a challenge to keep

Abby reined in. The mare was spirited this morning and kept shaking her head and setting off into a trot, so Andi would have to slow her back down to a walk. Luke only glanced at them, but didn't say a word.

After half an hour of riding in silence, Andi couldn't stand it any longer. "Listen, Luke. I know you didn't want me to come along, but I'm here so we may as well make the best of it. Okay?"

They rode side by side in an open field. Luke turned and looked at her with a surprised expression on his face as if he had forgotten she was there. "It just doesn't seem right, you coming along when you have a fiancé waiting for you."

Andi sighed. "I promise not to jump your bones, okay? Will that make you feel better?"

A slow smile spread across Luke's lips. "Sure you can control yourself?"

"I'm sure I can manage," she said. Once again, she pulled on Abby's reins to slow her down.

"That horse is acting up too much. We should have given you a more experienced horse for this far of a ride," Luke said.

"She's fine," Andi said. "I said I liked mine spunky, and she is."

Luke raised one brow at Andi. "Yes, I forgot you like yours spunky."

Andi rolled her eyes. "I think you'd better rein yourself in, Cowboy. Let's change the subject. Tell me a little about the ranch. How many acres are there?"

Luke laughed. "Okay. That's a safe subject. It's two thousand acres."

Andi's brows rose in surprise. "Really? That's a lot of land. Your mom said the ranch was started in the mid-1860s. Has it always been this large?"

"Nope. My three times great-grandfather, Kelvin Brennan, and his brothers came out here from Ohio in 1866 when land was being offered for homesteading. Each person was allowed one hundred and sixty acres if they lived on it and worked it for five years. One of Kelvin's brothers died on the trip here, so there was just the two of them left to homestead acreage. Between them, they started with three hundred and twenty acres. A few years later, more land was offered for homesteading, so they were able to add more property to their ranch. A lot of people came here at first to homestead and farm, but after a few years, many decided the life was too hard and wanted to go back east. So, our family bought up land little by little through the generations until we'd acquired the two thousand acres."

"That's incredible. Is the ranch house the first homestead on the property?"

Luke nodded. "But it was just a one room cabin to begin with. The sitting room is basically all there was, with the fireplace. Then the kitchen was added, and Ma's room behind the kitchen. Through the years the house has grown. The upstairs was added and the sitting room ceiling was raised up to a cathedral ceiling. It looks nothing like the one room cabin it was once."

"That is so neat," Andi said. "Your family has basically lived in the same house for over a hundred and fifty years and worked the same land. Not many people can say that anymore."

"Yeah, it is pretty amazing, I guess. I've never really thought about it."

"What about the cabin we're going to? Was that just built for staying in the summer pasture?"

"Actually, that was the other homestead cabin built by

Kelvin's brother to claim his land. That's why it's still so rustic. It's only used in the summer to check on the cattle, so it really doesn't have to be fancy. Usually, only men are there," he said, glancing over at Andi.

"I guess I'm breaking tradition then," Andi said. "I'm sorry I'm intruding on your 'male alone time'." She emphasized her words by making air quotes with her hands. "It wasn't my idea, though. It was your mother's."

"Yeah, I know. I'm not sure what she was thinking."

"Well, you shouldn't have called me a city girl again. Otherwise, I would have never said I wanted to come along. You know how mad that makes me," Andi said.

Luke frowned. "Really? That's what did it? I was trying to piss you off so you wouldn't want to come, not make you more determined."

"Ha! The joke's on you," Andi said with a wide grin.

Luke tossed her one of his wicked grins. "The joke may just be on you after all. Wait until you see the bathroom facilities."

Andi grimaced. She wasn't looking forward to using an outhouse.

They rode along through wooded areas that broke up into lush pastures. Soon, Andi saw cattle sprinkled among the green grass. A few turned into many. She saw several calves nursing as their mothers grazed. On a hill above the pasture, Andi pulled out her camera and started taking photos of the cattle against the rich, green grassland spotted with colorful wildflowers of yellow, pink, purple, and blue. Everything here seemed to have a richer, deeper color. She assumed it had to do with being up in the higher elevation where the air was cooler. After taking a few shots, Andi turned and slipped the camera back into one of the saddlebags.

They traveled among the cattle and then away from them

again and up a short hill. At the top of the hill, nestled among a copse of evergreens, was a small log cabin. There was a covered, plank porch in front and a stone chimney jutting up above the shingled roof on the right side. A small, square window with four panes was beside the door. Andi thought the cabin was adorable.

To the right side of the cabin was a small corral for the horses with a pole barn for shelter and a shed Andi assumed was for the saddles and other supplies. Luke rode Chance in the direction of the corral and Andi followed behind on Abby. As they neared the corral, something spooked Abby and she called out in a high-pitched whinny. Before Andi knew what was happening, Abby reared up on her hind legs and she was thrown off onto the hard ground.

Luke had turned just as Abby rose up and was off his horse before Andi hit the ground. He ran to her and dropped to his knees beside her prone body. "Andi? Andi? Are you okay? Andi!" he called out.

Andi lay still a moment, the wind completely knocked out of her. She heard Luke calling to her, but he sounded like he was far away. It took her a moment to get her bearings and open her eyes. As she focused, she saw the fear in Luke's eyes.

"Don't move. Just stay still. I don't want you hurting yourself even more," Luke commanded.

Andi took a deep breath. She lay there, waiting for some sign of pain, but she didn't feel any. Slowly, she pulled herself up on her elbows. Her arms didn't hurt, or her back.

"Don't move!" Luke yelled, kneeling over her.

"I'm okay," Andi told him in a shaky voice. "I just had the wind knocked out of me."

Luke reached down and placed his hands on Andi's left leg. He slowly moved them down her leg, squeezing gently at intervals. "Does this hurt? Does it hurt anywhere?"

"No," Andi said.

Luke did the same for her right leg. "What about here?"

"No, they're both fine," Andi said. "Just help me up, okay?"

Luke looked uncertain, but then finally put his shoulder under her left arm so she could circle her arm around his neck. He held her other hand and gently helped her up.

"See, I'm fine," Andi said, trying to smile. So far, she didn't feel hurt. "That's not the first time I've been thrown from a horse."

Luke didn't look convinced. "Let's get you inside. I want to check the back of your head for any cuts or lumps. It took you a moment to wake up. You may have a concussion."

"I'm fine," Andi insisted again. "I'm tougher than you think." With Luke still supporting her, she stepped on her left ankle. An involuntary groan escaped her lips and she winced.

"What's wrong?" Luke asked sharply.

"I'm not sure. I can't seem to stand on my left leg. I think it's my ankle."

Without listening to another word, Luke lifted Andi up into his arms. Surprised, she clasped her arms around his neck to balance herself.

"I shouldn't have let you ride that horse," he said angrily as he carried her to the cabin. "She's too young and spirited. I should have made you ride an older, milder mare."

"It's not Abby's fault," Andi said. "Something spooked her. And it's not mine, either. I didn't ask to be thrown."

Luke strode up the porch steps and set Andi down carefully for a moment to unlock the door with a key he'd pulled from his pocket. He opened the door wide, lifted her again, and carried her inside. There was a brown sofa in the center of the small room that faced the stone fireplace. Luke kneeled down and gently set Andi on the sofa.

"Was that really necessary?" Andi asked, a teasing smile on her lips.

Luke looked up at her, his eyes reflecting his fear. "This isn't funny. Do you know how scared I was when I saw you lying on the ground? You could have broken your back. Or your neck, for that matter. You could have hit your head on a rock. Anything could have happened to you." Luke's voice cracked and he bent his head down, shielding his face with the brim of his hat.

Andi was taken aback by the raw emotion she'd seen on Luke's face. Her heart swelled. He'd been afraid for her life, and she'd just laughed it off. Gently, she lifted his hat from his head and placed it on the sofa beside her. She ran her hands gingerly along each side of his face and through his hair, smoothing it back. It felt thick and silky on her fingers.

"Hey," she said softly. "I'm sorry. I'm all right, though. There's no reason to be upset, okay?"

She moved her hands gently down Luke's chiseled cheeks and under his strong jaw, lifting his face up. Blue eyes met green. "I'm sorry I scared you," she said. "And that I joked about it. But I'm fine."

Luke reached up and cupped the side of her face with his hand, rubbing his thumb gently across her cheek. It was as if he wanted to confirm she was indeed fine. His touch felt so intimate, Andi closed her eyes to feel its full effect. Luke sighed. "Okay," he said softly. "Okay."

Finally, Luke dropped his hand from Andi's face and rose to his feet. "Let's take a look at that ankle," he said.

"Shouldn't you take care of the horses first?" Andi asked. "I'll be fine."

Luke ignored her and walked over to the tiny kitchen that

consisted of a sink with a large, red hand pump, an old electric stove, a half-sized refrigerator, and only a few cabinets over and under the sink. He searched through a cabinet and found what he was looking for.

"You first, then the horses," he stated as he walked back to the sofa. He knelt in front of Andi again. "Here. Give me your boot."

Andi leaned back against the sofa and lifted her left leg. As Luke started to pull her boot off, she drew in a sharp breath. Luke stopped pulling and looked up at her with a frown.

"You're fine, huh?" he asked. "It must already be swelling if it hurts just to pull your boot."

Andi glanced at the pistol on his hip. "You're not going to shoot me, are you?"

"Only if it's broken," he quipped back.

Andi made a face at him, but kept quiet.

"Hang on," he said as he pulled the boot off. Andi bit down on her lip, but once the boot came off, the sharp pain subsided.

Luke set her boot down and then gently placed her foot in his lap. Slowly, he rolled down her sock to see her ankle. "It's already swelling," he said. "We should radio the house and have Colt come get you with the truck. You need to see a doctor."

Disappointment fell across Andi's face. "No. I rode all the way here and I want to stay. I'm sure it will be fine. A little ice and rest, and it will be back to normal."

"What if it's broken? You won't be able to ride home again. I'd feel better if you'd go see a doctor," Luke told her.

"It's not broken. It's only sprained," Andi insisted angrily.

Luke's eyes narrowed, but he didn't protest. "Fine. Give me your other foot," he said.

Andi looked at him warily, but lifted her right foot. Luke gently pulled her other boot off, and then held her legs just under her knees and slowly turned her so she was lying on the sofa. Andi carefully scooted herself up against the sofa's pillow.

Luke picked up the item he'd taken from the cupboard and twisted it in his hands. It made a cracking sound. "It's an ice pack," he said. He leaned over Andi's swollen ankle and propped it up on a pillow. Then he rolled her sock back up and laid the ice pack over it.

"Ice pack, huh," Andi said with a smirk. "Guess you cowboys sometimes need a little first aid up here."

"Hey, we work hard," Luke said defensively. "It's good to have ice and heat packs up here for swollen muscles."

"I was just teasing you, Luke. You don't have to get angry," Andi said softly.

Luke looked at her a moment, before nodding. "Now, let me take a look at the back of your head."

Andi sighed, but lifted her head up so he could take a look. Luke felt the back of her head and neck for any bumps, but found none. "Looks good," he said. Her ponytail had dirt and leaves in it from being on the ground. Gently, he pulled the band out and ran his fingers through her hair. "There's some dirt," he explained.

"Thanks," Andi said, not sure what to think.

Luke stood and came around the side of the sofa, looking down at Andi. "Are you sure you want to stay? I'm going to be gone half of today and all of tomorrow. You might need help."

"I'm sure," Andi told him. "I'll bet it will be fine by morning."

"Anyone ever tell you that you're a stubborn cuss?" Luke asked.

Andi grinned. "Speak for yourself. But I wouldn't mind some ibuprofen if you have it."

Luke turned and walked over to the kitchen cabinets again. He pulled out a small bottle and shook out two pills before stepping to the side of the refrigerator to pull out a bottle of water from the case sitting there. "Sorry, the water's warm," he said as he handed her the pills and bottle of water. "I'll get the generator going and put a few bottles in the fridge for you. The well water out of the pump isn't the best tasting."

"Thanks." Andi took the pills and water from Luke. She watched as he fussed around the room. He brought her a blanket from one of the two bunks that were on the other side of the room and spread it over her.

"I'll bet you've been bucked off a horse a dozen times," Andi said with a glint in her eyes.

Luke grinned that wicked grin of his. "Yeah, a few times. But that's different, because I'm a guy."

"Oh, really? You think you're so tough, huh? Well, I'm not the fragile little city girl you think I am. I can be tough, too."

"We'll see," Luke said with a wink.

Chapter Thirteen

Luke walked outside and found the horses grazing near the corral. He led them through the gate and began unsaddling Abby. He had to stop a minute to compose himself, because his heart still pounded and his hands shook. He'd never been so scared in his life as when he saw Andi lying there on the ground. What if she'd been hurt, or worse, killed? That thought made him shiver all over.

Luke took a deep calming breath. He carried the saddle, blanket, and bridle to the little shed and set them inside, then went back for the saddlebags and hung them over the fence rail. Going back to Abby, he rubbed his hands down her back and sides, searching for a burr or bump that might have caused her to rear up, but nothing was there. He checked her over to make sure she wasn't hurt and found her to be fine. Maybe a snake had scared the horse. He'd seen it happen before. Whatever it was, he was thankful that Andi hadn't been hurt too badly. Luke left Chance's saddle on, but took off his bridle so he could graze until Luke was ready to leave again. He pulled the rifle out of the case on the saddle and leaned it up against the fence where the saddlebags hung.

The sun was directly overhead. Luke estimated it was a little past noon. He could still check the cattle and fences for the next five or six hours if he was sure that Andi would be fine alone.

A water trough stood over by the pole barn with a hand pump beside it. Luke pumped water into it for the horses to drink, and then led them to it by their halters. Going back into the shed, he picked up a gas can and strode back to the cabin to start the generator.

As Luke worked on the generator, his mind kept turning back to Andi. He'd been so upset after setting her on the sofa, he'd had to bow his head so she wouldn't see his face. Here he was, a tough cowboy, and he had almost broken down in tears. The thought of what could have happened to her had nearly torn him apart. He'd been surprised when she'd gently taken off his hat and run her hands through his hair. But it had soothed him. That touch, so caring, had made him feel better. When she'd raised his eyes to hers, it was all he could do not to reach for her and kiss her. *Oh, God. I have it bad.*

This trip was supposed to get him miles away from Andi so he wouldn't have to face the feelings for her growing inside him. But here she was, and his feelings were so strong, he didn't know how he was going to contain them during these days alone with her.

The generator came to life and Luke tossed the saddlebags over his shoulder and picked up the rifle. He went inside the house, leaned the rifle up against the wall by the side door, and set the saddlebags on the small kitchen table. He plugged in the old refrigerator and began filling it with bottles of water and a few items his mom had sent along for them to eat.

"I'm sorry I'm no help," Andi said from the sofa. "I really didn't mean for this to happen."

"Don't worry about it," Luke told her. "I'll be right back."

Luke took the broom out of the small closet in the kitchen and went outside. The outhouse was only a few steps behind the cabin. He unlatched it, and used the broom to sweep out cobwebs that had formed since it was last visited. It was pretty clean for an outhouse, but the warm day didn't help the smell any.

Once again returning to the cabin, he went to the sink and pushed down the pump handle a few times before water began pouring out. He washed his hands with the ice cold water and dried them with a paper towel from the roll sitting on the counter.

Luke walked over to where Andi lay and stood over her. "Do you have a headache?"

Andi shook her head.

"Are you sick to your stomach? Dizzy? Light-headed?"

"No," Andi said, making a face. "I feel fine."

"Just checking," Luke said. "I want to make sure you don't have any symptoms of a concussion before I leave for the afternoon."

"I'm fine. My head doesn't hurt at all. I'm sure I didn't hit it when I fell. I'll just lie here like a good girl and rest my ankle."

"Are you hungry? I can make you something before I go," Luke offered.

"No thanks. If I get hungry later, I'll make something."

Luke frowned and looked around the room. He went to the broom closet and found a tall umbrella. After testing how strong it was, he brought it over and set it on the floor by Andi.

"Is it going to rain?" Andi asked.

"You can use this like a cane if you need to walk around. That way you won't put all your weight on your ankle."

Andi nodded. "Smart."

"Two more questions," Luke said. "Do you know how to fire a rifle?"

Andi's brows popped up. "No. Why? Will I have to shoot something?"

"Probably not, but there are dangerous animals roaming this area."

"Like what?" Andi asked.

"Mountain lions, bears, grizzlies, and wolves to name a few. We've seen them all in this back pasture since it's so isolated."

"Geez. Are they going to just walk inside the cabin?"

Luke chuckled. "Not likely, but not unlikely, either. The gun is loaded and the safety is on, so don't touch it unless you absolutely have to. I'll teach you how to shoot it tonight when I get back."

Andi bit her lip. "Okay. What's your second question?"

Luke cleared his throat. "Do you need to use the bathroom before I leave?"

"Luke Brennan, there is no way I'm going to let you escort me to the outhouse and wait outside while I do my business," Andi said with certainty. "If I need to use it, I'll go by myself."

Luke grinned. "Okay. I was just checking. But watch out for all those critters I told you about." He turned to leave, but when Andi's hand grasped his, he turned back around.

"Luke?" she said, looking up at him with those big, green eyes and holding his hand gently.

"Yeah?"

"Thanks. For everything. You're a good guy."

Luke smiled, and then did something that shocked even him. He leaned down and placed a soft kiss on her cheek. "You're welcome," he said. Then he strode out of the room.

* * *

Andi lay on the sofa for a long while after Luke left, still thinking about the kiss he'd given her. *Did it mean anything? Was it brotherly? Did she want it to be brotherly?* Her mind swirled with questions.

She closed her eyes and tried to block out Luke and think about her fiancé, Derek. She pictured him in her mind, his dark hair, his serious face, his chocolaty brown eyes. He didn't smile very often, but when he did, his eyes lit up and his serious expression softened. Usually, he was always thinking about work, even at home, and a small crease was beginning to become permanent between his eyebrows. No matter how hard Andi tried to conjure up Derek, though, the face that swam before her eyes was Luke's. That perfectly shaped face, those deep-set blue eyes, and that wicked grin that brought out a twinkle in his eyes. And that body. His wide shoulders attached to steel-hard biceps and forearms. His big, powerful hands. Muscles rippling from his chest down to his six-pack abs. He should be in a Bowflex commercial. He'd sell them faster than they could produce them.

Andi opened her eyes and tried to wipe the X-rated image of Luke out of her mind. What was wrong with her? She was engaged to Derek. She'd known Derek for almost three years. She'd only known Luke for less than a week. Yet, when he'd looked at her with fear in his eyes, her heart had melted. It was easy to see that he cared about her. And when she'd run her hands through his thick, silky hair, she hadn't wanted to stop. For one brief moment, she'd wanted to pull him to her and hold him close. She'd wanted to kiss that delicious mouth of his and feel his arms around her.

Geez. I must be the worst fiancé in history.

The long day, the fall, and the ibuprofen finally took their toll and Andi's eyelids grew heavy. Just a little nap, she told herself, and then she'd get up and go sit outside. Maybe bring the gun, just in case a grizzly bear or a mountain lion wanted to eat her. She giggled softly to herself as she fell into a deep sleep.

* * *

Andi slowly awoke to the sounds of cupboard doors opening and closing and a loud scraping. Her eyelids felt heavy and were slow to open, and her mind was blurry. What was making that noise? And what was it she smelled? Suddenly, she wondered if a bear had found his way into the cabin and was foraging through the cupboards. Her heart began to pound. Maybe if she pretended to be asleep, the animal would leave her alone. But her curiosity got the better of her. She turned her head slightly and looked toward the kitchen. She saw movement and a shadow, but the kitchen was too far behind her to see much else. *Crap. I'm here only a few hours and I'm going to be eaten by a bear.*

A shadow loomed across her and Andi jumped.

"How's the ankle feeling?"

Andi put a hand to her chest and sighed. "Geez, Luke. You scared me half to death. I thought a bear was in here."

Luke laughed. "You thought a bear was cooking supper?"

Andi made a face at him. "No, I thought he was looking for supper. What time is it? Why are you back so early?"

"It's not early, silly. It's after six. There were dark clouds rolling in so I figured I should get back in case it storms."

"After six?" Andi asked, pushing herself up to a sitting

position. Her ankle began to throb and she winced.

Luke went over to the other end of the sofa. "Let me have a look at that," he said. He took the now warm ice pack off and rolled down her sock. "It's only a little swollen, and it's not turning black and blue, so I doubt it's broken. We'll get some more ice on it, though. There should be some ready in the freezer."

Andi glanced around from her half-sitting position. "I can't believe I slept so long. I wasted the whole day."

Luke opened the freezer door, pulled out an ice tray, and began dropping cubes into a plastic bag. "Yeah, you were sleeping like the dead when I came in. I rattled the pans and slammed cupboards to see if I could wake you, but you just kept sleeping. I was afraid you were in a coma or something."

"Ha, ha. What do I smell cooking?"

"Pork and beans. Sorry, we have a limited choice of foods since everything is canned. But we also have fresh bread Ma sent along and a jar of her strawberry jam. Oh, and canned peaches, too."

"Yum," Andi said. "I'm starving, so anything sounds good."

Luke came over with the ice pack.

"Um, I hate to have to ask, but I think I need the bathroom," Andi said sheepishly.

Luke grinned. "I knew you'd have to go eventually."

"Just help me up, okay, smartass?"

Luke shook his head. He bent down and lifted Andi easily in one smooth motion.

"What are you doing? I can walk," Andi protested.

"It'll put less strain on your ankle, and it will be faster. Don't be such a stubborn cuss," he said, but he was smiling.

Luke carried Andi out the side door and to the outhouse.

He set her down gently, and unlatched the door before helping her inside.

"You can leave now," Andi said. "I think I can do this myself."

"I'll be right here."

Andi rolled her eyes and shut the door.

There was a clear piece of corrugated plastic slanted on top of the outhouse for a ceiling allowing light to filter in. While an outhouse wasn't her preferred choice of a bathroom, Andi had to admit that this one wasn't too bad. There was an actual "toilet" in there and rolls of paper, and by the door was a bottle of hand sanitizer. It was about as modern as it could be.

After she finished, Andi opened the door. Luke stood a few feet away. After latching the door shut again, he told Andi to stand still and began brushing the back of her T-shirt and jeans with his hand.

"What are you doing?"

"You still have dirt on your clothes from the fall," Luke said. "Looks like you skinned up your elbow pretty badly, too. We should put something on it."

"Oh." Andi hadn't even noticed her elbow hurting.

Luke lifted her up again and began walking to the cabin.

"Is this really necessary?" she asked.

"No," Luke replied, flashing a sly grin. "But I kind of like doing it."

When they returned to the cabin, Luke set her down by the sink and began pumping the hand pump until water flowed. Andi washed her hands in the ice cold water and rubbed some over the cut on her elbow. Luke went to the stove to stir the beans again and pulled the sliced bread from the oven where it had been warming. He let Andi lean on him over to the small, wooden table and chairs. He pulled out the first aid kit from the cabinet in the kitchen and took out some antiseptic and a bandage. He also took out a bandage roll for Andi to wrap her ankle with.

"Here," he said. "Sit still a moment." He used a cotton ball to apply the antiseptic to the scrape on her arm.

"Ouch. That hurts," she complained.

"Don't be such a baby." Luke put a small bandage over the cut, then he handed her the other bandage roll. "You can wrap your ankle with this later for support."

"Okay."

Luke served supper and they sat quietly eating their beans with bread slathered in Ginny's strawberry jam. Andi tried one of her canned peaches, too. "These are wonderful," she said, placing several more on her plate.

Luke nodded. "Can't argue with you on that."

Luke made Andi lie down and put the ice pack on her ankle while he did the dishes. He heated up water on the stove and filled the sink half and half with hot and cold water. Andi watched him with interest.

"Imagine actually living like this," she said. "Except without the generator. You'd have a woodstove for cooking and heating water and use oil lamps for light. No cold food storage except in the winter. Think of all the hard work it was, just to eat and keep warm. Most people today would never survive that."

"You're right about that," Luke said. "I sometimes wonder what it was like for my ancestors living out here over a hundred years ago. But that was all they knew while we've all gone soft."

"Soft?" Andi asked. "Not you, Luke Brennan. You'd survive in an instant. You're as hard as they get."

Luke turned and cocked one eyebrow. "Excuse me?"

Andi's face grew hot. "You have a dirty mind, Luke. You know that? You know exactly what I meant."

Luke chuckled and kept right on washing the dishes.

* * *

Before it grew dark, Luke brought Andi outside to teach her how to use the rifle.

"Are you sure I need to learn this?" Andi asked. "I'm not comfortable shooting a gun."

"If you're going to be out here, you'd better get comfortable with it," Luke told her.

He brought out one of the kitchen chairs for her to sit on so she didn't put pressure on her ankle. Then he carried her out and set her in the chair before retrieving the rifle.

"Can I at least stand?" Andi asked. "I feel stupid shooting a gun sitting down."

"Not tonight. If you are going to be moving around tomorrow, I don't want you taxing your ankle tonight. Now, just sit there and pay attention, okay?"

"Bossy," Andi said under her breath.

"I heard that," Luke responded.

Luke positioned her chair so she wasn't shooting in the direction of the horses or the livestock. In the distance was a fence. Luke placed four plastic water bottles he'd weighted down with dirt inside and set them on the fence. Then he ran back to where Andi sat with the gun in her lap.

"Okay," Luke said. "For starters, this rifle uses a magazine, but it only holds four shots in it. So, if you shoot at anything, make sure you get it right away because a wild animal isn't going to wait around for you to reload."

"Great. I'm toast for sure."

"Don't worry. The sound of the gun will usually make an animal run. Well, except maybe for a mountain lion. And a grizzly."

"You're not making me feel any better here," Andi said.

Luke ignored her and picked up the rifle. "See this, underneath? That's where the magazine goes." He snapped it out and then snapped it back in. "Got it?"

Andi nodded.

"Before I put a round in the chamber, I want you to hold it up to your shoulder so you can get a feel for it." Luke put the gun up to Andi's shoulder and told her to grab it. "Good. Now, see that scope on top? Look through it and sight in one of the water bottles."

Andi tilted her head, closed her left eye, and looked through the scope. "I can't find them."

"You should be able to see a deer on that mountain over there with that scope," Luke said. "Here." He got down on his knees behind her and put his hands over hers on the gun. Slowly, he moved it in the direction of the water bottles.

Andi's hair was still loose from when he'd run his hands through it earlier that day. It brushed against his face, and he caught the scent of her shampoo despite her having fallen in the dirt. He closed his eyes and inhaled the sweet scent.

"I see one," Andi yelled with delight, startling Luke.

"Oh, yeah. Good," he said. "Now, bring the gun down and I'll show you how to put a round in the chamber."

Andi did what he said.

"Okay. First, here's the safety button. Hit that. Now, you're going to lift the bolt lever up, pull it all the way back, then push it forward again and push down the bolt. That will put a round in the chamber."

Andi bit her lip. "Okay." She lifted, pulled, and snapped it back in place. "Now what?"

"It's ready to fire. Keep your finger away from the trigger until you're sighted in on your target." Once again, Luke kneeled behind Andi. He wrapped his arms around her and showed her exactly how to hold the rifle until she was ready to shoot. "Got a bottle in your sight?"

"Yes."

"I'm letting go, then you can push the trigger and shoot. Careful, though, it kicks."

Andi held the gun steady, then moved her finger over the trigger and squeezed. The gun shot loudly and the bullet flew past the bottle. Andi turned and smiled up at Luke, her eyes bright. "I did it! I missed, but I shot the gun."

Luke grinned. "Yeah, you did it. Now, keep your finger away from the trigger and pull out the bolt and push it in again. Keep the gun facing away from you, cause the spent shell will come popping out."

Andi did what he said.

"It's ready to shoot again. Want to try?"

"No. You shoot. I want to see you hit the bottle," Andi said.

Luke carefully lifted the gun from Andi's hands and aimed. He squeezed the trigger and shot. A bottle went flying off the fence.

"I want to hit one," Andi said excitedly. "Let me try again."

Luke reset the rifle and put the safety on. Then he handed it to Andi. "Okay, one more try. Turn off the safety, aim, and shoot."

Andi hit the safety button and aimed carefully. This time when she squeezed the trigger, a water bottle flew off the fence. "I got it!" she yelled. "Did you see that?"

Luke nodded. "You did." He looked up at the sky. The clouds rolling in were dark and the air felt heavy. "Looks and feels like a storm brewing," he said. "Let's get you inside. At least now I know you can handle the gun if you have to."

"Let's just hope I won't have to," Andi said.

Luke unloaded the last shell and snapped on the safety button before putting the rifle back in the cabin. He went back outside and helped Andi walk in. "How does the ankle feel?"

"Sore. I'll ice it tonight and see how it is tomorrow. If nothing else, I'll stay close to the cabin tomorrow and sketch."

No sooner had they gone inside when thunder rumbled across the sky and rain began to fall. Andi spread out on the sofa again with her ankle propped up and a new ice pack on it. "Will the horses be okay outside?"

"Yep. They can go under the pole barn for shelter if they want to."

The storm raged off and on. In-between heavy rainfall, Luke and Andi used the outhouse and got ready for bed. Luke gave Andi her things from the saddlebag and she set them on a small table by the sofa. She brushed out her hair while Luke lit an oil lamp.

"I'm shutting off the generator for the night," he said. "I'll turn it back on tomorrow before I leave so you have lights."

Luke went outside and the lights flicked off. He came back in and shook the water from his hair, then slipped off his boots and took off his outer shirt, leaving his T-shirt on. When his eyes adjusted to the soft light of the oil lamp, he saw Andi sitting on the sofa, slowly running the brush through her long hair. His first thought was to walk over and offer to brush it for her, like he'd done for Ashley so many times when they were married. But he stopped himself. It was too intimate of a gesture. *Keep your distance, you idiot. Keep your distance.*

"Want some help over to the bunk?" he asked.

Andi stopped brushing her hair and nodded. Luke came over and wrapped his arm around her waist and she slid her arm over his shoulder. He held her up as she walked slowly over to the bunk beds.

"Guess I'm on the bottom," she said with a grin.

"Yep. And I'm on top."

Andi giggled like a schoolgirl. "That sounded terrible."

"Hey. You started it," Luke said.

Andi sat on the edge of the bunk, pulled down the sheet, and crawled in under it. Luke retrieved her blanket from the sofa and spread it out over her.

"Thanks," she said softly.

Luke blew out the oil lamp, climbed up to the top bunk, and stretched out. They both lay there a moment, listening to the rain softly drumming on the roof.

"Why bunks?" Andi asked.

"Guess it made the most sense since men usually came here to stay," Luke answered. "The bunks have always been here."

"Are you still angry that I came along?" she asked.

"Yep."

"What?"

"I'm just kidding," Luke said. "Actually, it's been nice having the company."

"Better than Randy or Colt?"

Luke laughed. "Much better than Randy or Colt. You look and smell a lot better."

Andi chuckled, and then grew serious. "I'm sorry I scared you today. I scared myself, too."

Luke closed his eyes, remembering how terrified he'd been that first few seconds Andi lay on the ground, immobile.

Thank God she was okay. "It wasn't your fault. I'm happy it wasn't anything serious."

"Goodnight, Luke."

"Goodnight, Andi."

As Luke lay there, listening to the rain falling against the roof, he wondered what it would be like to be able to say goodnight to Andi for the rest of his life.

Chapter Fourteen

Andi was awakened by a gentle nudge on her shoulder. She opened her eyes slowly, trying to focus.

"Andi? Wake up."

She turned her head and looked up into a pair of gorgeous blue eyes. She smiled. What a lovely dream.

"Andi? Are you awake?"

Andi squinted and looked up again. The dreamy blue eyes were set in the face of a male model. She giggled. A hot cowboy super model.

"What's so funny?"

The deeply male voice made Andi realize she wasn't dreaming. She was looking up into Luke's perfect face.

"Are you awake or not?"

"What do you want? What time is it?" Andi asked. All she wanted to do was scrunch down under the covers and go back to sleep.

"It's just after five. Listen, I'm leaving. If the weather holds, I won't be back until six or seven. Is there anything you need before I go?" Luke asked.

"No. Just sleep."

"Okay. The rifle is by the door. The generator is on, and the umbrella is on the floor by your bunk. Use it. I want that ankle to heal. Do you understand?" Luke asked sternly.

Andi sighed. "Yes. Just go. I'll be fine."

She lay there a moment with her eyes closed. She sensed someone still looking at her and opened her eyes to see Luke smiling down at her with a twinkle in his eyes.

"What?"

"See you later," he said. He stood and strode out the door.

Andi watched him go and a small smile touched her lips. *Imagine waking up to that face every morning.* She sighed before curling deeper under her blanket and falling back to sleep.

An hour later, Andi awoke for good this time. She slowly climbed out of bed and tested her ankle. It felt a little better, but she heeded Luke's command and used the umbrella like a cane as she visited the outhouse and then washed up at the sink before changing into clean clothes. She warmed up a couple of slices of bread in the stove and ate them with a good helping of jam for breakfast. Then, with her sketchpad and pencils in one hand and the umbrella in the other, she headed out the front door to the porch to see what she could sketch.

The sun was shining, the sky was blue, and a crisp morning breeze caressed Andi's cheeks. With the aid of the umbrella, Andi walked down one of the two steps and sat down on the porch. She closed her eyes and inhaled deeply. The rain had left the pines around the cabin damp, emitting from them an earthy, sweet scent. Andi loved that scent. It reminded her of walking the wooded trails around Mount Rainier National Forest. Her parents used to take her and Carly hiking there, and Andi had always loved the serenity of the forest.

Andi opened her eyes and looked all around her. In

front of her were open pastures with cattle grazing off in the distance. A fence around the outer area of the yard kept the cattle from trampling around the cabin. To her left was the small corral where Abby grazed lazily. To her right was more pasture and the fence where they'd shot the water bottles. Far beyond that was a forest of pine trees. After looking around for a moment, Andi felt inspired. She hobbled into the cabin, picked up one of the kitchen chairs, and brought it outside so she could sit in the sun and sketch.

Andi settled in the chair and began preparing a page to sketch. Once it was ready, her hand flew across the page, drawing outlines of the trees, fence, and the field. The sun beat down on her and her jeans and fleece jacket absorbed its warmth. Luckily, Andi had rolled her sneakers into her extra pair of jeans, so she didn't have to try to get the riding boots over her swollen ankle.

After a time, Andi realized she should have her ankle elevated so it wouldn't swell larger than it already was. She pulled her chair up near the cabin, still facing the landscape she was sketching, and placed her foot up on the step. It wasn't up as high as it should have been, but it was better than being on the ground.

As Andi's sketch came to life, she smiled. She'd drawn the fence with three water bottles on it and one on the ground as if someone had just shot it and it had fallen. The thick forest of trees was in the background, and above those were puffy white clouds. While she knew it wasn't something anyone would ever want to buy, it had a special meaning to her. This sketch would always remind her that she'd once shot a rifle and knocked down the bottle.

It would also be another reminder of her time spent with Luke.

When Andi finished that sketch, she moved her chair away from the cabin and placed it facing the cabin at a side angle so she could also see the corral and Abby. She prepared a new page, and then began outlining the scene before her. Later, when the sun was at the perfect angle, she planned on bringing her camera outside and taking photos of the cabin and the surrounding area. But for now, the sketches were a template she could use if she decided to turn any of them into an actual painting.

The third sketch she worked on was of Abby. She sketched the mare's strong face and dark eyes framed with long lashes. Abby stood sideways, with her head turned, looking at Andi. She drew Abby's muscular body and long legs and sketched her thick mane and tail slightly darker than her body. Andi captured the spirit of the horse as well as her gentleness. When she was finished, Andi was pleased with her sketch.

After taking the chair back into the cabin and bringing her camera outside, Andi began taking photos of everything she saw. She zoomed in on the treetops far away in the distance and was rewarded by capturing an eagle sitting on a limb, staring straight at her. Turning slowly, Andi clicked photos as she scanned the land around her. Far off in the pasture, Andi snapped a photo of a calf suckling its mother as the cow grazed. Farther to her left, she caught a shot of another calf rolling around in the grass, its long legs wriggling in the air. Each turn to the left found shot after shot of something amazing until Andi had made a complete circle and was once again facing the cabin. Then she spent a few more minutes taking photos of the cabin at different angles, even one including the outhouse behind it.

Andi's last shots were of Abby. Close ups and distance shots. She caught Abby as she grazed and walked around the corral. She also snapped a beautiful close up of the horse's face. It didn't matter that Abby had thrown her yesterday or that Andi had only ridden the mare a few times. Andi had already fallen in love with her. Abby was yet another reason it was going to be difficult to say goodbye when her car was fixed.

Luke, Colt, Ginny, Bree, Abby, and even Randy. In only six days they had all found a place in Andi's heart.

Andi capped her camera and laid it carefully on her chest where it hung around her neck. With the umbrella in hand, she walked over to the corral fence and whistled softly for Abby. The horse came instantly, nuzzling Andi's outstretched hand with her warm nose.

"Is it really possible to fall in love with someone in less than a week?" Andi asked Abby softly. She thought about yesterday and how Luke had taken such good care of her. She remembered how he'd run his fingers through her hair. He'd said there was dirt in it, but she wondered if that were true. And the gentle kiss he'd placed on her cheek. Did it mean anything, or was he just being nice? Luke could be obstinate and stubborn, and he teased Andi mercilessly. But she gave it right back to him. She'd never known a man like Luke before. So strong and in control, yet so kind and gentle.

Andi sighed, placed a gentle kiss on Abby's nose, and walked slowly back to the cabin. The day had grown warm, and her ankle throbbed from overuse. She was going inside to make up an icepack, then lay on the sofa for a while with the ice on her ankle to soothe the swelling. Hopefully, her ankle would be fine by the time they left so she could ride Abby back to the ranch and not have to have Colt or Randy come and get her with the truck. She wanted to ride alongside Luke. She wanted to get to know him better. She wanted to know everything about him.

As Andi climbed the porch steps, she turned and gazed out into the distance, wondering where Luke was and what he was doing at that exact moment. Then she turned and headed into the cabin.

* * *

Luke had been riding all day, checking on the cattle, and making sure the fencing was secure. He was happy to find all of the cattle and the calves in this part of the pasture safe and in good health. The fence, however, was a different matter. The weather and the cattle took a toll on the fencing and he'd marked down several locations where new railings and wire were needed. A few new posts wouldn't hurt either. He kept a small notepad in his back pocket and made notes in it so he could let Randy and Colt know what supplies were needed and where the repairs were necessary. As soon as they could, they would come up here and work on it.

The sun was heading west when Luke turned Chance back toward the cabin. He had a long ride home. Tomorrow, he'd check everything along the other side of the pasture. When they came to do the repairs, he'd check the rest of the fencing at the back of the property. There was always something to repair or replace on a ranch this size, but he didn't mind. He loved living here and wouldn't trade it for anywhere else in the world.

Of course, he had traded it for a few years in California and working as an engineer. And even though he'd loved Ashley enough to stay in California during that time, he had missed the ranch dearly. When his dad became sick and Luke had talked Ashley into moving to the ranch, he'd never in a million years thought they couldn't live a happy life there together. He'd foolishly believed that love was enough to keep their relationship strong. But it hadn't been. Ashley had wilted like a flower in desperate need of rain, and he'd watched her lose all the energy and love for life she'd had when he'd first fallen in love with her. No matter what he did, he couldn't bring that spark back into her eyes again. So, he'd let her go. It had been the hardest thing he'd ever done, but he knew it was the right thing to do. He'd never be happy moving back to California, and Ashley would never be happy here. In the end, they had both lost.

Luke's thoughts turned to Andi as he made his way across the pasture. He wondered how she'd managed all day with the hurt ankle. He hoped it was healing. He felt terrible that she'd been thrown by one of their horses under his watch. She sure was a trooper, though. Andi was a city girl, and yet she seemed to embrace ranch life as if it was second nature to her. Andi rode well for not having been raised around horses and she could saddle a horse as expertly as he did. She pitched in at the house, too, happily, without a complaint. Yet, she was as stubborn as they come. She was also beautiful, intelligent, and talented as hell. He wished he'd found her first, before she'd met that Derek guy and become engaged. Before she'd started a road trip to join him in Buffalo. Yet, what did Luke have to offer a woman like Andi? Not much, and certainly not as much as her boyfriend had to offer. Luke would never make a ton of money, live in a fancy house, or be able to buy Andi beautiful and expensive things. He was just a cowboy who came home smelling of dirt, dust, and manure, who lived in a small cabin, and wore jeans every day. Andi deserved so much more than someone like him.

Not that any of this mattered. Despite their good-natured

teasing, it was unlikely a woman like Andi would ever fall in love with a guy like him.

Luke rode up to the cabin just as the sun dipped below the tree line. He led Chance to the corral and unsaddled him, then pumped more water into the trough for the horses. Luke was dirty, tired, and hungry. He didn't care what he ate for supper as long as it filled him up. He unbuttoned his shirt and slipped it off, then pulled off his T-shirt and hung them over the fence. He pumped some more water and washed his hands, face, and arms with it, even though it was ice cold, then leaned forward and ran water over his head, wetting his hair. Luke stood up and brushed his hair back with his hands. The warm air dried his skin quickly. He shook out his T-shirt and pulled it back on, picked up his other shirt and his hat, and strode to the side door of the cabin.

When Luke walked through the door, he immediately smelled food cooking. He looked over toward the stove and saw Andi standing there, stirring something in a pot. She smiled up at him.

"Hey there, Cowboy. How was your day?" Andi asked, her eyes twinkling mischievously.

Luke broke out into a broad smile. He couldn't help it. She looked adorable standing there by the stove, smiling over at him. "Just the usual. Riding fences, chasing outlaws, and playing poker at the saloon," he said with a grin. "What about you? Did you have a good day?"

"I did," Andi said. "I did some sketches and took a bunch of photos. Then I came inside and iced my ankle for a while."

"That's good to hear," Luke said. He hung his shirt and hat on the hook by the door and went to sit down at the table. It was all set for supper. "What are you cooking?"

"Stew." Andi continued stirring the contents of the pot.

"There's not a whole lot to choose from in the cupboard and we already had beans last night. Looks like soup will be on the menu for tomorrow night."

"Smells good. I'm glad you cooked. I'm as hungry as a bear."

"Do I need to get the rifle?" Andi teased.

"Don't worry, I won't bite."

Andi studied Luke a minute. "Why are you so wet?"

Luke reached up and ran his hands through his hair to push it back. "Sorry. I cleaned up out at the horse trough. I didn't want to come in and dirty up the kitchen sink.

Andi's brows rose. "The horse trough? Really? Well, you can't get any more cowboy than that, can you, Desperado?" She pulled two plates out of the cupboard, walked over, and set them on the table. Then she went back for the pot of stew.

"Hey, don't make fun of my favorite song," Luke said.

"I'm not. I happen to like that song," Andi said. She brought the pot over and began ladling stew onto Luke's plate. "Has it always been your favorite song?"

"No, but it is now."

Andi ladled stew onto her plate then returned the pan to the stove. She pulled a plate of sliced bread wrapped in paper towels from the oven and brought that and the jar of jam over to the table.

"This sure hits the spot," Luke said after eating a forkful of stew. He reached for the bread to sop up the gravy.

"Why?" Andi asked.

Luke looked at her, confused. "Why does the stew hit the spot?"

"No. Why is "Desperado" your favorite song now?"

Luke smiled and winked at her. "Because you and I danced to it."

Andi smiled at him but didn't say a word.

* * *

Luke insisted on cleaning the dishes after supper so Andi could rest her ankle. She lay down on the sofa and propped her foot up with the pillow. The swelling had gone down and the ankle wrap had helped all day to support it when she walked.

After Luke finished the dishes, he walked over to sofa. Andi had her sketchpad in hand and was putting a few finishing touches on one of her drawings.

"Do you mind?" Luke asked, pointing to the sofa.

Andi looked up, confused. "Mind what?"

To her surprise, Luke carefully lifted her legs up and sat down at the end of the sofa, setting her feet down in his lap. He lifted her hurt ankle and set the pillow under it so it would stay up high.

"Ah, no. I don't mind," she said, trying to ignore the fact that her feet were resting in his lap.

"Can I see what you sketched today?" Luke asked.

Andi sat there a moment, unsure. *What if he sees the other sketch of himself?* She decided it didn't really matter. At least he wasn't shirtless in it. "Sure. Here." She handed him the sketchpad.

Luke looked first at the sketch she'd been finishing. It was the one of Abby. He studied it a moment. "You caught her perfectly," he said. "The sharpness of her eyes, the strength of her body, yet her total beauty shines through. It's amazing."

"Thanks," Andi said, her cheeks heating up from his praise.

Luke lifted the page and studied the sketch of the cabin. Then he turned the page and stared at the fence and tree line sketch for a moment. He smiled. "Is that the water bottle you shot?"

Andi nodded. "That's probably the only thing I'll ever shoot. I had to capture it so I'll always remember."

Luke looked at her, his eyes warm. "You have an incredible talent, Andi. You can take a pencil and a piece of paper and make it come to life. You amaze me."

"Thanks, Luke. But they're just sketches. Templates, really. They aren't anything special."

"I'm serious. People would buy these. Don't you sell sketches?"

"Well, yes, but not ones like these. These are just what I draw for ideas for paintings. No one would want to buy these."

Luke shook his head. "I think you're wrong. People around here would buy them. They have a rustic appeal to them. They capture the heart of this country. They're beautiful."

Andi smiled at Luke. His opinion meant a lot to her.

Luke turned the page again. There, staring back at him, was a sketch of his face.

Andi put her hands over her eyes and groaned.

"You sketched me again?" Luke asked, sounding amused. "Well, at least I have my clothes on this time."

"I'm going to stop letting you look at my sketchpad," Andi said, reaching out to take it away from him.

Luke pulled it just out of her reach. "Why? Are you going to do more sketches of me?"

"No. I'm never sketching you again. I'm sure there are at least a hundred hot cowboys around here that I could sketch instead. Now give me that."

"A hundred hot cowboys around here?" Luke asked, chuckling. "So, you think I'm hot?"

Andi felt her face grow warm. "Just give me the sketchpad, Cowboy."

He flipped through the pages until he found the other sketch of him, shirtless. He turned it around for Andi to see. "Honestly, Andi. This looks like one of those fake cowboys on a romance novel. I don't look this good. No one looks this good in real life."

Andi shook her head. "Sorry, Luke Brennan, but that's you. You really look that good, as if you didn't already know."

Luke handed her back the sketchpad. "Aaah. I don't put much stock in looks. Looks fade fast. In a few years, I'll have a bald spot and a beer gut. You just wait and see. Then what will you think of me, Andi? Will I still be a 'hot cowboy'?"

Andi didn't answer. She didn't dare. Because as she looked across the sofa at Luke, all she saw was the most handsome man she'd ever met, and in her eyes, he'd always be that. No matter how bald he got or how big his beer gut was, he'd always be a hot cowboy to her.

Chapter Fifteen

The next day was much like the day before. Luke took off early and Andi spent the day close to the cabin, sketching. Her ankle felt much better, but she was still careful not to overuse it. Luke had told her that tomorrow morning they'd leave for home, so she wanted to be sure she could ride. First, though, he was taking her tonight to see the incredible valley view Ginny had talked about. She could hardly wait.

Luke returned a little earlier that evening and Andi had supper ready for him. As promised, they had vegetable soup with bread and also some of Ginny's canned peaches.

"I could get used to this," Luke teased as he walked in the door and hung up his hat.

I could too. Andi kept that thought to herself as she served up supper.

After they ate, Luke told Andi he'd get Chance ready so they could ride the short distance to the valley view.

"What about Abby?" Andi asked.

"I'd rather you not put pressure on your ankle until tomorrow when we leave," he said. "We can double up on Chance. It's a short ride."

Andi slipped her camera in its case and hung it across her body so it would stay in place. She stepped outside, walked carefully to the corral, and watched as Luke put on Chance's bridle. He then led Chance out the gate.

Andi frowned. "Where's his saddle?"

"We don't need it. We can ride bareback."

"I've never done that before," Andi said.

"Well, there's a first time for everything, City Girl," Luke said with a wicked grin.

"Watch it, Cowboy."

Luke chuckled and hopped up on Chance. He reached down to Andi. "Grab ahold of my arm and pull yourself up," he said. "Be careful of that ankle, though."

It took her two tries, but she made it up onto Chance's back behind Luke.

"Hold on tight," Luke said. "We can't have you falling off again."

"Hey. I didn't fall off. I was thrown."

"Either way, you ended up on the ground," Luke said.

Andi rolled her eyes even though he couldn't see her. There was nothing to hold onto except Luke, so she wrapped her arms around his waist.

Luke clicked his tongue and Chance started walking. They went around the back of the cabin and off on a trail that had a slow, but steady incline. Andi had to hang on tighter to Luke so she wouldn't slide off of Chance. The sway of the horse's body caused her to slip even closer to Luke, so their bodies touched with each motion of the horse. Andi had to admit, though, that it wasn't such a terrible thing to be up against Luke's rock hard body.

The trail ran through a forest of tall evergreens. Andi inhaled deeply. Their sweet scent smelled wonderful.

"I hope you're not smelling me," Luke said. "Or else you will fall off the horse."

Andi laughed. "No. I'm enjoying the scent of the pine trees. Don't you just love how they smell? Especially after a rain, when their scent is the strongest."

"Yeah, I do. I just never thought anyone else enjoyed it. The scent of evergreens reminds me of early mornings riding around the summer pasture with my dad. It was always the strongest up here."

"That's lovely. It reminds me of walking the trails around Mount Rainier National Forest with my parents and sister when I was younger," Andi said wistfully. "I guess childhood memories are the strongest."

"Adult memories can be nice, too," Luke said softly. "Maybe the smell of evergreen will remind you of today, too."

Andi closed her eyes and inhaled another deep breath. "I think it will," she said.

After riding up the incline for a time, the land flattened out and the trees opened up to a large field. Luke stopped Chance.

"Here is where we get off," he said. He put out his arm so Andi could grasp it and slide off of Chance. Then he slipped off, too. He led Chance to a lone tree and tied him to it so he wouldn't follow them. Chance happily stood there and grazed.

"Over here," Luke said. He held out his arm for support and Andi leaned against him.

They walked a short distance until the field became a rocky ledge that fell away to the most breathtaking view Andi had ever seen. Below was a lush, green valley painted in a burst of color with wildflowers, a sparkling river running through it, and pine trees sprinkled all about. In the distance were more rocky cliffs that also overlooked the valley. It looked like it went on for miles. With the sun making its way down through the clear sky, turning everything golden and orange, Andi felt like she was in Heaven, looking out over the world below.

She lifted her camera and began snapping photos of the valley and the surrounding area. It already looked like a scene that had been carefully painted to perfection. Andi knew in that moment that she wanted to capture it on canvas.

Andi turned to Luke, her eyes shimmering, nearly in tears. "Oh, Luke. Isn't it the most beautiful sight you've ever seen?"

"I beg to differ," Luke said, walking over to stand in front of Andi. He reached around her and slowly pulled out the band that held her hair back in a ponytail. Her hair fell loose. Luke ran his hands through it, fanning it out around her shoulders, and then he gently took the camera strap from around her neck and raised it up over her head. Andi stood there, watching him, unable to move, her heart pounding.

Luke stepped back a few feet and lifted the camera up to look in the view finder. He snapped a photo of Andi with the valley behind her. Then he walked back to her and slipped the camera strap around her neck once more. He reached behind her and slowly pulled her hair loose of the strap, letting it fall once more on her shoulders.

"Now it's the most beautiful sight I've ever seen," he said, gazing down at her.

Andi stood there, looking up into Luke's warm, blue eyes. She was speechless. Before she could react, Luke reached around her and placed his strong hands on her waist. She took a breath just as he ducked his head and claimed her lips with his.

* * *

Luke pulled Andi to him and kissed her with more passion than he'd ever kissed a woman in his life. He'd been right. Her lips were luscious. Her mouth opened and their tongues danced. She was as delicious as he'd imagined, except this was no dream. This was real.

Luke felt Andi's arms reach up around his neck and pull him closer. If it hadn't been for the camera hanging down between them, their bodies would have melted into one. With the setting sun as their backdrop, Luke and Andi kissed like two people desperately in need of one another. Neither hesitated. Both hungered for more.

Andi pushed the camera aside so their bodies could mold together. Luke ran his hands up her back and into her hair so he could run his fingers through its silky thickness. Andi's hands explored Luke's muscular back. It wasn't until Luke pulled back a moment to catch his breath that he realized what he'd done.

Andi's green eyes sparked with desire for him. It was all Luke could do to pull away and step back. If he kissed her again, he knew he wouldn't be able to stop.

Andi closed her eyes a moment and took a deep breath. She opened them when Luke spoke huskily.

"We should head back."

Andi nodded. They walked without a word back to Chance and Luke untied the horse. He pulled himself up onto Chance's back and offered his hand to Andi. She grasped his arm and he pulled her up in one smooth motion. Without hesitating, Andi placed her arms around Luke's waist and laid her head against his back. When she sighed, Luke's heart melted. He had never wanted a woman as much as he wanted Andi right now, but he knew he couldn't have her. She didn't belong to him. He turned Chance around and headed back to the cabin.

* * *

Once inside the cabin, neither said a word as they put away their things and readied for bed. They were leaving tomorrow morning, so Andi packed up her sketchpad, dirty clothes, and camera into the saddlebags and only left out her clean clothes for tomorrow. She also straightened up the cabin and made sure everything was put away for the next person who'd stay here. She wondered if it would be Luke again. She wondered if he'd think of her when he stayed here next. She knew she shouldn't care, but she did.

Luke turned off the generator and the cabin grew dark except for the silver light of the crescent moon shining through the small windows. Andi lay on her bunk and Luke lay in his. She wondered if he'd ever say another word to her. Was he embarrassed? Mad at himself? Or did he think she was angry. Of course, she hadn't said anything yet either. She was still getting her bearings after what had happened. Luke's kiss hadn't upset her—it had scared the bejeezus out of her. His kiss had unlocked more raw emotion in her than she'd ever felt before. And truth be told, she'd liked it.

Oh, my God. I kissed a cowboy! Just like Carly told me to do. And I liked it!

A nervous giggle escaped from Andi's lips into the dark room.

"What's so funny?" Luke asked.

"Nothing. Sorry. Were you sleeping?"

"No."

Because you were thinking of kissing me. This thought delighted Andi.

Luke said brusquely. "I'm not going to apologize for kissing you."

"I don't expect you to," Andi replied.

Luke rustled in his bed above her. She saw him lean over and look at her. "I liked kissing you, Andi," Luke said, his voice now soft and warm.

Andi closed her eyes as her heart swelled. "Me, too," she said quietly.

The room fell silent again as both lay there in their own thoughts. Finally, Andi spoke up. "Tell me about Ashley."

"Hmmm. I suppose my mother told you about her."

"Yes. A little. I'm curious about her."

Luke sighed. "Ashley is beautiful, intelligent, and talented. She had too much going for her to be tied to just a cowboy."

"Don't sell yourself short, Cowboy," Andi insisted. "You have an engineering degree, you worked for a major corporation in California, and now you run a two-thousand acre ranch with over eight hundred head of cattle. Ashley saw something in you that she admired or else she'd never have married you in the first place. Now, tell me about Ashley without putting yourself down."

"Fine," Luke said. "I met Ashley when I was in my second year of college and she was waitressing at a little burger joint where my friends and I ate regularly. She was adorable. She was short and petite and had the most amazing long, blond hair that seemed to sparkle in the sun. Her blue eyes were big and expressive. And when she smiled, well, it made you feel special. At least, it made me feel special. She was musical and was going to college for that. She played the violin and the piano beautifully. I never dreamed a girl like that would ever give me a second glance, but she did. We were married two years later, after I graduated, and we moved directly down to southern California where I'd been recruited by Boeing. Ashley loved it there and blended right in. She taught music in a middle school there, but her goal was to one day play for one of the larger symphony orchestras in Los Angeles. She practiced all the time and auditioned a couple of times for different orchestras. But then my dad got sick and I felt it was time to come home."

"Did Ashley want to move here?" Andi asked.

"She never told me outright that she didn't want to come here. She went along with it for me. Ashley had met my parents only a couple of times and she and my mother got along well, so maybe she thought she could live here. We moved here in the spring and I began building our cabin right away so she'd have a place of her own. I was excited to be back here and working on the ranch. I hadn't realized just how much I'd missed it until I came home. But Ashley never showed any enthusiasm at all. Even with the cabin. I'd ask her opinion on everything to do with it, and she just said whatever I did was fine with her. We moved into the cabin that fall, and by the next spring, she left."

"I'm so sorry, Luke," Andi said gently.

"It was for the best. I had to let her go. In that one year, she became a shadow of herself. She missed the big city, she missed being around a lot of people, and the opportunities a big city could give her. She just wilted here, and it broke my heart to watch her fade. I knew there was no way I could go back to the city and work. I belonged here. And I also knew that she'd never be happy here. We didn't fight about it, we just said goodbye and that was that."

"Do you know where she is now? Did she marry again?" Andi asked.

"She's somewhere in California, the last I heard. We don't stay in touch. That's for the best, too."

"Do you still love her?" Andi asked, nearly in a whisper.

"I don't know," Luke said. "I suppose I always will. But, I'm not holding out for her to ever come back. I know it's over.

She's a city girl and I'm a cowboy. Oil and water. It doesn't mix well together."

Andi closed her eyes. *City girl.* There were those words again. And that is what he thought of her. Just a city girl who could never be anything else. The thought made Andi sad.

"Now it's your turn," Luke said, interrupting Andi's thoughts. "Tell me about Derek."

Andi's eyes flew open. "Why?" she asked.

"I told you about Ashley. Now you tell me about your fiancé."

"But you already know about him. He works for a huge bank chain, he's on the fast track to management, he's ambitious, a hard worker, and he likes the good things in life. He won't stop until he gets what he wants."

"Are you one of those things he wants?" Luke asked.

"What do you mean by that?"

"It just sounds like he always goes after what he wants and gets it. Did he do that with you?"

"No. I mean, yes. Oh, I don't know," Andi said, frustrated. "I'm not a thing to him. Derek loves me. He's always looking out for me and wants what's best for me. He's supportive in my art career and he wants me to continue it wherever we live. There aren't many men who'd be so generous. I mean, I make money at it, but not the kind of money that Derek makes, and he's fine with me pursuing my art."

"That's very considerate of him," Luke said.

Andi frowned. Luke sounded very sarcastic. "You don't know Derek, so you don't understand. He's a good guy. He wants to take care of me. I think that's a good thing."

"Do you love him?" Luke asked. "I mean, really love him?"

"Of course," Andi insisted.

"And he'll make you happy for the rest of your life?" Luke asked.

Andi lay quiet for a moment, mulling over Luke's question. "Andi?"

"No one knows what the future holds. The rest of my life is a long time," Andi said quietly.

"Yeah, it is. Hey, Andi? I'm just giving you a hard time. I'm happy that you have someone to take care of you. I'm sure you two will be very happy," Luke told her.

Andi swallowed hard. "Thanks."

Andi lay in her bunk mulling over their conversation long after she heard Luke's steady breathing as he slept. Did she love Derek? Really love him? Like the way Luke had talked about loving Ashley. After she and Derek had met, they seemed to click, but Andi was never sure why. He loved power and money and she wasn't interested in either. She enjoyed her art and was fine with making enough money to pay the bills and maybe stash a little away. Derek, however, wasn't going to stop pushing until he lived in a penthouse and had more money than he could ever spend. But, he was sweet to her and encouraged her in her pursuits. And the day he'd proposed, he'd promised to take care of her for the rest of their lives. That was love, wasn't it?

Andi's mind returned to the kiss she'd shared with Luke. She'd never been kissed like that. There had been more passion in that one kiss than she'd ever felt before. And she'd responded in kind. Luke made her feel things that no man had ever made her feel before. Like butterflies in her stomach at the thought of just one kiss. Why didn't it feel the same way when Derek kissed her?

Andi had no answers, but she knew one thing for certain. If she wanted to marry Derek, she'd better stay as far away as possible from Luke's lips.

Chapter Sixteen

Andi and Luke left the cabin early the next morning. Andi had wrapped her ankle for support and it didn't feel too bad for riding. Occasionally, she'd feel a twinge, but then she'd put more weight on her other leg instead and it was fine.

Neither of them spoke much on the ride home. They were both lost in their own thoughts. Andi was just trying to digest everything that had happened since they arrived at the cabin. And the kiss. Had it meant anything or was it just one of those things that happen when two people spent too much time together alone? Luke had said he wasn't sorry, that he liked kissing her. What in the world did that mean? Andi had felt an underlying tension between them since the moment they met. They'd argued, they'd teased each other, and they'd even shared details of their lives with one another. Andi sensed that Luke would rather have a root canal than talk about himself or his past, yet he had when she'd asked. For some unknown reason, she and Luke had formed a deep connection, and Andi couldn't deny that when Luke touched her, she felt sparks. But she loved Derek, right? She was going to marry him and spend the rest of her life with him. Yet, she felt something more than friendship with Luke.

They stopped a couple of times for Andi to take photos. She loved the many faces of the ranch, from the green pastures dappled with color from wildflowers to the lush forests of pines. It was all so beautiful, and she wanted to have remembrances of it for when she was gone. She wanted so badly to take a picture of Luke, to have proof that the perfect cowboy did exist, but she thought better of it. At least she had her sketches of him. They were much more personal than any photo could be.

It was late afternoon when they arrived at the ranch and stopped outside the horse barn. Randy came out to meet them. By now, Andi's ankle hurt badly, but she still offered to unsaddle Abby. Randy told them both to go up to the house and he'd take care of the horses. Neither Luke or Andi argued with him. They were hot, tired, and hungry.

Luke grabbed both saddlebags and slung them over his shoulder. They walked together up to the house. Before they made it to the door, Ginny came out with a worried frown on her face. Bree bounded out to greet them, too.

"Hey, you two. Did you have a good time?" Ginny asked.

"Yeah, it was fun," Andi said.

"That's good," Ginny said. She came up closer to Andi and spoke in a quiet voice. "Your fiancé is on the phone. He's been calling every day since you left, and I wasn't sure what to tell him. I said you were away from the house and would call him back, but now he's getting impatient. I'm sorry, dear. I didn't know if I should tell him you were gone for a few days or not."

Andi placed her hand on the other woman's arm. "It's okay, Ginny. I'll go talk to him." She gave Ginny a weak smile and walked into the house. Luke didn't hesitate. He followed Andi inside.

Ginny stopped him in the mudroom. "Let's give them some privacy," she whispered. "He didn't sound too happy."

Luke frowned, but stayed put.

Andi walked over to the phone and stared at it a moment, then gingerly picked it up. She took a deep breath to muster up some courage, then said a cheery, "Hi, Derek."

"Where in the hell have you been?" Derek growled through the line. "I've been calling you since Monday and you never called me back. And that woman kept saying you were busy and that she'd tell you I called. Why didn't you return my calls?"

Andi's shoulders sagged. She wasn't going to lie to Derek, but she knew his response to the truth was going to be even angrier than he was right now. "I was gone for a few days to a little cabin they have in the summer pasture," Andi said. "Ginny wasn't sure if she should say where I was, so she didn't tell you. It's not her fault. It's mine. I should have messaged you before we left."

"We? Who was with you? And why would she lie to me?" Derek asked.

Andi took a breath. She ducked her head a little and spoke quietly into the phone. "I went with Ginny's son, Luke. He went there to check on the cattle and the fences, and I went along to take some photos and do a few sketches. It was beautiful there, Derek. Ginny thought I should go and see it, and she was right. No one meant to lie to you. I was going to tell you when I got back."

"You went off to some place alone with some guy? No wonder she lied to me. What the hell is going on there, Andi? Are you having some sort of fling with a ranch hand? Here I am, far away from you, worried as hell about you and you're out flitting around with some other guy."

"No, it's not like that," Andi said. From the corner of her eye, she saw Luke standing in the back porch, a deep crease between his brows. She turned her head away from him and pulled the phone cord as far as it would go around the corner of the doorway into the sitting room. She felt small, and she didn't want Luke seeing her that way.

"Then tell me what it's like," Derek said. "What would you think if I went off for three days somewhere with another woman? Would that be okay?"

"Derek, please, don't be angry. It wasn't like that. We're just friends. Everyone here is so nice and friendly. We're like family, nothing more."

There was a long silence that weighed heavily on Andi. Finally, Derek spoke in that calm, controlled way he had when he was trying to manage his anger. "We're engaged, Andi. Remember that. You're with me now. Who else is going to support you and your art career? Who will give you everything I can? That cowboy *friend* of yours? Ha! I doubt it. Remember that the next time you decide to go off with another man."

The line went dead.

As steady as she could, Andi walked back into the kitchen and hung up the phone. She turned toward the mudroom and caught a glimpse of Luke's angry face. It was more than she could take. Andi turned and ran up the stairs to her room.

* * *

Luke dropped the saddlebags onto the floor and took one step toward the kitchen before Ginny placed a hand on his chest.

"No, Luke," she said. "Leave her be. She needs to be alone."

Luke stood there a moment, looking like he was going to

push past his mother, then he stepped back. He turned and strode outside.

* * *

Andi lay on her bed and cried for a long time after her conversation with Derek. He'd been right. She shouldn't have gone off with Luke alone. She was engaged to Derek, and she put their relationship at risk when she spent time with Luke. She hadn't thought of it that way, because she'd felt so comfortable around Luke. But then there'd been that kiss, that amazing kiss, and that changed everything.

Derek had never been anything but good to her and he didn't deserve for her to disrespect him. He'd always been generous and giving. He may have gotten angry with her a time or two, but he was never unkind. Today's conversation was not typical of how he spoke to her. He was generally polite and considerate. For him to blow up at her like that just proved how worried he'd been about her.

Andi sat up and grabbed her phone. She sent an apology to Derek by email, telling him she was sorry she'd worried him and that he was right, she shouldn't have gone to the cabin with another man. She told him again that nothing happened, and she and Luke were just friends. She hoped Derek would believe her.

Andi showered and changed into clean clothes. It was almost suppertime and she knew she should go help Ginny. She was embarrassed that Ginny and Luke had overheard her conversation with Derek. She could only imagine what they were thinking. The look on Luke's face after she'd hung up had devastated her. He'd looked angry as hell. But he didn't understand. Derek had been right and she'd been wrong.

With a heavy heart, Andi went downstairs.

* * *

Luke was mad as hell and had every right to be. He'd watched Andi slowly unravel during her phone conversation with the man who was supposed to be in love with her. He'd wanted to grab the phone out of her hand and tell that Derek guy just where he could go. But, of course, he hadn't. When Andi ran upstairs, he'd wanted to follow her, hold her in his arms, and comfort her. But his mother had stopped him. Maybe his mom had been right. Maybe Andi had needed some time alone. But, damn if it hadn't broken his heart to see the pain on her face.

That's it, you idiot. You know it's true, so admit it. You're in love with Andi. And she belongs to someone else.

How could he have fallen in love with a woman he'd only known for seven days? It was insane, but it was true.

After Luke left the house, he'd driven his truck back to his cabin, turned on the generator, and drank a warm beer from the fridge. He'd showered away the three days of dirt and stink he'd accumulated and changed into a clean T-shirt and jeans. He didn't head up to the house for supper, though. He didn't trust himself to be in the same room as Andi with everyone else around. His emotions were too transparent right now. So, he sat on his sofa in his quiet cabin and ate crackers for supper and drank another warm beer. As the sun began to fall behind the hills, he slipped on his flannel shirt and walked up the road to the barn.

* * *

Luke was noticeably absent from the supper table that night. Ginny made the excuse that he was probably tired from working in the summer pasture, but Andi knew differently.

Randy and Colt ate without saying much, as usual, while Ginny tried to keep a steady stream of conversation flowing with Andi. She asked what Andi thought of the view at the summer pasture and if she'd done many sketches. Andi tried answering all of Ginny's questions, but her mind was far away. She was actually relieved when supper was over and she could escape outside after helping Ginny clean up.

Andi walked outside with Bree at her heels and stared out past the hills where the sun was slowly setting. She closed her eyes and inhaled deeply. The scent of evergreen and freshly cut hay came her way. She loved this ranch. She loved everything about it and everyone on it. There was a sense of calm that came over her when she stood here, overlooking the beauty of it all. And the people. They had all found a place in her heart. Cute, shy, Colt who could dance up a storm. Randy, who said few words, but always managed a kind smile. Ginny, who was so warm and caring and was the backbone of the entire ranch. Even Bree, who happily followed Andi around the ranch. And Luke. Andi took a deep breath when she thought of Luke, the hunky cowboy who irritated her one minute and warmed her heart the next. Andi had never felt as comfortable with a man as she felt with Luke. He'd seen her good side, and her stubborn, argumentative side. Yet, he had still kissed her.

Derek and she had never fought before. He just didn't tolerate it. It wasn't civilized. And they'd never had much reason to fight, until now. Andi had fit into his life easily, because she'd accepted the fact that his work was paramount to him and she came second. Standing here now, it wasn't a comforting thought that she came second to money for him.

She knew she could always count on him, though, to take care of her in every way possible. Maybe that wasn't what every girl dreamed of, but for her, it was important.

Sighing, Andi walked to the corral fence and searched the field for Abby. Her eyes adjusted to the growing darkness and she spotted the horse on the other side, grazing. When she left, Andi knew she was going to miss riding Abby. The thought made her heart feel heavy.

The barn door was slightly ajar and through the open crack, Andi saw a light on. She pulled the door open a bit more and entered, thinking that Colt must be working in the barn. A tall man in a blue plaid flannel shirt had his back to her as he pitched fresh straw into a stall. Andi recognized the long, muscular legs and broad shoulders immediately.

"I thought you'd gone home," Andi said softly.

Luke turned suddenly and stared at Andi. "Well, this time you startled me," he said, giving her a small grin. "I was at home, but I was restless. Thought I'd do a little more work."

Andi stared up into his blue eyes. They were the most gorgeous set of eyes she'd ever seen on a man. Frown lines appeared around them and Andi looked away. "I guess I should leave," she said, turning. The last thing she needed was to spend more alone time with Luke.

Luke dropped the pitchfork and was at her side before she could take a step. He placed a hand on her arm. "Don't leave," he said huskily. "I want to talk to you."

Andi stood still, the warmth of his hand radiating through her arm. *How can a single touch from this man bring chills up my spine?* She'd never felt anything like it before. Slowly, she turned and gazed at Luke. His face was mere inches from hers.

"Are you okay?" he asked gently.

Andi frowned. "Of course, I'm okay. Why would you ask that?"

"After the way Derek spoke to you, I figured you'd be upset," Luke said.

"I'm fine. Everything is fine," Andi insisted. "It was all a misunderstanding."

Luke's lips pulled into a tight line. "No man should ever talk to a woman the way that man talked to you."

Andi's eyes grew wide. "What do you mean? You couldn't have possibly heard what he said."

"I didn't have to hear the words to know how he spoke to you," Luke said. "No man ever has the right to make a woman shrink into herself. I watched you grow smaller and smaller as he talked to you. You are a tough, strong woman, Andi, but I saw you fade with every word he said to you. It's just not right."

Andi swallowed hard. Tears welled up in her eyes. She had felt small when she'd spoken to Derek. He had a way of making her feel that way sometimes. But the fact that Luke saw it so clearly cut deeply. "You don't understand. He had a right to be angry. I shouldn't have gone off alone with you when I'm engaged to him."

Luke's eyes burned like fire. "Dammit, Andi. He doesn't own you. You have every right to do whatever you want. You didn't do anything wrong. How can you let him talk to you that way?"

"Derek's a good man," Andi insisted as a tear trickled down her cheek. "You don't know him. He takes care of me. He worries about me. I'm lucky he even chose me."

"You're lucky?" Luke asked, astounded. "You're lucky he chose you? The way I see it, he's dammed lucky you said yes. Does he even know anything about you? Who you really are?

Has he ever seen your stubborn side? Or your ability to adapt to difficult situations so effortlessly? Does he realize how talented you are or how kind and caring you are?"

"Of course he knows me," Andi said. "He's known me for almost three years."

"No, Andi. I'm asking if he knows you. The real you. You're the most stubborn, strongest, opinionated yet kindest woman I've ever met. You have no qualms about showing those sides to me. Yet, you let him ride roughshod all over you today without a word. Why don't you fight back with him? Why do you let him treat you that way? You deserve so much better."

"You just don't understand," Andi said.

"Yes, I do," Luke countered. "He has to be in charge. He calls all the shots. Why do you let him do that?"

"It's not like that," Andi said.

"Really? Whose idea was it to move to Buffalo?" Luke asked.

"It's his job. He had no choice."

"Didn't he? Did he even ask if you'd want to move across country? Did he give you any choice at all?"

"It doesn't matter where I live. I can do my art anywhere. He has to move for his job," Andi insisted.

"Who picked out the place where you'll live there? Who chose the furniture?" Luke asked.

"He did. What does it matter? I don't care about all that stuff."

"That's the point, Andi. He runs every aspect of your life. How can you expect to be happy when he's always telling you what to do?"

Hot tears fell down Andi's cheeks as anger rose inside her. "You don't know anything about me," she yelled at Luke. "You've known me for a week. He's known me for three years.

I'm lucky to have someone like Derek who is willing to take care of me. He's dependable. He's responsible. And he'll be very successful someday. I will always be safe with him. I can do my art and not worry about paying the bills or keeping a roof over my head."

"Is that all you want?" Luke asked. "Someone to take care of you? What about love? What about respect? What about passion? Aren't those things more important?"

"You just don't get it, Luke. I've been taking care of everything since I was eighteen years old. I had to unravel my parent's financial mess, sell the business, make a living, raise Carly, and put both of us through college. Do you think that was easy? For ten years I've been the dependable one who worried, worked, and held everything together. I'm tired. Don't you understand? I don't want to be responsible for everyone else anymore. So, if Derek wants to be in charge of our life, that's fine with me. Because, I just can't do it alone anymore."

Andi dropped to her knees on the soft straw as tears fell fast and hard down her face. Luke was beside her in an instant. He wrapped his arms around her.

"I'm sorry, Andi," Luke said softly. "I shouldn't have pushed you. You're right. I don't know how it's been for you all these years. You deserve to be happy."

Andi's head dropped onto Luke's shoulder as he held her close. Her shoulders shook. Hot tears stained his shirt. Now that the dam had opened, it was hard for her to stop. They sat on the floor like that for several minutes until Andi could contain herself. Luke held her gently. Beside them on the floor, Bree came over, snuggled up against Andi, and whimpered.

Andi finally pulled away from Luke and patted Bree gently before rising.

"I don't want to fight anymore," Andi said. "I'm so tired of fighting."

"I'm sorry," Luke said. "I seem to do nothing but give you grief. I won't do that anymore. At least, I won't try to."

Andi took a deep breath and sighed. She turned to leave. "Come on, Bree. Let's go." The dog stood and followed.

"Andi, wait," Luke said.

Andi stopped, but didn't turn around.

"I care about you, Andi. I think you already know that," Luke said sadly. "And I don't want to do anything to make you unhappy. I'll try not to butt in anymore. It's just that, maybe Derek isn't the man I think he is. Maybe he is a good person, I don't know. But I sure as hell hope he's the man you think he is before you tie yourself to him forever. For your sake."

Andi dropped her head and walked out into the night.

Chapter Seventeen

Breakfast the next morning was just Andi and Ginny. Randy and Colt had eaten earlier and left in the truck for the summer pasture. They were going to repair the areas of fence that Luke had noted were weak or broken. Luke had eaten earlier, too, as usual. That was fine with Andi. She wasn't ready to run into him any time soon.

After breakfast, Andi helped Ginny put labels and ribbons on the dozens of jars of canned peaches she'd made while Andi was at the cabin. They were halfway through when the phone rang. Ginny got up to answer it.

"Hon, it's for you," she told Andi.

Andi frowned. "Is it Derek?" she whispered. She hadn't heard back from him yet after sending the email.

Ginny shook her head. "I think it's the man from the garage."

Andi took the phone from Ginny and listened to what Jeff had to say. With a sigh, she hung up and returned to the kitchen table.

"More bad news?" Ginny asked.

"Good and bad news. The transmission finally arrived,

but the bolts from the old one broke when they took it out. I guess they were rusted pretty badly. So, now they have to order those and wait for them."

"Huh," Ginny said. "Wouldn't you think they would have pulled it out first before ordering the new transmission? Then they would have known about the bolts and ordered those, too."

Andi shrugged. "You would think. But Jeff said they always wait until the new one comes in before pulling out the old one. Something about not wasting the mechanic's time in case they can't get a new one. I guess that makes sense."

"So, how much longer do they think before your car is ready?"

"Probably another week, maybe sooner, he didn't know for sure. I'm sorry, Ginny. I can always go and stay at a hotel. I hate to keep imposing upon you."

"Bite your tongue," Ginny said. "You're not imposing upon us and I would never let you go stay at a hotel. You can stay here as long as you need to. Or as long as you like. Whichever is longer." Ginny grinned. "I'd keep you here forever if I could. I love having you here."

"Thanks, Ginny." Andi stood and walked to the other side of the table to give the older woman a big hug. "But watch what you say. I might take you up on the forever part. I'm getting attached to this ranch."

Ginny laughed. "You always have a room here, Andi. Although, I'm not sure your fiancé would appreciate that."

Andi sighed again.

After they had finished with the jars, Andi helped Ginny make sandwiches for lunch. There were only the three of them, so they didn't have many to make.

"Andi? There's something I wanted to run by you," Ginny said.

"Okay. Shoot."

"I know you're worried about how much money it's going to cost to fix your car, and I thought of a way you might be able to earn some money while you're here."

Andi looked at Ginny with interest. "How?"

"Well, you know how I said that some ladies and I share a booth at the fair in Missoula for the week. We sell our preserves and one of the ladies makes a few craft items to sell. I was thinking you could have some of your prints sent out here and sell them."

"Huh," Andi said. "That's an idea. But most of my prints are of seascapes and landscapes. Would anyone be interested in those here?"

Ginny's eyes lit up. "I think so. Remember when I told you that there are a lot of people who have summer homes here from all over the country? Not everyone wants only western pictures in their homes. Plus, we get tourists from all over, too. Just think about it, dear. It couldn't hurt to try."

Andi nodded. Ginny was right. It wouldn't hurt to have a few there to sell. At least she'd make a little extra money.

Ginny brought out a small cooler and packed up sandwiches, homemade cookies, and sodas. "Here, dear. If I know that son of mine, he'll work all day on that stable of his and won't come in for lunch. Do you mind taking this out to him? I packed enough for the both of you."

"Oh." Andi hesitated. Spending time alone with Luke wasn't something she was eager to do. But she didn't want to have to explain why to Ginny.

"It's beautiful out, Andi. You don't want to be stuck inside here. Go ahead. Have a picnic outside. You can drive my truck over to Luke's place. He's working on the stable out back. The keys are in the ignition."

Reluctantly, Andi picked up the cooler. "Okay. Thanks." She headed outdoors to the white pick-up truck and drove over to Luke's cabin. She saw a narrow road that went around back and followed it. Out in the fenced-in field, she saw Luke, shirtless, up on the roof of a small building, pounding nails.

Andi sighed. He just had to be shirtless, didn't he?

Luke looked up when the truck stopped at the fence. Andi hopped out with the cooler, climbed over the short fence, and walked over toward the stable.

God he looks good. No man has a right to look that perfect.

"I brought lunch," Andi hollered up to him.

Luke climbed down the ladder and pulled on his T-shirt before walking over to Andi. "That was nice," he said, smiling. "But you didn't have to."

"It was your mom's idea, not mine," she said. She glanced around. "Where can we sit and eat this?"

"There's a blanket in the back seat of my mom's truck. I'll go get it," Luke offered. He retrieved the old, plaid blanket, brought it over to a grassy spot under a lone tree, and spread it out. "Does this work?"

Andi smiled. "Are you guys always so prepared?"

"The blanket is for the winter in case she breaks down. We all have one in our vehicles."

"Oh. I usually don't drive too far, so I guess I never thought of that," Andi said, sitting down on the blanket and opening the cooler. "I'm sure it gets a lot colder here than in Seattle, too."

Luke grinned. "A little bit, I suppose."

They both sat there in the shade, eating turkey sandwiches and drinking sodas. It was a warm day, but it felt good sitting under the tree.

"I'm sorry…" Luke began.

"I'm sorry..." Andi said at the same time.

They looked at each other, startled, then laughed.

"Go ahead," Andi told Luke.

"I was going to say I'm sorry about last night. I shouldn't butt into your business, and I'll try not to again. I guess I was pulling that big brother thing again," Luke said.

Andi cocked her head. "Is that what it is? A big brother thing? What about when you kissed me? Don't tell me that was brotherly."

Luke frowned a moment, then let out a sigh. "You're right. I can't hide behind that big brother excuse. I just felt like I had to protect you. I hate seeing a man bully a woman. Correction. I hated seeing him bullying you."

Andi looked down at the ground. Luke's honesty triggered her already fragile emotions. She took a deep breath. "I'm sorry I reacted the way I did last night. I don't want to fight with you. We seem to do that a lot."

Luke ducked his head and looked into Andi's eyes. "We get along really well, too."

"Yeah." Andi gave him a small smile. "We do, don't we? Why do you think that is?"

"Well, maybe because we're always completely honest with each other. We are who we are. There are no games between us. It's not like when people are dating and trying to impress each other. We show each other who we really are."

"Are we always completely honest?" Andi asked, her eyes sparkling with mischief.

Luke looked at her seriously. "I did kiss you, didn't I? That's about as honest as it gets."

Andi sat there, not knowing how to respond. She decided it was best to change the subject. "The garage called today."

"Yeah? What did they say?"

"It's going to take even longer to fix my car. They had to order new bolts. Looks like I'll be staying here a while longer."

"I think we can put up with you for a bit longer," Luke teased.

"Your mom had an idea. She thought I could sell my prints at the fair. What do you think?"

Luke sat there a moment, considering. "Can you have them here in time? The fair is next week."

Andi nodded. "I can have Carly ship them two-day delivery. Or overnight, if it's absolutely necessary. It's pricey, but I have to ship them to Buffalo anyway, so I might as well send them here first."

"Then I think it's a great idea. I'm sure you'd sell a lot of prints at the fair," Luke said.

"And you're basing that off of what? My sketch of you shirtless?" Andi asked with a wicked grin.

Luke rolled his eyes. "You better not sell that sketch," he said. "I'm basing it off of your painting of the Lone Cypress. It's amazing, Andi. If your other prints are as beautiful as that, then you will sell quite a lot."

"Thanks," Andi said softly. Her eyes turned devilish. "You know, if I framed that sketch of you shirtless, I'll bet I could get a lot of money for it. Maybe a couple hundred dollars. I'm sure the girls would line up to bid on it."

"Don't you dare. Don't even tease about it," Luke warned. "And don't show it to anyone. It's embarrassing."

"Then you should keep your shirt on," Andi said, laughing.

Luke joined in laughing with her.

* * *

As soon as Andi returned to the house, she called Carly at the gallery and asked her to sort through the prints and box up a good selection to send out.

"You're going to be there another week?" Carly asked. "Lucky you. I want to spend a summer with hunky cowboys."

"I'm not spending the summer with hunky cowboys," Andi said. "I'm waiting for my car to be fixed. Hopefully, I'll sell enough prints to pay for the bill. At the very least, I'll make a little extra money."

Carly promised to box up the prints and send them out right away. After chatting a few more minutes, the sisters hung up. Andi was suddenly excited by the idea of selling her work here. She sat there, lost in thought, when the phone rang and shook her out of her trance.

Cheerfully, she answered, "Brennan Ranch."

"Andi? Is that you?"

The smile on Andi's face faded. "Hi, Derek."

"Are you answering their phone for them now? Like a secretary?" Derek asked.

"No. I was just talking to Carly, so I was close to the phone."

"Oh." Derek hesitated a moment. "I got your email last night. I should have called you right back, but I thought I should wait a day so I'd have a clear head."

Andi frowned. Was he going to break up with her?

"I owe you an apology. I shouldn't have overreacted the way I did yesterday. I'm sorry, Andi."

Andi's mouth dropped open. She hadn't expected Derek to apologize. He rarely admitted when he was wrong. "Thank you, Derek," she said softly. "And I'm sorry that I worried you."

"I appreciate that," Derek said. After a moment's pause, he asked, "Is everything okay with us, Andi? I feel like we've become disconnected ever since you decided to take the road trip to Buffalo instead of flying out here with me."

Andi sat there a moment, pondering his question. She had to admit that since she'd been staying at the ranch, she'd started questioning her relationship with Derek. More specifically, ever since she'd met Luke. Her feelings for Luke confused her. She had thought she loved Derek, but now she wasn't completely sure if he was the man she wanted to spend her life with. Yet, she didn't know what had changed.

"Andi? Are you still there?" Derek asked.

"Yes, I'm still here," Andi said. "Can I ask you a question first?"

"Sure."

"Where do you see yourself in ten years? Where do you see us?" Andi asked.

"You know my plan as well as I do," Derek said. "In the next few years, I see myself as the manager, or at the very least, accounts manager, of a bank in Manhattan. You and I will be living in an upscale apartment with a view of Central Park, giving dinner parties for important clients, and living the high life. Our place will be big enough for you to have a room just for your art, so you can work on it undisturbed as much as you want. I even see you showing your work in quaint little galleries around Manhattan. We're going to have everything we've ever wanted, Andi. Everyone will envy us."

Andi did know that was Derek's dream, and until now, it hadn't bothered her as long as she could continue with her art. But, hearing him say all that as she sat in the cozy ranch kitchen made it all seem so ridiculous. Andi wasn't an upscale socialite. She was a down-to-earth girl.

"Derek, what if I don't fit into that plan? What if I'm more SoHo than Manhattan? I'm not sure I can be happy catering to your rich clients and putting on a show."

"What are you talking about?" Derek asked. "Of course, you'd fit into that world. I would never have asked you to marry me if I'd thought we couldn't be happy together. Andi, you're beautiful, intelligent, talented, and educated. You'd fit in anywhere."

"What about children? Do they fit into your plan, too?" Andi asked.

"I'll be honest, Andi. I don't know. I know you've mentioned having children before, but we never seriously discussed it. That's something we can negotiate after we get married. Is having a child that important to you?"

"Maybe. I think I might like to have children one day."

"Sweetie, we don't have to make all these decisions in one day. When you get here, we can talk about all of this. Once you get here and see how wonderful it is, I'm sure all your reservations will disappear."

"Maybe," Andi said without enthusiasm.

"Have you heard about your car yet? When will it be fixed?" Derek asked.

"They had to order more parts. I'll be here another week," Andi told him.

"Well, okay. But please come here as soon as it's fixed. Our being separated has put stress on our relationship. We are meant for each other, Andi. Believe me. I can take care of you like no other man ever could. We'll be happy together."

After saying goodbye, Andi thought about what Derek had said. *They were meant for each other.* She was no longer sure of that. They could *negotiate* having a child after they were married. That hadn't settled well with Andi at all. She wasn't sure if Derek had actually listened to her. He just talked circles around all the concerns she'd brought up. Their conversation had left her even more confused about their relationship instead of feeling more secure about it.

As of this moment, Andi wasn't sure she wanted to marry Derek. She had a lot to think about over the next week.

Chapter Eighteen

The three of them ate an easy supper of grilled chicken, baked potatoes, peas, and strawberries from the garden topped with whipped cream for dessert. They talked about safe subjects, like the upcoming fair in Missoula, the weather, and how Luke's stable was coming along. Andi felt the tension from her phone conversation with Derek slowly fade away and enjoyed Ginny and Luke's company.

After helping Ginny clean up, Andi headed outside. The temperature was dropping, but the air felt heavy and damp. There were no storm clouds in the sky, but Andi suspected there would be later if the humidity was any indication.

She looked around and noted that Luke's truck was still in the driveway. She walked down to the barn and peeked inside, but Luke wasn't in there. In the corner of the barn was a sack of grain and a bucket, so Andi scooped some up and walked outside. She climbed up to the top of the fence and sat, then shook the bucket. Abby and another horse came running, recognizing the sound of the grain.

Andi let Abby eat grain out of the bucket before letting the other horse have some. She ran her hand along the side of Abby's neck. Andi would have loved to go riding tonight, but her ankle was still a bit sore and she didn't want to risk it quite yet.

"What are you feeding my horses?" Luke asked, coming up to the fence.

Andi noticed he had a smudge of grease on his cheek and some stains on his shirt. His hair was damp with perspiration and curling up around his neck. She wanted to reach out and wipe the smudge off of his face, but she restrained herself from doing so. "Just a little grain," she told him.

Luke nodded and climbed up onto the fence to sit beside her. "How's the ankle? Are you ready to ride again?"

"It's okay, but I think I should wait another day or so to ride. Just to be on the safe side."

"Good thinking. Here, I'll take that." Luke took the empty bucket from her. They sat there in silence while Andi stroked Abby's neck. The other horse had left as soon as the grain was all gone.

"Feels like rain is coming," Luke said. "Probably a thunderstorm."

"Yeah, I thought so, too," Andi said.

"Want to walk a bit?" Luke asked.

"Sure."

Luke hopped down from the fence and reached up, encircling Andi's waist with his hands to steady her as she climbed down. The went to the barn to put the bucket away, then started walking slowly down the driveway in the direction of Luke's house.

"Derek called this afternoon to apologize for the way he spoke to me yesterday," Andi said, purposely leaving out the fact that she'd emailed him and apologized first.

"That's good. Does he do that often? Apologize, when he's been an ass to you?"

"Luke," Andi said reproachfully.

"Sorry."

"Actually, no, he rarely believes he's in the wrong. Derek is a perfectionist and he's a very confident person. He didn't get as far as he has by being a pushover. So, it's hard for him to admit when he's wrong."

"I get it, he's tough in business," Luke said. "But there's a time and a place for that. He shouldn't be tough with you."

Andi sighed. "He did apologize though. He's not as bad as you think."

Luke nodded.

"He's worried that something has gone wrong between us," Andi said.

Luke looked over at her, one brow cocked. "Really? Like what?"

Like you. The words came to Andi's mind quickly. She was relieved when she realized she hadn't said them out loud. "I'm not sure," she lied. "It's just that we've never really argued before. We've never had any reason to. He feels like we've become disconnected."

"Have you?" Luke asked.

"I'm not sure," Andi said honestly. "I had every intention of moving to Buffalo when I loaded up my car and started driving east. But, ever since I've been here at the ranch, I'm starting to question if that's what I really want."

Luke stayed silent. Andi figured he was just thinking over what she'd said. They had walked the entire way to his cabin and they stopped in front of the porch. Andi was surprised they'd walked this far without her even realizing it.

"Do you want a beer?" Luke asked.

Andi nodded. "Sure."

Luke stepped up onto the porch and opened the door. He

nodded to the porch swing. "Have a seat and rest your ankle. I'll be right back."

Andi sat on one end of the porch swing while Luke entered the house. A minute later, she heard a humming sound and figured he must have turned on his generator. Luke appeared after that with two bottles of beer and handed one to Andi.

Luke sat on the swing and began moving it slowly back and forth as they both took sips of their beers. Andi smiled as she remembered as a child she'd always wanted a porch swing like the ones she'd see on the porches of older homes. Luke's swing was stained light oak. She'd wanted a white one, but her parents liked new, showy homes and a porch swing was not the type of thing you hung in front of a contemporary house.

"What are you grinning about?" Luke asked.

"Was I?" Andi asked. "I didn't realize I was. I was thinking about how much I've always wanted a porch swing. They give a house a warm feeling."

"Really? Ashley thought it was sort of corny. Very country, I guess. I figured what was a porch without a swing?"

Andi shook her head. "There's nothing corny about your place, Luke. I love your cabin. It's cute and cozy. It's a real home. Don't let anyone tell you differently."

They sat there a while longer before Andi turned to Luke. "Can I ask you a question?"

Luke shrugged. "Sure."

"Where do you see yourself in ten years?"

"What is this? A job interview?" Luke teased.

"No. I'm just curious. What do you want in your life in the next ten years?"

Luke sat silent for a moment as the swing moved back and forth. Andi waited patiently.

"Well, for one thing, I'm sure I'll still be here, running the ranch. I'll be here until the day I die," Luke said.

"Nothing wrong with that," Andi said softly.

"And I'd hope that I'd have found someone to share my life with by then, maybe have a little boy or girl, or both, running around here. I know my mom would love to have grandchildren."

"She would love that," Andi agreed.

"I'm not sure if all that will happen, but I can always hope," Luke said.

Andi gazed over at Luke. "Why shouldn't it happen? I'm sure you could have your pick of any woman you wanted."

Luke looked directly at Andi, his blue eyes warm. "I don't want just any woman. I want someone who will understand me and accept me for who I am and not want to change me. A woman who will want to be a rancher's wife, and who won't mind living in a cabin instead of a big, new house." Luke's voice deepened. "I want a woman who will be my friend, confidant, and lover, all in one."

Andi swallowed hard. "I'm sure you can find someone like that."

"Are you?" Luke asked.

Andi looked away, but Luke placed his fingertips on her chin and gently turned her face so their eyes met.

"What do you want, Andi? How do you see your life in the next ten years?" he asked.

"I want the same things," Andi whispered. "I want a husband who understands me, children, and a cozy place I can call home. And my art, of course. I'll always need my art."

They sat there, staring at each other for only a moment, but it seemed like forever. Andi wanted Luke to kiss her again. She wanted to get lost in all the passion she'd felt the first time he'd kissed her. She wanted to feel that way for the rest of her life.

Luke finally dropped his eyes to his lap. The moment was gone.

"We should walk back," he said, rising from the swing. "It'll be dark soon." He offered Andi his hand, and she accepted. He pulled her up from the swing and they both stood there, facing each other.

Andi reached up and slid her thumb gently across Luke's cheek, wiping the grease smudge away. Luke looked down at her, stunned.

"You had a smudge on your cheek," she said.

Luke blinked. He took her empty beer bottle and placed both bottles on the porch railing, then they turned and walked side by side up the driveway, back to the main house.

* * *

By the time Luke drove back to his cabin that night, a thunderstorm was brewing and rain was beginning to fall. He ran between raindrops to the porch, grabbed the empty beer bottles off the railing, and headed inside the cabin.

The air outside had cooled considerably, so Luke started a fire in the fireplace to take the chill off in the cabin. He sat on the sofa after that, watching the flames, thinking about his talk with Andi this evening.

Andi's demeanor had been thoughtful, as if she'd been trying to figure something out. She'd said she was questioning if she wanted a life with Derek in Buffalo, but she didn't say outright that she didn't want to marry him. Luke had tried not to read too much into it, but it was difficult not to.

When Andi had asked him what he wanted in his life

in the next ten years, he'd wanted to answer *you*. It was the first answer to come into his thoughts. And it was true. But it wasn't realistic. He'd never fallen for a woman so hard and so fast. Not even Ashley. Their relationship had grown over time. With Andi, though, he would have asked her to marry him in that first few days. It was insane, but he couldn't help it. Unfortunately, he'd already been beaten to the punch by Derek.

At least he had another week to spend with Andi while she waited for her car and while she sold her prints at the fair next weekend. One more week, and then she'd be gone. And his life would go back to how it had been before she'd knocked on his door that fateful night.

As the thunder rumbled and lightning lit up the sky, Luke walked into his bedroom and crawled into his bed, alone.

* * *

Saturday evening Randy and Colt returned from the summer pasture and talk around the supper table was about fencing and cattle. Andi smiled. If she hadn't been up there, she'd have never understood anything they were talking about. It made her feel like an actual member of the family, and she liked that.

Sunday afternoon, Andi and Luke went for a long ride up the center trail and around pastures that they hadn't ridden through before. Bree followed along, running here and there, sniffing out a rabbit or a squirrel and chasing it. She never caught one, thank goodness, but it was fun watching her try.

Andi and Luke kept their conversation light and on safe topics. No talking about Derek, marriage, or life plans. It was a relief to Andi to just enjoy the beautiful day and not think about anything other than having fun. Andi took photos as they rode along and Abby behaved this time and didn't buck her off. That, also, was a relief.

After a couple of hours, they headed back to the ranch. As they rode closer to the barn, Andi noticed a vehicle parked near the house. It looked oddly familiar.

"I wonder who's visiting at the house," Luke said. "I don't recognize the car."

Andi studied the car as they drew closer. There was no way it could be who she thought it was. But the beads hanging from the rearview mirror were as familiar as the car. *No. There is no way it's her.*

Colt came out of the barn as Luke and Andi rode up. He took Abby's reins while Andi slid out of the saddle. Luke also stepped down from Chance.

"Who's here?" Luke asked Colt, nodding toward the car.

Colt shrugged. "I don't know. I heard the car drive up a few minutes ago, but I never saw who got out of it." Colt grabbed Chance's reins, too. "I'll take the horses into the barn," he offered.

"Thanks," Andi said, still staring at the silver-blue Honda CR-V. She walked up closer to the car with Luke right behind her. Bree followed them and began sniffing the car's tires.

"It can't be," Andi said. She cupped her hand and looked in through the tinted windows. The back seat was folded down and there were several boxes inside the car.

"It can't be what?" Luke asked, staring at Andi. "Do you know who owns this car?"

"Andi!"

Andi and Luke turned simultaneously to see who had called her name. There, on the steps of the house, stood a slim girl with long blond hair wearing a red T-shirt, short denim skirt, and brown cowboy boots. Andi couldn't believe her eyes. It was her sister, Carly.

"Carly? What in the world are you doing here?" Andi asked, stunned.

"Carly? Your sister?" Luke asked.

Carly came flying down the stairs and pulled Andi into a big hug. Andi hugged her back. She was happy to see her sister, but shocked, too.

Carly pulled away and gave her a big, red lipstick grin. "I decided it would be more fun to bring you the prints myself. That way I could bring more than I could ever have shipped. Are you surprised?"

"Of course, I'm surprised. You drove all this way by yourself? Was that safe?" Andi asked.

"You did it. I figured I could, too. Besides, my car is a lot newer than yours so it was safer for me to drive than it was for you," Carly said. "So, how do I look?" she asked, twirling around for Andi to inspect her. "Do I look like I belong on a ranch?"

Andi stared at her in amazement. She looked adorable, but she was a little overdressed, or underdressed, for a ranch. "You look cute, as always," Andi said, pulling her sister into another hug. "And I'm really happy to see you."

Carly smiled wide. "I'm glad you're happy. I was afraid you'd be mad at me."

Andi shook her head. "No, I'm not mad. Just very surprised."

Carly glanced up at Luke who stood there, watching the whole scene. Her eyebrows rose and she smiled sweetly. "So, you must be the hot cowboy that Andi has told me all about."

"Carly!" Andi felt her face grow warm.

Luke chuckled. "I suppose I am," he said, offering his

hand in greeting. "I'm Luke. It's nice to meet you, Carly."

Carly bypassed his proffered hand and pulled him into a hug. Luke's eyes opened wide at the familiar greeting. At only five feet, five inches tall, Carly looked half the size of Luke.

"We're practically family," Carly said. "A handshake won't do."

Bree came around from the back of the car to see what was going on.

"Well, who's this?" Carly asked, bending down to scratch Bree behind the ears.

"That's Bree. She's the cattle dog," Andi said. "She's become my best friend."

"Hi there, Bree. Aren't you a pretty girl," Carly cooed.

As Carly stood up, Colt came out of the barn to see what was going on. Andi watched his mouth drop open when he saw Carly.

"Well, yee haw," Carly said when her eyes locked on Colt. "Who's the cute cowboy by the barn?"

Andi stared from Carly to Colt and back again. She frowned. "That's Colt, Luke's younger brother."

Carly ran her hand through her straight blond hair, fluffing it up. "Isn't he just about the yummiest thing you've ever seen?" she asked. "Is he old enough?"

"For what?" Luke asked.

Carly gave him a flirty smile. "For everything."

Andi rolled her eyes. "He's your age, Carly. But he's shy. Don't play any games with him."

Carly pouted. "Oh, Andi. You're such a killjoy. You have a cowboy, so I can have one of my own, too." She bent her head close to Andi. "Should I act like I know nothing about horses so he can teach me, or should I let him know I can ride?"

"Be yourself, Carly. They like honesty around here."

"Okay," Carly said, and then she sashayed her way across the yard toward Colt. "Hello, Cowboy," she sang.

Andi and Luke stood there, staring at her in disbelief.

"Your sister is a bit…" Luke paused.

"Wild? Pushy? Forward?" Andi finished for him.

"Well, I was going to say, friendly," Luke offered.

Andi shook her head and sighed as she watched her sister sidle up to Colt and flirt shamelessly.

Luke chuckled. "Colt isn't going to know what hit him."

"Sorry," Andi said, glancing at Luke. "Should I tell her to stay away from him?"

Luke shook his head. "Nope. He's a grown man. He can take care of himself."

"Let's hope so," Andi said.

"So, what's this about you having a cowboy of your own?" Luke teased.

Andi swatted his arm. "Don't even start. Carly talks crazy sometimes." She turned to the car, opened the back door, and looked inside. It looked like Carly had brought every print Andi owned.

"Want some help unloading those?" Luke asked.

"Yeah, thanks," Andi said.

Andi and Luke began pulling boxes out of the car and carried them to the house. Andi glanced once more to where Carly and Colt were and watched them walk into the barn. She sighed again and went into the house.

Chapter Nineteen

Ginny told Andi and Luke to place all the boxes in the sitting room.

"You'd never believe how surprised I was to see your sister pull up to the house," Ginny told Andi.

"Probably as surprised as I was," Andi said.

"She sure is a pretty girl," Ginny said. "And so sweet. She apologized right away for not calling in advance and said she really wanted to surprise you. Then she offered to help me make supper."

"I'm so sorry about this, Ginny," Andi said. "I had no idea she was coming."

"Sorry? Don't even think about it. I'm happy to have her here. As long as you two don't mind sharing your room, it's not a problem. She's a breath of fresh air."

"I think Colt would agree with you on that," Luke said, his eyes sparkling with mischief.

"Yep. I kind of wondered how long before those two saw each other," Ginny said with a grin. "Things could get really interesting around here."

Andi let out a big sigh.

Once they brought in all the boxes, Andi helped Ginny finish making supper. Luke had gone back outside to check on Colt and see if the horses had been unsaddled. Just as they were getting ready to put the food on the table, Carly came running in, her face flushed, a smile on her lips.

"Colt said he'd take me riding after supper," she announced, her voice full of excitement.

On a horse, I hope. As soon as Andi thought it, she admonished herself. She wasn't being cruel, just honest. Her sister was a wild child, always had been, and probably always would be. Even as a little girl, she was the shining star in any crowd. She'd been popular in school, and that had trickled over to her college days and adult social life. She was the life of the party, and she went through men like water. Yet, somehow, women were never jealous of her and she managed to stay friends with every man she'd ever dated. It all amazed Andi, who was much more quiet and reserved.

They all sat down to supper and Andi was relieved that Randy wasn't here tonight. He'd meet her sister soon enough, but at least tonight it was just the family. Andi sat there and listened as Carly bubbled on. She loved how cute the ranch was, and my but the men in Montana were delicious, and she'd met the nicest man at a gas station in Idaho who helped her check her oil, and weren't the horses in the corral just adorable? She rattled on and on as Colt hung on every word, Ginny grinned, Luke stared at her with glazed-over eyes, and Andi's head spun.

Carly jumped right in after supper, helping Ginny and Andi clean up. Then she asked where she could change into jeans so she could go riding.

"I already took your bag up to my room," Andi told her. "I'll show you where it is."

Carly followed her up the stairs and into the bedroom. "This is adorable!" she exclaimed. "So cute and country looking." She turned to look at Andi and her smile faded. "Are you mad that I came here without telling you first?"

Andi sat on the bed. "No, I'm not mad. But I do wish you'd told me. I feel bad that we're imposing on Ginny."

Carly brushed her hand through the air. "You're such a worrywart. Ginny seemed fine about me staying a few days. She was very nice to me, and it's obvious she adores you."

"Ginny's a sweetheart. The feeling is mutual. So, please, let's not take advantage of her, okay? While you're here, help out whenever you can."

Carly pushed out her bottom lip. "I did. I helped with the supper dishes. And I'll help with whatever she needs me to."

Andi shook her head and grinned up at her sister. "I am happy to see you, even if you're a whirlwind blowing in here so unexpectedly."

Carly bent down and gave Andi a hug. "I knew you'd love seeing me." She tossed her bag on the other side of the bed, opened it, and rummaged through it for a pair of jeans.

Andi looked at the overstuffed bag full of clothes. "Just how long do you expect to stay?"

"Just a couple of days. I have to be home by the weekend for work. They gave me a few days off when I told them I wanted to bring your prints out here. I needed a vacation anyway, and what better place is there than a ranch with hot cowboys?"

"That's another thing," Andi said sternly. "No playing around with Colt. He's a nice guy and he doesn't need to have his heart broken by you."

"Andi," Carly whined. "How bad do you think I am? I'll be nice. I'm just having fun."

As Carly changed into her jeans, Andi hoped that her idea of fun didn't include letting Colt fall head over heels for her.

* * *

After Carly and Colt left on their horseback ride, Andi got down to business sorting through her prints. Ginny came in to see if she could help.

"I'm being nosey," Ginny said. "I want to see all your prints."

Surprisingly, Luke had hung back and stayed at the house after supper. He sat on the sofa in the sitting room and watched as Andi pulled out prints of various sizes from different boxes and began shuffling them around. She wanted to put a few of each print in separate boxes so all she'd have to bring is one box of each size to the fair every day.

Andi prints included small 5x7s and 8x10s and larger sizes going up to 16x20s and 24x36s. They were all laid out on cardboard sheets with shrink wrap to protect them from people handling them. Carly had also brought a few framed prints to display.

"Oh, Andi, these are all so beautiful," Ginny exclaimed as she looked at each print that Andi pulled from the box. There were prints of downtown Seattle at night with the buildings lit up, one of Puget Sound, another of Mount Rainier, and some of woodland trails around Mount Rainier. There were also ones of ocean scenes along the northern California, Oregon, and Washington coasts. And of course, there were prints of the Lone Cypress that Andi had painted. All were vivid and rich in color and so true to life.

Luke came over and inspected each print along with his mother. "Andi, you continue to amaze me with your talent.

These are all so wonderful."

"Thanks, Luke." His words warmed Andi's heart. Luke's praise meant so much to her.

Luke left soon afterward and Ginny helped Andi sort her prints. They had made a big dent in their sorting by the time Carly returned with Colt from their ride.

"Did you both have a good ride?" Ginny asked when they came inside the sitting room. Carly's face was flushed and she had a big grin as she nodded. Colt said he had, too, but Andi noticed that his face was also red. She also noted that his eyes never left Carly.

They all went to bed soon after that. Andi's room had a full-sized bed that she and Carly shared. Andi didn't mind. They'd shared a bed often throughout the years. When Carly was little and would get scared at night, she'd sometimes crawl in with Andi for protection. Right after their parents' died, they sometimes shared a bed at night for comfort. They were adults now, but they were, after all, sisters. After they both got ready for bed and turned out the lights, they started whispering to each other and giggling, just like the old days.

"Colt sure is a cutie," Carly said dreamily. "And he's so nice and polite. They don't make men like that anymore. At least, I never meet men like him."

"He's adorable and sweet," Andi agreed. "I hope you were just as nice and polite as he was. You two looked awfully flushed when you came in tonight."

Carly giggled. "That's because Colt showed me the hayloft and it was really hot up there."

"It *was* really hot or it *got* really hot up there?" Andi asked, disapproval in her tone.

"Oh, Andi, you're not my mother, you know." Carly giggled. "But he sure is a good kisser."

"Carly, you just met Colt today!" Andi exclaimed.

"Don't be such a stick in the mud, Big Sis," Carly said. "I'll bet that hunky Luke is a good kisser, too."

"Leave Luke out of this," Andi told her, but in her mind she thought, *he sure is.*

"Oh, Andi, Luke is one hot cowboy and he looks at you like you're a piece of apple pie that he wants to take a bite out of."

"Carly!"

Carly ignored her. "I think you should dump Derek and grab up Luke. He's more man than Derek will ever be."

Andi lay there, stunned. "What is it with you and Derek? Why don't you like him?"

Carly grew serious. "I just don't think, no, I know he isn't the man you think he is, Andi."

"Why? Do you know something about him that I don't?"

Carly took a deep breath, but didn't answer.

"Carly? Tell me if you know something," Andi insisted.

"Okay, but you're not going to like it. I never told you this, because I didn't want to tarnish your view of Derek, but he's such a jerk, maybe you should know."

Andi sat up in bed. "What?"

"One night, about a year ago, I was in a bar with my friends and I saw Derek there with some "clients". They were two older men in suits, and they were all sitting in a big corner booth. You know, the type that makes up a half-circle? It was so dark and noisy in there that I wouldn't have even noticed them if they hadn't been near the bathrooms."

"And?" Andi asked.

Carly sat up and looked at her sister in the dark room. "They weren't the only ones there. There were three women with them. Tall, slender, dressed to the nines, a bit slutty. They were young, so there was no way any of them were the mens' wives. The women were hanging all over the two men and they were all laughing and drinking and having a good old time."

Andi frowned. "What are you saying? Were those women hookers?"

"No, I don't think so. More like escorts, but I wouldn't be surprised if they were paid for other things as well. Derek saw me as I passed the table and he was just furious. He pulled me aside and told me he was with clients and nothing else was going on. Well, I told him that I knew exactly what was going on, and he got even angrier. He said that I'd better not tell you what I saw or I'd be responsible for ruining your life. I just walked away."

"Why didn't you tell me this before?" Andi wanted to know.

"I didn't want to be the one to break up your relationship with Derek," Carly said. "You seemed happy with him. After all those years of you having to take care of me, I wanted you to be happy."

"Was Derek with any of the women?" Andi asked quietly.

Carly shook her head. "Not that I saw. The women were hanging all over the other men, like they were there to entertain them. The thing that bothered me, though, was the fact that Derek would actually pay for women to entertain clients who were from out of town. It's disgusting. Those guys were probably even married. Maybe that's how he does business, but it's wrong."

Andi lay back down against her pillows. She had no idea that Derek was involved in doing business that way. Then she thought back to when she'd called him from The Depot that Saturday night and the woman's voice in the background, telling him to hurry up. Had that been an escort? It was all starting to make sense. That must have been why he'd never invited her to business dinners unless the wives were along. He supplied entertainment to these men. She agreed with Carly—it was disgusting.

Carly lay down beside Andi. "Are you mad at me for telling you?"

"No," Andi said. "I'm just disappointed in Derek. He always comes off as this straight-laced businessman who works hard for his success. But now, I'm not sure if he's even the man I thought he was."

"I'm sorry, Andi," Carly said sincerely. "Maybe that's how everyone does business. Maybe it's not Derek's idea."

"I'm sure it's something that goes on all the time," Andi said. "But that doesn't make it right. Derek is so career driven, and I knew that, but the fact that he'd do something like that to get ahead doesn't settle well with me. I'm just not sure we are a good fit anymore."

"He's always been career driven," Carly said. "What's so different now?"

Andi sighed. "I'm not sure. It's like I just ignored it before when I was living with you and focused on my art. But since I've been here at the ranch, I've had a lot of time to think. I'm just not sure that I still want the same things Derek wants."

"It's Luke, isn't it?" Carly asked. "He's changing your mind."

"No, Carly, it's not Luke," Andi insisted. *Well, maybe it is, a little.* "It's just everything about living here. The slower pace of life. The beauty of the surroundings. A simpler way of looking at things. It's making me reevaluate my choices."

"Well, you can deny it all you want, but I think that hunky cowboy has gotten under your skin," Carly teased.

"Carly! Is that all you ever think about? Men and sex? I just don't understand you. We're so different."

"Oh, we're not really all that different," Carly said. "I just say out loud what other people are thinking. That's the only difference."

Andi lay there and thought about what Carly had said. Maybe she was right. Maybe she wasn't so different from Carly. She only kept it to herself instead of being so outspoken. Andi thought of the many times she wanted to say something to Luke, but she'd held her tongue because it wasn't proper. Heck, she'd said many things out loud to Luke that weren't proper. She tried thinking of Derek as she lay there, growing drowsy, but she failed miserably. All she could think of was Mr. Tall, Dark, and Handsome standing up on the roof of the stable the other day, shirtless. Hmmm, maybe she was as bad as Carly after all.

Chapter Twenty

The next day was Monday and everyone on the ranch was hard at work again. Randy showed up for breakfast and got his first dose of Carly and all her charm. She had cozied up to Colt at the table, but she still flirted shamelessly with Randy. Andi was embarrassed, although she noticed that Randy took it all in stride, not reacting to anything Carly said. Ginny just grinned at the scene, seeming to find a great deal of humor in it all.

As promised, Carly helped around the house that morning and then helped Andi sort the rest of her prints as well as make sure all were priced properly. When it came to art, organization, and sales, Carly was a pro. She was a good manager at the gallery and she could talk anyone into buying anything. Andi almost wished she were staying the entire week to help sell prints at the fair. Almost.

In the late afternoon, Carly disappeared to find Colt and see if she could "help" him with whatever chores he was doing. Bree decided to follow along after her. Andi just shook her head at her little sister.

Andi spent the time alone sitting outside near Luke's

cabin, sketching it in detail, porch swing and all. Behind the cabin, in the small pasture, Andi heard the sound of a hammer pounding and knew it was Luke. She closed her eyes and listened to the steady, rhythmic sound of hammer hitting nail. She heard birds chirping in the trees and smelled the now familiar scents of fresh cut hay and evergreen. She imagined what it would be like to live here, every day, for the rest of her life. Early morning breakfasts at the house, horseback rides in the evening, sitting on the porch swing with Luke right before sunset, enjoying a beer. Waking up to his handsome face. *Yikes! Stop it, you idiot!*

"Daydreaming?"

Startled, Andi opened her eyes. Luke stood there, damp with sweat, wiping the back of his neck with a rag. *Damn, he even looked good all sweaty!* "You have to stop scaring me like that. I thought you were working on the stable."

"I was, but it's almost supper time. I came home to shower before going up to the house. What are you doing? Spying on me?" Luke grinned.

Andi grinned back. "Believe it or not, you're not that interesting," she lied. "I'm sketching your cabin. See?" She turned the sketchpad around so he could look at it.

Luke leaned closer and inspected the sketch. "Looks good. Especially since I'm not in it, shirtless."

Andi turned the sketchpad back around. "Smartass," she said, her eyes glinting mischievously.

Luke chuckled. "Want to come inside and wait while I shower? I have the generator on and the air conditioning running. We could ride up to the house in the truck after."

Andi shrugged. "Sure. Mind if I sketch the inside?"

"Knock yourself out," Luke said.

Andi followed Luke into the cabin, and as promised, it

was much cooler in there.

"Do you want something to drink? A soda or water? A beer?" Luke asked, walking over to the refrigerator. He pulled out a bottle of beer and waggled his eyebrows.

Andi laughed. "As tempting as that sounds, I think I'll pass. Thanks."

"Suit yourself." Luke popped off the twist top and took a long swig of it. "I'll be back in a few minutes. Make yourself at home."

Andi watched Luke walk away down the hall before turning slowly in a circle around the room. She stopped when she was facing the dining table. She walked over to it and ran her hand along the smooth wood. Everything from this heavy, wood dining table and chairs to the leather sofa screamed one hundred percent male. It was obvious that Luke had picked out all the furnishing for the entire house. He'd told her as much that night at the summer pasture cabin. Ashley hadn't been interested in any of the process of building the house. She obviously hadn't cared about the furnishings, either. But as Andi looked around, she liked everything she saw. It may be a masculine home, but it still felt warm and cozy. If it were her place, though, she'd add little touches, like a warm, fuzzy, throw blanket over the back of the sofa, a few pillows, and a rug under the coffee table and dining room table. Just a few touches would make this cabin even cozier.

Andi pulled out one of the dining room chairs and sat down, deciding to sketch the back of the sofa and the fireplace. She methodically prepared the paper, and then started sketching. As she worked, she heard the water running in the shower at the back of the house. She hadn't seen inside the master bathroom, but she could almost imagine it had a big shower with clear glass doors, a huge tub, and a double sink.

Luke would have designed it modern for Ashely. What she tried hard not to imagine was Luke taking a shower just a couple of rooms away from her. His rock hard abs, his powerful shoulders, his long, muscular legs.

Stop thinking of him in the shower! Andi felt her face grow hot, embarrassed by her thoughts. But a sigh escaped her lips just the same.

By the time Luke was dressed and back in the living room, Andi had almost finished her sketch of the sofa and fireplace. She added a throw on the back of the sofa, just as she'd imagined, and also a painting on the mantel. The painting she'd added was similar to the one she'd painted of the Lone Cypress.

Luke walked up and looked over Andi's shoulder. He studied her sketch. "I like it," he said. "Your painting looks good on my mantel. Maybe I should buy a print of it."

Andi inhaled deeply and was rewarded with the clean scent of Luke's soap and aftershave. *God, he smells good.* He smelled fresh and spicy, just like a man should.

"I'll give you a print if you really want one," Andi said. "It's the least I could do for all your family has done for me."

Luke shook his head. "I always pay my way."

"We can work something out," Andi said, closing her sketchpad.

"I'm sure we can," Luke replied with that adorable wicked grin of his.

"Dream on, Cowboy," Andi said, laughing.

Luke chuckled. "Ready to go?"

"Yes."

They drove up to the house and entered just as supper was being served. Carly was helping Ginny bring food to the table. Everyone looked up and stared at them.

"What?" Andi asked, as she stood next to Luke.

"Where have you two been?" Carly asked, smirking.

Andi rolled her eyes. She walked over to the refrigerator and poured a glass of iced tea, then came back to sit down. Carly had already sat down beside Colt on the bench seat, so the only spot left was the chair next to Luke. "We just came from the cabin," Andi said, sitting down. "I was waiting for Luke so he could drive me here."

"So, why is Luke's hair wet?" Carly asked.

"He showered. What's the big deal?" Andi asked, annoyed.

Carly raised her brows, but didn't reply. Colt concentrated on his supper and Randy chuckled softly. Andi looked over at Ginny, who looked slightly amused at the whole scene.

"What?" Andi insisted.

"Just ignore them," Luke said. "They're trying to get your goat."

Andi sighed.

Ginny piped up. "I've been living around men for so long, I've forgotten how sisters tease each other. Sorry, Andi, but it's kind of fun to watch."

"I'm glad we didn't have any sisters then," Luke said. "It would have been annoying."

"Hey." Andi hit him on the arm.

Colt looked up at Andi. "I don't know. I think it's been kind of fun having Andi around here. It's been like having a sister for a while. I'm going to miss her when she leaves."

Andi's heart melted. "Thanks, Colt. I'm going to miss you, too."

"Hey, what about me?" Carly asked, giving her best pout.

"I doubt Colt thinks of you as a sister," Andi said with a grin.

Luke chuckled and almost choked on his potatoes.

Ginny laughed.

Carly ignored them all. "Colt and I are going riding after supper. Do you two want to go along?"

Andi looked up at Luke, her eyes twinkling mischievously. "Want to go riding, Big Brother?"

Luke glanced at her. "Sure, Little Sis."

"Oh, brother," Randy said under his breath.

Ginny let out a laugh and everyone joined in.

* * *

Luke and Colt went out to the pasture to round up the horses while Andi and Carly waited in the barn. As the two men walked toward the horses, Colt asked, "What do you think of Carly?"

Luke looked at him evenly. "She's a pretty girl, no doubt. Why do you ask?"

Colt shrugged. "Just wondering."

"Do you want my advice?" Luke asked.

"Maybe."

"Take it slow. You've known Carly for one day. She's only staying for a couple more. Don't fall for her too quickly," Luke told him.

Colt stopped walking and looked directly at Luke. "What about you? Will you take your own advice?"

"What?"

"It's obvious there's something going on between you and Andi. Not that I care, but you haven't known her all that long, either. And she's engaged," Colt said.

Luke frowned. Were his feelings for Andi that obvious? "There's nothing going on between Andi and me."

"Right. You just keep saying that," Colt said, turning to

walk away.

Luke grabbed Colt's arm. Colt turned back and stared hard at him. "I don't care if you believe me or not," Luke said. "I'm just asking you to be careful. Carly likes to flirt, and from what Andi says, she's not looking for a steady boyfriend. I just don't want to see you get hurt, okay? From one brother to another."

Colt glared at Luke a moment, then his features softened. "Okay."

They rounded up the four horses and brought them back to the barn. Colt saddled his and Carly's, but Andi saddled Abby herself. Soon, they were on the trail that led up the middle of the ranch so Carly could watch the sunset from the top of the hill. Andi had brought along her camera to snap photos of it.

Colt and Carly rode side by side in the lead and Luke and Andi followed behind. Andi was quiet, but Carly rattled on to Colt as he smiled at everything she said. Luke figured she could sing the alphabet and Colt wouldn't even care, he was that much in awe of Carly.

Luke purposely slowed his horse down so there was some distance between them and the two lovebirds. Andi had yet to say a word to him.

"Is everything okay?" Luke asked.

Andi looked over at Luke. "Oh, yeah. I was just thinking, that's all."

Luke nodded his head toward Colt and Carly. "Colt's really falling fast for your sister."

Andi sighed. "I know. Carly's always had a way with men. She's always been the shining star and everyone wants to get close to her. The funny thing is, even if she dumps a guy, he still thinks she's some sort of a goddess. I've never understood it."

Luke gave a lighthearted laugh. "Colt seems to think there's something going on between you and me."

Andi looked up at him. "Is there?"

Yes, there most certainly is. He wanted to tell her that, but he didn't know if he should. He hesitated too long, because Andi put her hand up as if to ward off an answer.

"Forget I asked that," she said quickly. "Things have just been, well, confusing. I'm saying stuff that I shouldn't." She looked away.

"Do you want to talk about whatever's wrong?" Luke offered. "I'm a good listener."

Andi shook her head. She gave him a small smile, but her eyes didn't reflect it. "Let's just enjoy the ride," she said. "I don't want to think about anything else right now."

Luke nodded and they rode on. Soon, they caught up to Colt and Carly as they reached the top of the hill. Carly was giggling about something and reached out to touch Colt's leg. Colt smiled wide. Luke wished it could be as easy as his brother and Carly made it look, but for him, it was a lot more complicated.

They turned at the top of the hill just as the sun touched the treetops in the distance. Yellow and gold filled the sky.

"It's beautiful," Carly said. She reached over and took Colt's hand in hers.

Luke watched as Andi pulled out her camera and began taking pictures. Expertly, she snapped photos at different angles. He wondered how she saw it with her artist's eye. Unfortunately, he'd never see if she painted this view on canvas. She'd be far away in Buffalo, or maybe Manhattan, by the time she did. Or maybe she'd never paint it at all.

After that, they rode home. Carly was nonstop chatter and laughter with Colt, but Luke and Andi were silent. Luke wished he knew what Andi was thinking, but he reminded himself that it wasn't really his business.

* * *

Later that night, Luke lay in bed thinking about his conversation with Colt. He couldn't blame Colt for falling fast for Carly. After all, hadn't he done the same with Andi? How do you fall in love with someone in a matter of days? It seemed impossible. But it had happened, so he was the last person in the world to tell Colt to be careful. No matter how the cards fell, Luke knew he'd have a broken heart one way or the other. Just like Colt would.

Luke sighed and ran a hand through his hair. He wondered what had caused Andi to become so serious tonight on their ride. Earlier in the day, they had been teasing each other as they usually did. The whole brother/sister thing at supper had been her teasing him about saying he felt like a big brother to her days before. It was obvious now that he felt anything but a brotherly fondness for her. The kiss they'd shared had been too passionate to deny that he had strong feelings for her.

Tonight, however, she'd been quiet and far away. Like an idiot, he'd told her that Colt thought there was something going on between them. Cripes, what had he been thinking? It was like he'd been testing the waters, and it was so obvious. But when Andi had asked him, "Is there?", he'd been so caught off guard, he couldn't answer right away. He should have blurted out what he'd been thinking, *Yes! There most certainly is.* But he'd waited too long and the moment was lost. Probably the only chance he'd have to let Andi know exactly how he felt.

What an idiot I am.

Time was ticking away to the moment when Andi walked out of his life and he'd never see her again. He had no clue what he was going to do about it, if anything. Should he lay down his pride and tell her exactly how he felt and hope to God that she felt the same way about him? Or should he just be the gentleman and let her go, without a fight? Like he'd done with Ashley. He had less than a week to decide.

Chapter Twenty-One

"So, what do you guys do for fun around here, except riding?" Carly asked Tuesday evening as they were all eating supper. She'd spent the entire day following Colt around and being a nuisance, Andi suspected, although Colt probably didn't think so.

"We work," Randy said in-between shoveling forkfuls of peas and potatoes into his mouth.

Andi suppressed a grin. She got a kick out of how Randy spoke to Carly. She'd never met a guy in her life who didn't succumb to Carly's charms, so this was a first.

Carly wrinkled her nose at Randy, then cuddled up closer to Colt and put a pout on her full lips. "But it's my last night here," she said in her sweetest, 'give me what I want' voice. Andi resisted the urge to roll her eyes.

"On weekends we go to The Depot and dance," Colt said. "But they don't have a band there during the week, only a jukebox.

Carly's eyes lit up. "Is that the place you took Andi the first weekend she was here?"

"Yep," Colt said. "I taught her how to line dance."

"Can we go there tonight?" Carly asked, excited now. "We can have a couple of beers and dance to the jukebox music."

"Carly," Andi started to protest, but Carly cut her off.

"Come on, Andi. At least let me see the place. We don't have to stay long. It'll be fun."

"I'll take you," Colt offered. He looked over at Luke. "Do you want to come?"

Luke shrugged. "I don't know. Andi? What about you?"

Andi didn't really want to, but she was always being the 'stick in the mud' as Carly put it. "Maybe for a little while," she said.

Carly clapped her hands in delight. "I can't wait. We're going to have so much fun." She turned to Ginny. "You should come with us, Ginny."

"Oh, that's sweet of you to ask, honey, but I think I'll just stay home and get some work done. You young people go and have fun."

Carly turned her eyes on Randy. "What do you say, Randy? Are you up for a little fun for a change?"

"Nope," Randy said. "I'll pass on being the fifth wheel."

Andi figured he was more than likely passing on seeing Carly after she'd had a few beers in her.

A while later, the foursome stood in the parking lot at The Depot. They had taken separate trucks in case Luke and Andi wanted to leave early. Carly had dressed up in her short denim skirt and cowboy boots again, with a bright red T-shirt that scooped down low. She'd also snagged one of Colt's cowboy hats from the mudroom and Andi had to admit, it looked adorable on her. But then, everything looked adorable on Carly.

Carly linked her arm through Colt's and they headed to the door. Andi held back. "You three go on ahead," she said.

"I have to make a call. I'll be inside in a minute."

Luke frowned. "Is everything okay?"

"Oh, yeah. Everything is fine. I'm just going to touch base with Derek," Andi said with more enthusiasm than she felt. She saw a look cross over Luke's face before he turned and walked away. Had it been disappointment?

Sighing, Andi clicked on Derek's name in her contacts and waited. He answered on the second ring.

"Andi? Hi. You're using your phone. Is your car fixed? Have you left the ranch?"

"Hi, Derek. No, my car won't be ready until next week. We're at that restaurant down the road from the ranch where I get reception," Andi told him.

"We?" Derek asked.

"Yeah. Some of the people from the ranch, and Carly," Andi said. It was a little white lie, but she didn't want to fight about being out with Luke. "She drove out here with my prints so I could sell them at the fair this weekend. She wanted to go out for a couple of hours tonight. You know how Carly is."

"Yes, I do," Derek said dryly. "So, what's this about selling your prints at a fair?"

Andi told him about the fair booth and selling the prints so she could make some extra money to pay for the car.

"You know, I would be happy to give you the money to pay for the car," Derek said patiently. "In fact, I did tell you I'd buy you a new one. You shouldn't have to go hock your wares at some podunk country fair."

Andi's mouth dropped open. Sure, Missoula wasn't Manhattan, but it certainly wasn't a podunk town. "I don't expect you to pay for my car to be fixed or to buy me a new one," she said sharply. "I do earn my own money."

"Of course, you do," Derek said. "But we're getting

married, remember? I'm happy to buy you things."

Andi softened. Maybe she was being too hard on Derek. Then she remembered why she'd called in the first place, and she hardened her resolve. "Derek, I have to ask you about something, and I want you to be completely honest with me, okay?"

"I'm always honest with you," Derek said.

"Do you pay for escorts to entertain your male clients when you take them to dinner?" Andi asked. She took a breath as she waited for his answer.

A long silence settled over the line. Finally, in a harsh voice, Derek said, "Carly told you that, didn't she?"

"It doesn't matter how I found out. Is it true? Do you pay women to entertain your clients?"

"Okay. I'll be honest. Yes, sometimes I supply entertainment for male clients who are from out of town. But it's not as seedy as it sounds. Some clients are swayed to invest in our bank by just going out to an expensive restaurant and drinking expensive wine. Others may want theater tickets to a sold out show or box seats at a ball game. Some may want a little companionship. If it gets the deal done, it's worth the cost of a little entertainment."

Andi couldn't believe what she'd just heard. Not only was he admitting it, but he was justifying it as a way to do business. "Derek, buying tickets to a baseball game for a client is a lot different than buying a hooker for him. How can you condone such practices? Does the bank really tell you that you should do this sort of thing?"

"Building a client base is the most important thing for a bank to do well, Andi. And if it takes buying a little entertainment, then that's what we do. You have to understand, the business world is tough. People will back out of a deal for something as ridiculous as not giving them season tickets to their favorite football team. Sure, it has nothing to do with the actual deal, but they want the perks. And some men want a night of fun when they are out on the town. Do I condone it? No, of course not. But it's the price of doing business in a competitive market. If you worked at a real job, you'd understand that."

Andi's heart raced. *I do work at a real job and I earn real money.* She wanted to yell that at Derek, but she remained calm. Fighting with Derek just wasn't worth it, and she never won anyway.

"Andi, please, try to understand," Derek said, his tone softer. "These aren't my ideas. They're just business practices that men have been doing for years and years and I'm expected to keep up the traditions. This is a tough business and if I want to reach my way to the top, I have to do what is expected of me. I know it sounds terrible, and I'm sorry it upsets you. But I want the brass ring, Andi, and I won't get it if I don't play the game."

"Derek, is it really worth it? Is selling out worth sacrificing your own ideals? Or have you just been doing this for so long, you no longer feel that this kind of thing is wrong?"

"I don't understand you, Andi. I thought you wanted the same things I do," Derek said, frustration lacing his voice. "How do you expect me to succeed if I don't do what is expected of me? So what if I have to entertain a few men by bringing beautiful women along for dinner who make them feel special. If it helps us realize our goal of the perfect life, then what does it matter?"

The perfect life. Is that what Derek called his version of their future? Andi didn't think it was so perfect after all. "I'm not so sure I want to build our perfect life that way," Andi said sadly.

"Andi. You just don't understand the amount of stress I'm under daily to build up the numbers and keep them rising. Bringing in new clients with big money is what they hired me for, and that is what I need to do. I'm doing it for us. For me and you. We're going to be so happy when we finally make it to the top. Just wait and see."

"I'm not so sure, Derek," Andi began to say, but he interrupted her.

"Andi, I love you. I'm doing exactly what we both dreamed of when we talked about building a life together. It's all going to be wonderful. Please, don't back out on me now. You'll see. We're going to have an amazing life."

Andi wasn't so sure it was going to be that amazing after all. "I have to think about this, Derek," she told him. "Just give me a little time to let this all sink in, okay? I'll call you in a day or two."

"Fine," Derek said sharply. "But I don't understand what there is to think about. A million people would give their right arm to be in the position I'm in. And a million women would want to live the life I'm offering you. What more do you want, Andi?"

"I can't discuss this any longer. I have to go. Goodbye, Derek." Andi hung up before he could respond. She leaned against Luke's truck and mulled over everything they had said to each other. She couldn't believe the things Derek had said. She'd always thought Derek got ahead quickly because he was a hard worker and an honest, sincere person. But his business life was built on deceit and backroom deals. What if that same way of dealing with people began to filter into his personal life? What if it already had? Would she ever be able to trust him one hundred percent?

Inside the bar, music began playing from what Andi

assumed was the jukebox. She sighed, slipped her phone into her pocket, and slowly began walking toward the bar. After her conversation with Derek, she wasn't in much of a partying mood.

* * *

Luke sat in the booth, his jaw set in a tight line and his fingers strumming steadily on the wooden table. The jukebox music had started up and Carly and Colt danced along with two other couples. Luke took a swig of his beer and stared hard at the mug beside him that he'd bought for Andi. What in the hell was taking her so long? What could she possibly be talking about with that damned Derek for this amount of time? The longer he waited for her, the angrier he grew. Didn't she know that Derek was a jerk? Hell, he'd never even met the guy and he knew he was an ass. What did she see in that money hungry fool? Andi wasn't about money or status or even possessions. So, why did she want to marry an idiot who was?

Slow footsteps came up behind Luke and he turned to see Andi walking to the table. The forlorn look on her face wiped his angry mood away instantly. He wanted to jump out of the booth and hold her in his arms until she smiled again. Instead, he scooted over so she could sit down beside him.

"Is this for me?" Andi asked, pointing to the beer.

Luke nodded. He watched as Andi lifted the mug and drank down half of its contents. His brows rose in question. "I take it your conversation with Derek didn't go well."

Andi turned her green eyes up to Luke. He was a sucker for those eyes. Damn, he was a sucker for everything about Andi.

"We just don't seem to have the same ideas or ideals," Andi said. "I was blind to it before. I just don't understand what's happened. Did he change, or did I?" She drank down the rest of the beer and asked Luke if he would get her another one.

Luke hesitated, and then decided if Andi needed a beer, who was he to tell her no? He waved the waitress over and ordered another round.

"Do you want to talk about it?" Luke asked.

Andi sighed. "Aren't you tired of listening to my problems?"

Luke shook his head. "Not yet."

Andi gave a small smile. Luke smiled back. She began telling him about Derek and the escorts and the way he conducted business.

Luke sat and listened to it all without saying a word. The beers came and Luke paid for them. Andi took another long swig of hers. Luke grimaced. He knew Andi wasn't much of a drinker. He hoped she wasn't drinking more than she could handle.

"So, am I being too naive about this whole thing, or is he wrong?" Andi asked. "I don't even know anymore. Maybe he's right. I don't work in the 'real' world. I'm an artist who sells paintings. I don't have to kiss up to idiots or bribe them to buy my paintings. They either buy them or they don't." Andi looked at Luke. "What do you think?"

I think you're beautiful. Luke sat there a moment, hoping he hadn't said that out loud. From the look on Andi's face, he decided he hadn't. "I think you're an intelligent, competent woman who knows herself well and knows right from wrong. You are not naïve, Andi. You have every right to question his ethics."

Andi giggled. She took another long drink of beer. "You're only saying that because you think I'm cute."

Luke pulled back in surprise. "Oh, yeah? Who says I do?"

"I do. And that kiss you gave me said so, too." Andi giggled again, covered her mouth with her hand, and then giggled once more. "Uh, I think I drank my beer too quickly."

Luke chuckled. "Yeah, I think you did. At least you're not a mean drunk."

They both laughed again.

"I like it better when you're happy," Luke said. He ducked his head and caught her eyes with his. "And you're right," he whispered. "I do think you're cute."

Andi smiled wide.

"Hey, what's going on over here?" Carly asked as she and Colt sat on the other side of the table. Both of their faces were flushed from dancing, and they both took a hearty sip of their beers.

"Andi and I were just talking about her conversation with Derek," Luke said, sitting back against the booth.

"Ugg. Derek." Carly sneered. "He's a big jerk."

"Carly!" Andi said, then a big grin spread across her lips. "Yeah, he kind of is sometimes." Andi giggled, setting Carly off giggling, too.

Carly shook her finger at Luke. "You got my sister drunk, didn't you? Well, it's about time. She needed to loosen up a bit."

"I'm not drunk," Andi protested. "I'm just relaxed."

Carly laughed. "Relaxed. Right. That's what you call it." A slow song started up on the jukebox and Carly sprung out of her seat and pulled Colt to her. "Come on. Let's dance again."

Andi frowned as she listened to the start of the song. "No, it's not, is it? Not again."

Luke nodded. "Yep, it is. 'Desperado.' Want to dance?"

Andi took another sip of her beer, then scooted out of the

booth. "Sure. Just like brother and sister, right?"

Luke stood up and pulled Andi into his arms, guiding her to the dance floor. "No. Nothing like brother and sister," he told her.

Andi looked up at him, the teasing in her eyes now gone. Their bodies touched as they swayed to the music. She sighed, and laid her head on his shoulder.

Luke pulled Andi even closer, enjoying the feel of her against him. If only, he thought. If only life were a romance novel and ended just like this with the hero getting the girl. If only it were like a romantic movie and this was the final scene. Because if life was fair, he'd be the one to win the fair maiden and live happily ever after this time around.

Chapter Twenty-Two

Andi awoke feeling a little fuzzy, but not full-blown hung over from all the beer she'd drank the night before. After she showered and dressed, she felt better. Carly wasn't in the room, so Andi figured she'd gotten up early to spend every last minute she had here with Colt.

When Andi went down to breakfast, Ginny, Carly, and Colt were at the table.

"Good morning, Andi," Ginny said with a smile. "I heard you had a fun time last night."

Andi poured a mug of steaming coffee and walked over to the table. "Yeah, I guess I did. I think I had too much to drink though. I never do that."

"Oh, no," Carly said with a grin. "You weren't drunk, you were *relaxed*." She giggled and Colt even let out a chuckle.

"Ha, ha," Andi said. She began filling her plate with eggs and bacon. "Where's Randy? Am I that late getting down here for breakfast?"

"No, he and Luke ate earlier. They went up to the summer pasture to work on fences for a couple of days. Luke said he wanted to take advantage of the dry weather. You never know around here when the weather will turn."

"Oh." Andi was disappointed, yet relieved. She'd wanted to talk to Luke this morning about last night, but maybe it was best if she didn't. She'd acted silly last night. Maybe Luke had thought so, too, and that's why he'd high-tailed it out of here for the summer pasture.

After breakfast, Andi helped Carly pack her bag and take it down to the car. Ginny gave Carly a goodbye hug and told her she was welcome to visit any time. Both Ginny and Andi waited inside to give Carly and Colt privacy while they said their goodbyes outside.

Once Colt had left to go to the barn, Andi went outside and hugged her little sister goodbye. "I'm happy you came," Andi told her. "It gave me one more chance to see you before I go out east."

Carly looked at her sister seriously. "Andi, listen to me. Please, don't marry Derek. I know you think of me as your wild little sister, but I do know a little about love. Derek doesn't love you the way you want him to. You don't love him like you should. Not enough to spend the rest of your life with him."

Andi stared at her sister, considering what she'd said. "I know Derek and I have our differences, but I'm sure he loves me. He tells me he does all the time. We just have to work out our issues."

"Derek may say he loves you, but believe me, he doesn't know the first thing about love. He wants to own you, Andi. He wants you on his arm to show you off to all of his colleagues. You're beautiful and talented, the perfect trophy wife for him. He wants to own you like all of his possessions. Like that stupid expensive sports car he drives and those ridiculously expensive suits he wears."

Andi frowned. "How can you say that? I'm not some

airheaded trophy wife."

"No, you're not. But that's what you are to him. Derek loves Derek. Derek loves money, power, and possessions. Derek will never be able to make you feel loved the way you want. The way you deserve," Carly said adamantly.

"So, what am I supposed to do? Just turn around and go home after investing almost three years of my life in a relationship with Derek?"

Carly shook her head. "No. Stay here at the ranch. Fall in love with Luke. I've never seen a man more in love than he is with you."

Andi's mouth dropped open. "Now you are being crazy. Sure, I get along really well with Luke, but he's never shown any sign of being in love with me." *Except for that kiss. That fabulous, delicious kiss.*

Carly grinned. "Are you kidding? All I see from him are signs that he loves you. The way you two tease each other. How upset he was last night at the bar when he knew you were talking to Derek. The way you two danced together last night. He's attracted to you. Andi, he's in love with you."

Andi thought about last night and how silly she'd acted after drinking too much beer. He'd only been humoring her. He hadn't really meant anything he'd said. Why should he? He was a handsome man who could have any woman he wanted. He'd made it very clear that the last thing he wanted was a city girl like her.

"Luke doesn't love me, Carly. We just have some sort of connection, but that's all. Besides, you can't fall in love in a couple of weeks. It's crazy."

Carly winked at Andi. "Speak for yourself, Big Sis." She reached out and hugged Andi hard. "Luke or no Luke, at least think about what I've said. You deserve to be happy and Derek is not the one who'll make you happy."

Carly hopped into her car and drove away, waving at Andi.

Andi stood there a moment, thinking about what her sister had said. Her life was getting more confusing by the day. She had left Seattle thinking she was heading toward her future with Derek. And now? Well, she had no idea what the future held.

Ginny came outside and put an arm around Andi. "You're going to miss your sister, aren't you?"

Andi nodded. "Yeah, I will. She's wild and crazy sometimes, but we've been through a lot together. It's hard saying goodbye."

Ginny nodded toward the barn where Colt stood, watching Carly's car drive off in the distance. "Colt's going to miss her, too. I've never seen him so infatuated with a girl before. I think he's crazy in love with her."

Andi stared at Ginny, her brows furrowed. "They only knew each other a couple of days. Don't you think it was more like a crush than love? No one falls in love that quickly."

Ginny shot Andi a sly grin. "Some people do." She turned and headed back toward the house.

Andi stood there in the driveway wondering if everyone around her was crazy or if it was just her.

* * *

An hour later, Ginny and Andi were on the road to Missoula after having packed Ginny's homemade goods and a couple of boxes of Andi's smaller prints in the back seat of the truck. The fair had started on Tuesday, and Ginny's friends had the booth up and running, so Ginny wanted to get her goods there to sell. She told Andi she should bring along at least a few of her prints for her friends to sell. "The smaller ones will be easy for them to keep track of. Then you can bring the larger ones when we watch the booth Friday through Sunday," Ginny had said.

An hour later, they arrived at the fairgrounds. Ginny spoke to a man at the entrance gate and he allowed her to drive in so she could unload her vehicle.

The fairgrounds weren't very busy because it was still early in the day. Ginny maneuvered her truck outside a tall, white, barn-like structure with a sign on it stating it was the Commercial Building. They stopped and parked near a large entrance door. A few people were milling in and out of the building.

Andi and Ginny quickly began unloading the boxes of preserves and prints. They walked into the building and down the wide aisle past several booths selling all types of home-made gifts, furniture, crafts, and artwork until they were near the center of the building. They stopped at a booth that had a brightly decorated front table and tables and shelving along the side and back walls with several varieties of preserves and jams displayed. Baskets of dried flower arrangements sat among the jars and dried flower wreathes hung on the walls. In addition, there were jars of dried herbs, including rosemary, thyme, sage, oregano, mint, and a variety of others. The booth was only a ten by ten foot square, but they managed to display a large quantity of merchandise.

A woman who looked to be much older than Ginny sat on a chair at the front table. She had short, straight, gray hair, was slightly plump, and wore a flowered shirt, jeans, and sneakers. She smiled warmly when she saw Ginny.

"Hello, Ginny," the woman said as she walked around the table to give her friend a hug. "And this must be your young artist friend," the woman said, smiling over at Andi.

"Yes, it is. Andi, this is Mary. She, Sharon and I have been running a booth together here at the fair for ten years."

Andi held her hand out to the older woman. "Hi Mary, it's nice to meet you. I appreciate you letting me share your booth with you to sell my prints."

Mary waved a pudgy hand through the air. "Not a problem, dear. Happy to do it. We just had to get the okay from the fair committee to add additional items and they were fine with it. It's always nice having a professional artist's work among all the local items."

The three women went to work setting out Ginny's preserves and making room on a back table for Andi's prints to be displayed. She kept them in the boxes so people could easily flip through them. Mary suggesting hanging a few on the wall to attract the attention of customers.

"My, but aren't you a talented young lady," Mary said as she looked through the prints. "I may have to buy a few of these for myself. I'll certainly tell all my friends. Your work is just beautiful."

"Thank you," Andi said, a little embarrassed by the praise.

A tall, slender woman with a short blond bob appeared at the booth with coffee and sandwiches for her and Mary. Ginny introduced her to Andi as Sharon. She immediately started looking through Andi's prints. "I love all of them," she told Andi. "It's so nice to see ocean scenes for a change instead of ranches and cows."

After everything had been unloaded and set out, Ginny and Andi waved goodbye to the two women. On their way out of town, they stopped at the dealership garage to check on Andi's car and she met Jeff in person. He assured her that the car would be ready by Tuesday of next week at the very latest, and because it had taken so long, he offered to have it delivered out at the ranch that day. Andi gave him her credit card to pay for the repair, and then the two women began the hour-long ride home.

As they rode along, Andi stared out at the open spaces around her. Wildflowers of yellow, purple, and pink grew in the ditches and the terrain was a variation of hills with evergreens and rolling pastures. Wood rail fences strung with barbed wire ran along both sides of the road to prevent cattle from roaming onto the busy highway. Andi wondered where in the summer pasture Luke was and what he was doing. She smiled. *Riding fences, chasing outlaws, and playing poker at the saloon.* That's what he'd said that night when he'd come back to the cabin and she had supper waiting for him. So many memories in such a small amount of time. By Wednesday of next week, she'd be on her way to Buffalo. Andi's smile faded at the thought. She was already missing everyone at the ranch, especially Luke.

* * *

Luke stood, bent at the waist, pounding a nail into a fence rail while Randy held the other end. He'd been working on fencing all day, and his back ached. Worse yet, as hard as he tried, he couldn't keep his mind on what he was doing. He kept thinking of Andi and her big, green eyes, and how it felt to have her lean against him when they danced last night.

"Shit!" Luke yelled as he slammed the hammer on his thumb instead of the nail.

A low chuckle came from Randy across the way. "What was that, the fourth or the fifth time you hit yourself with the hammer?"

Luke stood up straight and glared at Randy who just grinned back. He pulled off his hat and pushed his hand through his hair. The sun had been beating down on them all day and Luke was hot, thirsty, hungry, and tired. His back was sore and his neck was tense. He set his hat back on his head and picked up his hammer and the box of nails. "That's enough for today," he yelled over to Randy. "I'm hungry. Let's go back to the cabin."

Randy strode over and kept pace alongside Luke as the two men headed to the truck. "So, you cooking tonight or are we ordering take-out?" Randy asked.

"What do you think, smartass?"

Randy laughed. "Guess I'm stuck with your cooking."

"Hey, you can always drive back home tonight and come back in the morning. Doesn't matter to me."

"Naw, I'm too tired. I'll choke down whatever you cook," Randy said.

The two men climbed up into the truck and Luke drove back to the cabin.

"Where has your mind been all day, anyway?" Randy asked as they rode along. "I must have heard you swear a hundred times when you either hit yourself with the hammer or dropped something."

"I have a lot on my mind," Luke said.

Randy nodded. "Yep, I'm sure you do. And all of it has to do with Andi. Am I right?"

Luke turned and glared at Randy. "Don't go there, okay?"

"Listen, Luke. I've known you my whole life. Your family has been good to me since I was just a kid in need of a real family. You and I are as close as any brothers could be. You can't hide a thing from me, so you might as well spit out what's bothering you so you don't harm yourself tomorrow when we're working."

Luke sighed. "There's nothing to talk about. Andi's special, that's for certain, but she's engaged to another man and she'll be leaving as soon as her car is fixed. End of story."

They pulled up to the cabin and Luke made sure to store all the tools in the lockbox in the bed of his truck. Randy went ahead inside the cabin and Luke walked around the side and started up the generator. He stood there a moment, staring at the cabin door, remembering when he'd walked inside and found Andi cooking dinner at the stove. He remembered holding her as he helped her around the cabin with her hurt ankle, and when they'd sat on the sofa together as he'd looked at the sketches she'd done that day. There were so many memories of Andi in this cabin alone, let alone at the ranch. Long after she was gone, he'd still think of her in almost every place he went on this ranch.

Luke walked inside and washed up before heating up stew on the stove and cutting up bread his mother had sent along. Randy sat at the table, playing solitaire with an old, worn out deck of cards. After supper, the two men played a few rounds of poker before settling into the bunks for the night. Randy hadn't brought up Andi again, until the room was dark and they were both in their beds.

"I'm going to say one more thing whether you want to hear or not," Randy said into the quiet room. "Then I'll shut up."

"What?" Luke asked.

"I know how you are, Luke. You and I are a lot alike. We don't talk about feelings and we keep to ourselves. But, I can't just sit back quietly and watch you lose again. Andi's the best thing that's happened to you in a long while. Don't stay quiet and let her get away. Tell her how you feel. Otherwise, she'll drive away and you'll never see her again, and then it will be too late."

"She doesn't belong to me, Randy," Luke said, sounding defeated.

"She doesn't belong to anyone, you idiot," Randy said. "Andi is her own person and will make up her own mind. But she won't know her choices if you don't tell her how you feel. Luke, believe me when I say, if any woman has ever been worth begging for, Andi is that woman. Do whatever is necessary to keep her here. Otherwise, you're going to be sorry for the rest of your life."

"Randy," Luke said.

"Yeah, I know. Shut up and mind my own business."

"No. Thanks for caring. But I'm not sure it's as easy as all that," Luke told him.

"Nothing worth having is ever easy, right?"

Luke mulled that over as he lay there in the dark cabin. Randy was right. Nothing worth having was usually easy. But convincing a city girl that her life would be so much better out here in the middle of nowhere was not only difficult, but almost near impossible. He'd tried it once, and failed. Even if Andi actually loved him, and loved him enough to stay, would she want to stay forever? Ashley had loved him, but she hadn't stayed. Maybe he'd be better off not knowing if Andi loved him in the first place. It would hurt less when she left.

Chapter Twenty-Three

Thursday was a quiet day around the ranch with Luke and Randy gone and only the three of them eating meals together. Colt was moping around, missing Carly, and Andi had no idea how to make him feel better. More than likely, Carly would forget about him the minute she returned to Seattle and her bevy of men who adored her. Carly had a short attention span when it came to men, and poor Colt was going to learn that the hard way.

Friday morning, Ginny and Andi headed off for the fairgrounds right after breakfast. They arrived just as it opened at nine in the morning and soon afterwards, people started streaming past the shops ready to buy souvenirs and gifts. Andi had brought along the boxes of her larger prints and had hung up a couple of the framed prints for display. She was surprised at how many of the smaller prints Mary and Sharon had already sold, and she was excited to see how the larger ones would sell.

As the afternoon wore on, the shops grew busier, and many people streamed in and out of their little stall, looking over the many jars of preserves for sale as well as looking through Andi's prints. She sold several prints of various sizes of her Mount Rainier landscapes and many ocean prints as well. A few of the customers who purchased prints were either from the west coast or had visited and wanted a picture of a site they had seen. Her prints of the Lone Cypress were very popular, too. By the end of the first day, Andi was pleasantly surprised at how many prints she'd sold and how much money she'd made.

They closed up at nine o'clock that evening and drove the hour home and were back again bright and early the next morning. Andi had sold so many prints the day before that she'd loaded up the remainder of them and brought them along. Ginny had told her Saturday would be their busiest day, so she'd probably sell the majority of prints today.

Ginny had been right. Their stall was busy all day long and they barely had time for one of them to leave for a few minutes to grab drinks and something to eat. Right away, two people asked to purchase the two large, framed prints Andi had hung up for display, so Andi sold them and had to hang up unframed prints instead. Not only was Andi selling her prints quickly, but all of the ladies' jars of preserves were selling out fast. Andi and Ginny would replenish the shelves from stock under the tables as quickly as they could, but the items sold as fast as they replaced them. It got so busy at times that Ginny stayed at the front table with the cash box selling purchases while Andi walked around answering questions and restocking. After one especially busy half hour, both women looked at each other and started laughing. They were surprised at how crazy the day was.

Later in the afternoon, after Andi returned from a quick bathroom break and food run, she saw a nice looking, older gentleman standing in their booth talking to Ginny. He was tall and had thick, wavy, silver hair and looked to be in good physical shape. He also had a kind smile as he listened to Ginny.

When Andi set down the drinks and food on the front table, Ginny waved her inside.

"Andi, this is Glen Parker. He's a regular customer of ours every year."

Andi walked over and shook Glen's hand. "Nice to meet you."

"Happy to meet you, too," Glen said with a friendly smile. "I've been admiring your prints. I used to live in the Seattle area and I love the ones of Mount Rainier."

"Thank you," Andi said appreciatively.

"Glen was a real estate developer in Seattle before he retired," Ginny offered. "Now he lives here in the summer and in San Diego in the winter."

"That sounds nice," Andi said, noting that Glen didn't look old enough to be retired yet. He looked to be in Ginny's age range.

"Yes, I was lucky enough to retire a little early," he said. "I hit the market when it was at a high and left right before it bottomed out. I'm so glad I left early or else I would have lost everything like many of my friends in the business did."

Andi nodded. "Does your wife like living summers in Montana?"

Glen shook his head. "I'm not married, I'm afraid. I was, many years ago, but we divorced. I'm not lucky enough to have someone as talented as Ginny to make homemade preserves for me, so I always come here to stock up for the year."

"That's nice," Andi said.

Andi watched as Ginny took Glen around and pointed out the different preserves he might like. Ginny boxed up a dozen different ones for him. From the way Glen watched Ginny, Andi thought he might be interested in her.

When they came back to the table with his box of preserves, Glen caught Andi's attention again. "I really do love that one print of Mount Rainier. Tell me, do you still have the original painting or have you sold it?"

Andi's brows rose. She couldn't believe he was asking about the original. Most people never did. "Yes, I do still have the original. It's hanging in a gallery in Seattle."

Glen's eyes lit up. "Can you tell me how it's framed?"

Andi thought a moment. "Actually, I can get a photo of it for you in a minute. My sister works at the gallery and she could send me one."

"That would be wonderful," Glen said.

Andi quickly texted Carly to send a photo of the painting and an up close picture of the frame. Within minutes, Carly sent her the photos. Andi handed the phone to Glen. "It's a rustic type of frame. I thought it looked nice with the subject of the painting."

Glen studied the picture. "Yes, it does look nice. It would go well with the décor of my home here." He looked up at Andi. "Prints are nice, but I enjoy owning the original paintings. I've become a bit of a collector. Can you tell me how much it is?"

Andi tried not to look as surprised as she felt. She glanced at Ginny, whose eyes were wide and she looked as if she was going to burst. Andi usually never sold her paintings herself—she always left it to the gallery to sell them. But this was an opportunity she couldn't pass up.

"This one is priced at eighty-six hundred," she said as calmly as possible.

"Hmmm." Glen looked at the photo again, and then turned

his eyes back to Andi. "Sold. If it's as beautiful as the print, it's well worth it. It will look wonderful over my fireplace."

Andi's face broke out into a wide smile. Behind Glen, she saw Ginny smile big and pump her fists up and down in a gleeful way. "That's wonderful," Andi said. "You'll have to go through the gallery to buy it since it's being shown there, but if you give me your number, I'll have my sister call you with the details."

"That'll be fine," Glen said. He gave Andi his number and she stepped away to call Carly and tell her the good news. Just as she came back, Glen had finished paying for his jars of preserves and was asking Ginny if she'd like to go out for dinner sometime.

"I'm only about ten miles from your ranch," Glen said. "I could pick you up and we could come into Missoula for a nice dinner. Or even one of the smaller towns, if you'd like."

Ginny looked like she was thinking about it. "That's very nice of you to ask, but I'm always so busy at the ranch and I cook all the meals for the boys. It's difficult to get away."

Glen nodded. "Maybe we can meet for lunch sometime then. On a Sunday afternoon? Surely the boys can fend for themselves for a few hours."

Ginny nodded. "Maybe we could do that," she said.

Glen looked like he'd won the lottery. "I'll call you, then." He turned to Andi. "Andi, you are a very talented artist. I wish you all the best with your career."

"Thank you, Glen. And I hope you enjoy the painting. I love all my paintings, so I'm happy when they find a good home."

"Oh, you can be sure it will be taken well care of," Glen said with a smile. He waved goodbye and left.

Ginny came over to Andi and pulled her into a big hug. "I

can't believe you just sold that," she said with delight. "Isn't it amazing?"

"I can't believe I just sold it, either," Andi said. "Who would have thought I could sell an original painting out here? At a fair? It's incredible."

"Well, now you have more than enough money for your car and your trip. Isn't it wonderful how things work out? We just never know when an opportunity will knock on our door, do we?" Ginny asked.

Andi grinned. "Do you think he bought my painting just to impress you?"

"Heavens, no," Ginny said. "What a silly thing to say. He bought it because you're a talented artist. You heard him."

"Yeah, but he sure has a crush on you," Andi teased. "Are you going to dinner with him?"

Ginny waved her hand through the air to brush Andi's question away. "He was just being nice. He'll never really call and ask me out. Besides, I'm too busy to date anyone. I've had my happiness. It's someone else's turn now."

Andi thought about Ginny's words long after they'd closed up shop and headed home for the night. Ginny may have already had her happiness with her husband, but didn't she deserve to find happiness again if it was offered to her? Andi thought about her own life. If she married Derek, and it didn't work out, would she have lost any chance at finding happiness again? *Maybe you should choose the right man the first time around instead of the wrong one.* The problem was, who was the right man? She had believed Derek was, but then Luke had come into her life. Carly had told her to not marry Derek and to stay on the ranch and fall in love with Luke. Ha. Falling in love with Luke was the easy part. Making a life with someone you hardly knew, that was the risky part.

"Besides, he's never actually told me he loves me," Andi said aloud in her dark room that night as she lay in bed. "We tease, we flirt, and that's it. Maybe, that's all it is."

As she lay there, Andi realized she hadn't seen Luke since Tuesday night when she'd been tipsy and acted silly. If he was back from the summer pasture, he hadn't made his presence known. Her car was supposed to be ready by Tuesday at the latest. That meant she'd be leaving Wednesday morning. *Just three more days, and I'm gone.* The thought made Andi very sad.

* * *

Sunday was the last day of the fair, and although Andi was pleased at all she'd sold, she was happy this was the last day they'd be at the booth. Carly called her that morning and told her the sale of the painting had been finalized and the gallery would transfer her portion of the earnings into her account on Monday. Andi was happy to hear that. It was a lot more money than she had hoped to make at the fair, and now she felt a little more secure about continuing to travel out east.

The morning sales were steady, but by afternoon, they began to dwindle. Many of the merchants were already packing up and getting ready to leave by three in the afternoon, even though the fair was opened until six. Andi and Ginny had very little to pack up as far as merchandise was concerned. After ten years of selling at the fair, the ladies had become pros at this, so they could estimate how much they would sell, and there wasn't much left. Even the craft items had sold out completely. Andi had sold dozens of prints, so she consolidated the leftovers into fewer boxes. She could now pack the remaining prints in her car and bring them to

Buffalo instead of having to ship them.

Just before four o'clock, a familiar face showed up at their booth. Andi smiled as she looked up into Luke's handsome face. He smiled back, his blue eyes twinkling. They hadn't seen each other since Tuesday night, but to Andi, it had felt like a lifetime.

"What are you doing here?" Andi asked when Luke came into their booth.

"I thought I'd come and help you two pack things up in the truck. I figured there'd be a couple of heavy tables and some shelving. Then I can take you both out to supper," Luke said, grinning.

Goodness, he looks adorable. Luke was freshly showered and smelled deliciously spicy. He'd worn a simple cotton, plaid shirt in blue, which set off his eyes, and his usual jeans, cowboy boots, and hat, but he was way too good looking to be considered ordinary. And that wicked grin of his. It made his face even more handsome, if that was possible.

"I knew I raised my boys right," Ginny said cheerfully, interrupting Andi's thoughts. "You can start by folding up these tables and bringing them outside. I'll go pull my truck around to the door so we can start loading."

Together they loaded up the tables and shelving as well as the few boxes of product left. By then, most of the merchants had left, so they decided to leave also.

"I heard you had an amazing sale the other day," Luke said to Andi as they walked out to Ginny's truck for the last time.

Andi's eyes lit up. "Yes. I sold one of my paintings. It was incredible. I never expected that to happen."

"It doesn't surprise me at all," Luke said. "You're very talented. That's obvious, even to someone like me who knows nothing about art."

"Glen Parker bought it for his home," Ginny piped up. "You know Glen. He buys preserves from us every year."

Luke's eyes sparkled mischievously. "You mean your would-be boyfriend?"

Ginny hit Luke's arm. "Stop that. I don't know who is worse, you or Andi. She was teasing me about it, too."

"Well, he did ask you out," Andi said in self-defense.

"He actually asked you out this time?" Luke asked, surprised. "What did you say?"

"She never answered him. She was very vague," Andi said.

Ginny shook her head. "I don't have time to go on dates. I'm too busy with the ranch. Speaking of which, what are Colt and Randy eating for supper tonight?"

"They're going to The Depot for a burger. Randy's going to try to get Colt to stop brooding over Carly. That kid sure has it bad," Luke said.

"Sorry," Andi said. "My sister seems to do that to men a lot."

"Well, I'm tired," Ginny said as she hopped up behind the wheel of her truck. "I think I'll just head home. You two go along and have a bite to eat."

Luke looked over at Andi. "Want to go eat supper?"

"Sure."

Ginny gave them a ride out to Luke's truck in the parking lot before she headed for home. Luke and Andi drove to the outskirts of town to a little place by the river where they served upscale meals, but everyone dressed casually.

"I feel kind of grungy after working all day," Andi said as they walked inside. "Hope I'm not too underdressed for this place."

"You're fine. And believe me, you don't look grungy. And

you smell a great deal better than Randy did after a couple of days at the summer cabin."

Andi laughed as they were shown to a corner booth and handed menus. The restaurant had a rustic décor, but everything looked nice. There were white table cloths and red, cloth napkins were folded under the silverware. A single lit candle sat on every table.

"Are you saying that you enjoyed my company at the summer cabin more than Randy's?" Andi teased.

"Yes, by a longshot." Luke smiled over at Andi.

They ordered their meals and Luke ordered a bottle of red wine to share with Andi.

"Wine?" she asked. "I thought you were a beer drinker."

"I can be fancy when I want to," he teased.

They sat there drinking wine and eating their salads, talking about the fair and how much the women had sold. Luke told Andi about the work he and Randy had done in the summer pasture, and that he'd finally finished the stable by his cabin so he could now house Chance there. By the time their meals came, they had exhausted all the safe topics of conversation.

Andi was careful to not drink too much wine so she wouldn't get tipsy. "Sorry I was so silly Tuesday night. I don't hold alcohol very well."

Luke looked up at her over his meal and smiled. "I'm not sorry. I enjoyed dancing with you."

"Me, too," Andi admitted.

After another pause in the conversation, Andi said, "I dropped by the dealership garage earlier this week. They said my car would be ready by Tuesday at the latest."

Luke's gaze dropped. He picked at his food. "So, you'll be needing a ride there to pick it up, I suppose."

"No. They're going to drop it off at the ranch. They said they would because it had taken so long to fix."

Luke nodded. "We'll have to go riding one more time then, before you go," he said somberly.

Andi nodded. "Yeah. I'd like that."

The cheerfulness of the evening had faded. The thought of leaving the ranch made Andi sad. She noticed that it had affected Luke as well.

They rode home in almost complete silence. Any attempt at chatter seemed forced. When they arrived at the ranch, it was already dark outside. Luke stopped at the main house to drop off Andi.

"Thank you for the nice meal," Andi said as they sat together in the truck's cab. "I really enjoyed it."

"You're welcome," Luke said, looking everywhere but at Andi. "I'm glad we went."

Andi reached for the door handle, but Luke stopped her. "Just a minute." He stepped out of the truck and came around to open her door. He held her arm gently as she climbed down. They stood there, staring at each other.

"Remember that first night when I knocked on your door and you drove me to the house?" Andi asked softly.

Luke nodded. "How can I forget?"

"That night you wouldn't even tell me your name and you jumped out of the truck like I had cooties and strode into the house. I had to run to catch up with you. A lot has changed since then, hasn't it?" Andi asked.

Luke's expression softened. "Yeah, it has. I was a jerk that night. Sorry."

Andi smiled. "That's okay. I was just some crazy city girl who interrupted your evening. I guess I can't blame you."

"It turned out you weren't such a crazy city girl after all,"

Luke said softly. "You do pretty well on a ranch."

"Thanks. You turned out to be pretty nice for a cowboy," Andi said.

Luke put his hands on Andi's arms and stood there a moment, looking down into her eyes. He bent down and placed a soft kiss on her cheek. "Goodnight, Andi."

"Goodnight, Luke," she said, a lump caught in her throat.

Luke stepped up into his truck and drove away. Andi watched him until the red taillights were no longer visible.

Chapter Twenty-Four

Luke lay in bed that night, alone as usual. He was tired of sleeping alone. His thoughts were always of Andi now, when he was working, when he was riding, and most of all when he was alone. Tonight had been nice, taking her out for supper and talking about everyday things as if they'd known each other for a very long time. That's how it felt to him, at least. But then Andi brought up the subject of her car and all pretenses were gone. Luke was slammed back to reality, the reality that Andi was leaving him very soon.

"Do whatever is necessary to keep her here. Otherwise, you're going to be sorry for the rest of your life." Randy's words echoed in his mind and Luke knew he was right. He'd never felt this way about any other woman before, not even Ashley. Luke was always honest with Andi, and she was with him, too, and they both respected the other's opinion. They teased each other mercilessly, and they both enjoyed it. Best of all, just being around Andi warmed his heart. He not only loved her physical appearance, he loved her soul. She was a good person with a good heart. He knew he'd never meet anyone like her ever again.

But could he ask her to stay after knowing her for only three weeks? She'd think he was crazy. And worse, what if she didn't feel the same way he did? That would be harder to bear than watching her go.

I knew it was idiotic to fall in love with Andi, but I did anyway.

Luke tried to fall asleep, but it was useless. He tossed and turned, then gave up. He didn't care if he was tired in the morning. What did it matter? Every day was the same and would be for the rest of his life. What was one day of being tired out of so many to come?

He lit an oil lamp beside his bed and walked out to the kitchen. Pulling a beer out from the refrigerator, he stood there in the semi-dark and took a long drink from it. He could lie on the sofa a while and read, like he used to before bed, but he didn't really want to. He could try going back to bed, but what was the point? He took another drink of beer, walked back into his bedroom, and quickly dressed into work clothes. Then he grabbed his flashlight and headed out to the stable. Chance was still up at the corral by the house. Earlier today, Luke had brought bales of fresh straw and hay down to his stable, but he hadn't had a chance to put either in Chance's new stall. Once he entered the stable, he turned on a large, battery powered lantern and began breaking open a bale of straw and shoveling a layer into the stall. Work would tire him out. It would help him sleep. He'd always have work here on the ranch, if nothing else.

* * *

Andi couldn't sleep. She'd gone up to her room after Luke had driven off with every intention of collapsing after her long day, but sleep eluded her. Her mind was filled with Luke.

She'd enjoyed the dinner they'd shared at the restaurant. It had been such a nice, comfortable evening, talking to each other and sharing their day. She wondered what it would be like to do that every day with someone. Or more specifically, with Luke.

Andi and Derek never did that. Sure, they went out to dinner countless times, but Derek was usually the topic of conversation when they talked. He would share every detail of his day, but when Andi mentioned something about hers, he'd just nod and turn the conversation back to him. Andi had always figured it was because his job was much more interesting than her painting was, but now she realized it had more to do with how self-centered Derek was. Carly was right about one thing—Derek loved Derek. Andi used to think it was good that he was so focused on his career, but now she wondered if it was. Shouldn't he be focused on their relationship as well?

Andi's thoughts turned back to Luke and the sweet kiss he'd placed on her cheek tonight. She knew he'd wanted to kiss her on the lips, she could see it in his eyes. But he'd refrained. That was good, right? Then why did she wish he'd kissed her like he had at the summer pasture? Andi sighed.

Unable to sleep, she slipped out of bed and pulled on a sweatshirt and her jeans. She walked quietly down the steps to the kitchen and turned on the small light over the stove. Bree's head popped up with interest, but the dog didn't leave her bed. Andi patted Bree on the head a moment, then rummaged through the refrigerator, but decided that she wasn't really hungry, just restless.

She thought that a short walk outside in the cool night air would help her sleep. She slipped on her sneakers that were in the mudroom, found a flashlight, and headed out the door.

The air was definitely cool as she maneuvered her way slowly down the gravel road that led to Luke's cabin. She figured she'd walk a short distance, and then turn back. Stopping for a moment, Andi looked up into the night sky. The moon was full and bright and the sky was filled with twinkling stars. She was in awe of its beauty. She hadn't even turned on her flashlight because the moon lit up the sky. At home in Seattle, the city lights blurred out the night sky and she never really looked up. But here, the sky was an endless display of tiny twinkling lights.

Andi walked a little farther until she saw Luke's cabin outlined in the moonlight. Behind it, she saw a light on and wondered where it was coming from. Walking even closer, she realized the light was coming from the new stable.

Luke couldn't sleep either.

Andi stared at the lit up stable for a long time. She considered going to see Luke, but decided against it. It was best if they kept some distance between them. With a heavy heart, she turned and walked back to the house.

* * *

After breakfast the next morning, Andi helped Ginny work in the garden for most of the afternoon picking beans and peas. She was surprised at how many there were and how long it took. Once finished, the two women cleaned them in the sink and began the process of shelling the peas. Andi didn't mind the work. She enjoyed helping Ginny and it kept her mind off of a certain hot cowboy.

Late in the afternoon, after Randy and Colt had come in for lunch and left, there was a knock on the door. Ginny went to answer it. It was a man from the garage, delivering Andi's car. Andi signed the paperwork and the man left. Both women walked outside and stared at Andi's blue Escape as if it was something from another planet.

Ginny found her voice first. "I guess this means you'll be leaving us soon."

Andi swallowed hard. "I guess so."

They looked at each other and Andi saw tears in Ginny's eyes. She couldn't blame her, though. Andi wanted to cry, too.

They turned and went back into the house and continued their work without saying another word.

Luke walked into the house with a long face right before supper. Randy and Colt were already sitting at the table and Andi and Ginny were serving the food. Andi looked up and caught Luke's eye.

"I see your car came," Luke said.

Andi nodded. The forlorn look in Luke's eyes made her want to break down in tears.

They all sat and started filling their plates.

"Does this mean you'll be leaving tomorrow?" Colt asked. He also looked somber. Andi wasn't sure if it was because she was leaving or he was still heartsick over Carly.

All eyes turned to Andi.

"I think I'll wait until Wednesday," Andi said. "That will give me time to pack up and get ready to leave."

Colt nodded. "It'll be strange without you here. You fit in so perfectly with all of us, it's like you've lived here forever."

Andi's heart swelled. She was sitting right next to Colt and she reached over and hugged him. "Thanks, Colt. It will be strange to leave."

Everyone was quiet after that. At one point, Andi could have sworn that Randy kicked Luke under the table, and then she saw him glare at Luke. Luke stayed silent though. Andi wondered what all of that was about.

That evening, Andi consolidated all the prints she had left and packed them in as few boxes as possible. Colt helped her put them in her car, and then he carefully carried out the painting of the Lone Cypress and laid it on top of the boxes, making sure it wouldn't shift around. All that was left to do was for Andi to wash some of her laundry, pack, and then leave on Wednesday morning.

* * *

Luke was behind the barn, splitting wood. It was cooler this evening and he needed something to take his mind off of Andi leaving. If he didn't wear himself out splitting wood, he wouldn't be able to sleep tonight any more than he had last night.

He picked up a piece of cut wood, set it on the chopping block, then swung the ax and hit the wood perfectly in the center. It split in one chop. Again and again, he did this until his back and arms ached. And then he did it some more.

Luke was just about to split another piece when a voice startled him.

"What in the hell are you going to do?"

Luke looked up into Randy's angry brown eyes. He dropped his arm, the ax still in his hand. "I thought you went home already."

"No. I'm here and I'm damned mad at you. What are you going to do about Andi? Have you talked to her yet? Have you told her how you feel?" Randy asked.

A crease formed between Luke's brows. "It's none of your business. Go home, Randy."

Randy stood there, rigid. "You're right. It's none of my

business, and I wouldn't have to be here yelling at you if you'd just done what you need to do. Tell her, Luke. Tell her you want her to stay."

Luke leaned the ax against the woodpile and crossed his arms over his chest. "What the hell am I supposed to tell her? That I want her to stay even though she's only known me for a few weeks? That I want her to forget about that fiancé of hers, who will definitely give her a life of luxury, and stay here with me so she can become a rancher's wife? I have nothing to offer her, Randy, so what the hell is it I'm supposed to tell her?"

"That you love her, you idiot. Tell her that you love her. That's all she needs to hear. From everything I've witnessed, that's all she wants to hear from you."

Luke sighed, all the bluster escaping from him. His shoulders sagged. "Love isn't always enough, Randy. I know that better than anyone."

Randy walked over and put his hand on Luke's shoulder. "Maybe not. But you're never going to know for certain unless you tell her."

Luke nodded, but he wasn't completely convinced. "I know you mean well, but sometimes things are just not that easy. Go on home, okay?"

Randy took a step back. "You have one more day, and then she's gone," he said quietly. "Don't lose her, Luke. Tell her how you feel." He turned and strode off to where his truck was parked, and then drove away.

Luke continued splitting wood.

* * *

Andi sat at the table with Ginny and Colt, eating a piece of peach pie and drinking a glass of iced tea when the phone on the wall rang.

"Who could that be?" Ginny asked as she answered the phone. She turned to Andi. "It's for you, dear. It's Derek."

Andi sighed, but stood up and took the phone from Ginny. She stepped into the sitting room as far as the cord would allow her and said, "Hi, Derek."

"Andi. Hi. I thought I'd call and find out if your car was fixed," Derek said, sounding cheerful.

"Yes, they brought it out here this afternoon," Andi told him.

"Great. So you'll be leaving tomorrow?" Derek asked hopefully.

"Not exactly," Andi said. "It didn't get here until late, so I wasn't quite ready to leave tomorrow. But I'll be leaving early Wednesday morning."

"Oh," Derek sounded disappointed. "Well, okay. At least you'll be leaving and heading here. How long before you think you'll get here? By Saturday or Sunday, maybe?"

Andi didn't know how to respond. She hadn't thought that far ahead. Since staying here on the ranch, she'd lost all interest in her trip across country to Buffalo. Suddenly, it was becoming all too real. She was leaving. She was heading to Buffalo to be with the man she was supposed to marry. It all was happening way too fast.

"Andi? Are you there?"

"Yes, I'm here," Andi said softly. "I'm not sure how long it will take me to drive there. I'll call you Wednesday night to let you know where I am."

"Wonderful." Derek sounded excited again. "I can't wait for you to get here. I know you're going to love the townhouse I'm renting, and the furniture I picked out, too. There's a little nook with windows that will be perfect for you to set up an area to paint. And I can't wait to show you off to all my new friends here. They will be so jealous that you belong to me."

Andi frowned. *I belong to him?* Derek sounded so excited, though, which was rare for him, that she didn't have the heart to say anything.

"Hurry here, okay?" Derek said. "No more adventures. I can't wait to see you."

"I'll try to hurry," Andi said without enthusiasm.

She sighed after they'd hung up. Her heart felt heavy. This was it. She was leaving the day after tomorrow. If Colt and Ginny hadn't been in the other room, Andi would have dropped her head and cried.

Chapter Twenty-Five

Tuesday morning Andi awoke to the early morning sun filtering through her bedroom curtains. She showered quickly and dressed, then pulled her hair up into a thick ponytail. This was her last day on the ranch. The thought made her sadder than she'd ever felt in her life. She'd been unhappy when she'd left Seattle and her sister behind to follow Derek to Buffalo, and this felt just as bad. It was strange how quickly this place had found its way into her heart, but it had. And the people had, too. One in particular.

Andi joined Colt, Randy, and Ginny for breakfast. Ginny tried keeping the conversation cheerful, but no one really felt like talking.

Before Randy headed outdoors, he asked Andi quietly, "Have you spoken to Luke?"

Andi frowned and shook her head. "Not since yesterday. Why?"

Randy just shook his head and walked out the door, leaving Andi to wonder why he'd asked her that.

After the dishes were washed, Ginny turned to Andi. "Honey, I don't want you spending your last day here working.

Go outside, wander around, visit the horses, or do some sketching. Do whatever makes you happy. Take Bree with you since she's become so attached. I'll take care of the rest of your laundry. Just enjoy your day."

Andi reached out and hugged Ginny hard. "Thank you for everything. I don't know how I'll ever repay you for all you've done for me. There aren't many people who'd take in a stranger and let her stay for three weeks in their home. You are a very special lady. I hope you know that."

Ginny pulled away and smiled up at Andi. "It's easy to be nice to you, hon. Now, don't say another word or I'm going to start crying. It'll be bad enough seeing you leave tomorrow. I don't want to cry all day today, too."

Andi hugged Ginny again, then ran upstairs to retrieve her sketchpad and headed outside with Bree at her heels. It was a warm day and the air felt heavy. Andi looked up into the sky, but there were no nasty clouds looming above. If it didn't rain later, she'd be surprised.

Andi walked down to the corral and stood on the fence a moment to pet Abby's sleek neck. She didn't see Chance in the corral, which made her wonder if he was down at the new stable by Luke's cabin. She climbed down from the fence and headed on into the barn to see if anyone was in there.

The barn was empty. Andi looked down at Bree and asked, "Where do you think all the men are?" Bree cocked her head, which made Andi smile. She reached down and rubbed the dog behind the ears. "I'm going to miss you as much as everyone else."

Andi sat on a square hay bale by the barn door and looked around. She inhaled deeply, and was rewarded with a sneeze. When she opened her eyes, she saw Luke standing in the doorway on the other side of the barn.

"Bless you," he said, grinning. "Don't inhale too deeply in a barn. If the dust from the hay doesn't get you, the smell of manure will."

Andi's face lit up. "I was just trying to remember everything. Scents are as good as images. Like the evergreens we smelled up at the summer pasture."

Luke walked over to where Andi sat. He reached down and patted Bree who sat beside Andi. "I hope you don't remember me as smelling of horse sweat and manure," he teased.

Andi thought of how he smelled fresh out of the shower. Clean soap and spicy cologne. "No, that isn't how I'll remember you," she said softly.

Luke straightened up. "Do you still want to go riding one last time?"

Andi nodded. "I'd like that."

"Let's go after supper, then. That'll give us a couple of hours. Hopefully, it won't rain until late tonight, like it's supposed to," Luke said.

"Okay."

Luke turned and strode toward the barn door.

"Hey, Luke?" Andi called after him.

He stopped and turned. "Yeah?"

"Is that what you wanted to talk to me about? Riding?"

Luke frowned. "What?"

"Randy asked me at breakfast if you'd talked to me yet. What was that about?" Andi asked.

Luke stood there a moment, his lips partly opened as if he was going to say something. He took a deep breath, and then let it out softly. "Yep. Just about riding," he said, before walking out the barn door.

Andi sat there and watched him leave. For a brief moment, it had looked as though Luke was going to say something to her, and then changed his mind. She sighed. Maybe she'd only hoped he'd had something more to say.

Opening her sketchpad, Andi prepared a sheet of paper, and then she began to sketch the interior of the barn. She sketched the stalls, the straw on the floor, and the hay bales stacked in the corner. She added Bree, lying on a pile of straw. Then she added Luke, standing as he had in the doorway when he'd entered. His jean clad legs, white T-shirt, and unbuttoned red plaid shirt. His dusty, black hat was on his head, cocked at a bit of an angle, and his face held that wicked grin of his. Andi smiled when she finally got the grin just right. She was going to miss that grin.

Unfortunately, the day went by quickly and soon Andi was inside the house helping Ginny with supper, despite the older woman's protests. They were having mashed potatoes that were home grown, green beans, homemade bread, and steaks on the grill that Colt was cooking outdoors for them. Everything was fresh and delicious and everyone enjoyed the wonderful meal despite the fact that Andi was leaving them tomorrow.

* * *

After supper, Ginny shooed Luke and Andi out the door so they could go riding. Earlier, Luke had gone home in his truck to clean up for supper and had ridden Chance up to the corral from his pasture. Andi insisted on saddling Abby, and then they were on their way up the center trail toward the high pastures.

The air was still thick and the wind had started whipping up. There were still no storm clouds in the sky, but it felt like rain was on the way.

Luke spoke up as they rode side by side. "Are you all packed and ready to go?"

Andi nodded. "Yeah. Ginny was sweet enough to finish my laundry and I packed up most of my clothes this afternoon. Colt helped me put my other stuff into the car last night. There's not much else left to do."

"This place is going to seem different once you leave," Luke said.

"Really?" Andi asked, giving Luke a sideways glance. "You mean you're going to miss me arguing with you, and teasing you?"

Luke grinned. "Yep. And I'll miss you calling me 'Cowboy', and drawing naked pictures of me."

"They are not naked," Andi insisted. "I would never sketch naked pictures of my *brother*."

Luke chuckled. "I'm most definitely not your bother," he said.

"Definitely not," Andi agreed.

"Colt's going to miss you. And Randy, and Mom. Bree and Abby will miss you, too," Luke said.

Andi's eyes turned sad. "I'm going to miss all of them, too."

"What about me?" Luke asked, trying to sound light-hearted.

"Yes. I'm going to miss you, too, Desperado," Andi said softly.

They rode on, stopping for a moment in a copse of evergreens. Andi inhaled deeply. "I'm going to miss that scent when I'm living in the city."

Luke stayed silent. He didn't trust himself to speak. He wanted to do what Randy had said and tell Andi he loved her and wanted her to stay, but he just couldn't make himself do it. It was best to just let her go, like he'd let Ashley go. It would save them both a lot of heartache in the end.

They rode a little farther and were halfway around the trail when the first rumble of thunder rolled through the sky. Luke looked up and saw dark clouds moving toward them from the west.

"We'd better head back before we get wet," Luke said. "The trail to my place is closer, let's head there."

Luke picked up the pace with Chance and Andi followed suit. They rode through the trees and then down the trail that ran alongside Luke's pasture. The wind whipped around them, moving the clouds faster in their direction. Thunder rumbled louder. They were almost to Luke's stable when the first big raindrops began to fall.

Luke hopped off of Chance at the fence and quickly opened the pasture's gate. He held onto Chance's reins and pulled him through and Andi followed, heading for the stable. After locking up the gate, Luke hurried with Chance to the stable as rain began to pelt him hard.

Once inside the stable, Luke and Andi quickly unsaddled their horses and hung the tack up after putting the horses each into a stall.

"I'm glad I got these ready last night," Luke said as he filled a bucket of grain for each of the horses and put them into their stalls.

"I saw the light on in the stable last night," Andi said. "Couldn't you sleep?"

Luke cocked his head. "How could you see that from the house?"

"I didn't. I went for a late night walk and that's when I saw the light on. I couldn't sleep either."

Another roll of thunder made them both look up toward the sky.

"I don't think that's going to let up soon," Luke said. "We'd better make a run for the cabin. I can drive you back to the house in the truck."

Andi nodded.

They stood at the door of the stable and watched the rain fall. It was starting to come down heavy and fast. Luke grabbed Andi's hand. "Ready?"

"Ready," she said.

They ran out into the rain and through the wet pasture toward the fence. Luke quickly helped Andi over the fence, then climbed over, too, grabbed her hand again so she wouldn't slip on the wet ground, and they ran to the side door of the cabin. Luke pushed the door open and Andi ran inside. He followed her in and shut the door. When he pulled his hat off, water fell from the brim onto the rug.

They both stood there in the small hallway, dripping wet and out of breath, staring at each other. Suddenly, they both broke out into laughter.

"I can't believe how hard it's raining out there," Andi said. "I'm soaked."

The rain began hitting the roof of the cabin even harder. "If we had waited any longer, we would have needed a boat to get here," Luke said, still laughing.

Andi stood there, laughing with him. Luke noticed that she started to shiver. She was only wearing a short-sleeved T-shirt, and the rain had soaked through it.

"You're cold," he said, sobering up. "Here." He reached around her to the hall cupboard beside the washing machine and pulled out a large towel that he wrapped around her shoulders and arms. Stepping closer, he began rubbing his hands up and down her arms to warm her.

Andi raised her green eyes to his. Her hair was wet and

there were tiny droplets of water glistening on her cheeks. Luke's heart pounded. She was so beautiful, so inviting. He could no longer resist. He dipped his head and caught her lips with his own.

Luke's arms encircled Andi as his kiss deepened with passion. Andi didn't resist. She stood on tiptoe and raised her arms up around his neck, opening her lips to his. The towel around her shoulders dropped to the floor, but neither noticed. Their bodies pressed together, warming each other despite their rain soaked clothing.

Luke pulled back. "Andi," he said, his voice husky.

Andi ran her hand along the side of his face. "Don't stop," she begged, her eyes shimmering with passion.

Luke bent down and kissed her again as shivers of joy slid up his spine. She was just as delicious as the first time he'd kissed her, maybe even more. He wanted her desperately, more than he'd ever wanted another woman in his life.

Pulling away again, he reached behind Andi and gently slid off the band that held her hair up, letting it fall loose. He ran his hands through it, as he'd imagined doing a million times. Even damp, her hair was soft and silky.

In one swift move, Luke lifted her up and sat her on the washing machine. Andi opened her mouth in surprise, but he clasped his own over hers. After a moment, he drew away and reached down to pull one mud soaked boot, and then the other, off of her. After quickly shucking his own boots, he reached for Andi, pulled her into his arms, and carried her to the bedroom.

Luke gently set Andi down beside him, reached over, and pulled the bedcovers down in one swift motion. Then he claimed Andi's lips once more as they stood there on the rug beside the bed. Andi ran her hands up Luke's strong back as he explored her curves with his own. She pulled away just enough to unbutton his shirt, finally releasing the last button and pushing the shirt away, off his arms, to fall on the floor. Luke heard Andi sigh as she ran her hands over his taut chest. He dipped down and kissed her neck until he found the sweet spot at the base of her throat that made Andi moan. His hands pushed up under her T-shirt, caressing her bare skin. She was just as soft as he'd imagined, and it only made his desire for her grow.

Andi stepped back and raised her arms, an invitation to pull her shirt off. Luke obliged. She then pulled up his T-shirt and Luke finished pulling it off and dropping it on the floor next to hers. Greedily, they clasped together, skin to skin, exploring every inch of each other until they both yearned for more. Luke reached around Andi and unclasped her bra, pulling it away.

"Oh Andi," Luke moaned as he gazed down at her. "You're so beautiful."

She reached for him again and he kissed her, down her neck, on her shoulder, then he gently pulled one nipple between his lips. Andi sighed with delight. Luke did it again with the other nipple and she reached around the back of his neck and ran her hands through his hair, pulling him closer.

Andi reached down and unbuttoned the top button of Luke's jeans. That was all it took. They both discarded their jeans and fell back on the bed, their tongues and hands exploring every inch of each other.

Luke pulled away only once to look down into Andi's eyes before he lost all sense of reasoning. "Andi, are you sure?" he asked, breathlessly.

Andi ran her hand along his beautiful, chiseled face, and smiled up at him. "Yes."

Luke kissed her once more, soft and sweet until desire overtook him. He drew her to him and their bodies melted together in a sweet release of passion.

* * *

Later, Luke and Andi lay together under the covers as the flicker of the oil lamp's flame danced on the ceiling above them. Luke had left Andi only long enough to light the lamp, and had returned to her side to hold her close. Neither had said a word. They didn't have to. They had shared a passion that both had deeply desired. Now, lying in each other's arms, Luke felt as if he'd finally found his place in life. He belonged with Andi.

The rain had softened to a gentle patter on the roof. Andi sighed as her head lay on Luke's chest. "I love the sound of the rain," she said softly. "Hearing the rain while we're all snuggled under the covers with the golden light of the oil lamp painting the room makes me feel like I'm safe and sound in a cocoon of warmth. I could stay this way forever."

Luke's heart swelled. Now was the moment. Now was the time to tell Andi to stay forever and let him love her. "We can," he said simply.

"If only it was that easy."

"You don't have to leave tomorrow," Luke said.

Andi rose up on one elbow and looked down at Luke. She ran her hand over his chest. "Let's not talk about tomorrow. I want only to think about this very moment with you." She bent down and kissed him gently on the lips.

Luke grinned. "Are you trying to seduce me, City Girl?"

"You bet I am, Desperado," Andi replied with a mischievous glint in her eyes.

Luke reached up and pulled Andi to him. "You're doing a really good job of it," he whispered into her neck. They made love again, slow and sweet, savoring every kiss and touch as if it were the first time, or the last.

Chapter Twenty-Six

Andi awoke slowly in the darkened room feeling the comforting warmth of Luke's body curled around hers. She lifted her head to read the clock on the nightstand. Four-thirty a.m. She lay her head down again and snuggled deeper into Luke's arms. Today was the day she was supposed to leave. To drive away from the ranch and all the people she loved on it, forever.

Andi thought back to last night, and the beauty of making love with Luke. Never had she felt so much passion for a man. Their desire had been building since the night she first knocked on Luke's door, and last night, they could no longer deny it. Did Andi regret it? Absolutely not. But did one night of passion make it possible to share a lifetime together? Andi wasn't sure.

Last night, neither of them had said the one word that may have persuaded Andi to stay. They had not said, "I love you." In her heart, Andi knew she loved Luke. She'd have never let last night happen if she hadn't felt love for him. But, it would have been insane to say the words out loud. No one falls in love in three weeks. Do they?

Andi turned carefully in bed and gazed at Luke. Even in

the dark, she could see the outline of his beautifully chiseled face and his thick, wavy hair. He looked peaceful and happy. All the tenderness Andi felt for him rose up inside her and tears welled in her eyes. Gently, she reached out and ran her fingers through his hair. "I love you, Luke Brennan," she whispered into the quiet room as her tears fell. She then slipped out of bed, retrieved her clothes, and left the room to dress.

Andi thought it best to go up to the main house before Ginny or Colt awoke. She slipped on her now dry clothes and picked up her boots from the hallway as she made her way to the living room. She figured it would be quieter to leave by the front door. Before reaching the door, Andi took one last look around the cabin. It was a beautiful place, warm and cozy, built with love. She was not the woman the house was built for, but she loved it just the same. She loved it because Luke had built it with his own two hands. With one final glance, she gently opened the door.

"Andi?"

Luke's deep voice startled her. She froze, not daring to turn around and look at him. He was just too damned hard to resist.

"Are you leaving?" Luke asked.

Andi stared at the door. "Yes. I thought I should go up to the house before your mom and Colt wake up."

Soft footsteps walked up closer behind her. "No. Are you still leaving the ranch today?"

Andi's heart dropped. "Yes," she said in a whisper.

"Don't go."

"I have to," Andi told him, tears rising in her eyes again. "Derek is expecting me."

Luke drew even closer. "Andi, please, look at me."

"I can't."

"Please," Luke pleaded.

Andi swiped away the tears that had fallen on her cheeks and turned around. Luke stood there, wearing only his jeans. His hair was tousled and his face looked strained, yet he was still so handsome.

"Stay, Andi. Please," Luke said, his deep blue eyes pleading with her. "I love you. I know that sounds crazy, because we've only known each other a few weeks, but I love you. I've never met a woman as strong, confident, stubborn, and beautiful as you are. I love every part of you."

Andi closed her eyes and shook her head as each word Luke said broke her heart. He'd said it. He'd said he loved her. But did it make a difference now? She had thought it would, but there was still the fact that she was committed to another man. Andi swallowed hard. "Luke, no," was all she could manage to say.

Luke took another step toward her. They were now only inches apart. "Please, Andi. Someone told me that if any woman was worth begging for, it was you. And he was right. Please stay. I will do anything to keep you here. We can build a room onto the cabin for you to use as an art studio. I'll add electricity, a phone, heck, we can even have internet. Anything you want, Andi, it's yours. But most of all, I'll love you more than anyone has ever loved a woman. I'll love you every day of my life until the day I take my very last breath. Please. Stay."

Andi stood there, tears streaming down her face. "Luke, I don't know what to do. Before I met you, I thought I was driving toward my future with Derek. I promised him I'd marry him. I thought I loved him. Now, I just don't know how I feel anymore." She lifted her eyes to his. "How do I leave the man I've been building a life with for three years for a man I've only known for three weeks?"

Luke dropped his head, defeated.

Andi wanted to throw herself into his arms, but she remained rooted on the spot. "I have to go up to the house," she said, her voice cracking. "It'll be light soon." She turned back toward the door.

"Take the truck," Luke said quietly. "The keys are in there. I'll bring the horses up later."

"Goodbye, Luke," Andi said, her back to him. When he didn't respond, she walked out the door.

Andi cried the short drive up to the house and wiped away her tears before she quietly entered. The kitchen was still dark and silent, with only Bree rising from her spot by the stairs to greet her. Andi gently patted the dog on the head and then climbed the stairs.

Once in her room, Andi fell down on the bed and cried. Her heart ached. Walking away from Luke was the hardest thing she'd ever done. But, she'd made a commitment to Derek. She knew him well, and she knew what kind of life to expect with him. Derek had his faults, but he'd also been good to her and had promised to take care of her. She could count on that, for the rest of her life.

With Luke, everything was different. She was drawn to him in ways she'd never been drawn to any other man. He was stubborn, pig headed, strong, steadfast, and downright gorgeous. He could infuriate her one moment and then make her want to kiss him breathless the next. Was that everlasting love? Or was that just something that happened to two people when they are thrown together? In truth, Andi knew very little of Luke, yet, she felt she knew him completely. But could she build a life with a man she'd only known a short time?

Finally, spent from crying, Andi gathered her things and went to the bathroom to shower. She dressed and packed up the last of her clothes, leaving the room she'd spent the last three weeks in exactly as it had been that very first day.

As Andi carried her bag downstairs, she heard Ginny moving around in the kitchen, beginning to make breakfast. Andi set her bag at the bottom of the staircase and walked over to help Ginny make the last meal she would eat at the ranch.

Ginny turned and smiled at her. "Good morning, sweetie. You sure were up early this morning. Are you in such a hurry to leave us?"

Andi shook her head. "No. On the contrary, I'm in no hurry at all. Leaving here is the last thing I want to do."

Ginny came over and hugged Andi. "I wish you could stay, but I know you have your future waiting for you in Buffalo."

Andi nodded, then went directly to work setting the table for breakfast and helping Ginny cook.

"Did you get caught in that rainstorm last night?" Ginny asked as she stirred the scrambled eggs and flipped bacon.

"Yes, we did," Andi said as calmly as possible. She didn't want the memories to come flooding back or else she'd start crying again. "We left the horses in Luke's stable and waited out the storm at his cabin."

Colt had come downstairs just as Andi finished speaking. "That must be why I didn't see you before I went to bed last night," he said, snitching a piece of bacon from the plate Ginny was putting it on and then heading over to the table. "That sure was some storm."

Andi agreed, but said nothing else. She had to get through breakfast without breaking down. It wasn't going to be easy.

Soon, Randy joined them and they all sat and ate. The men talked about work they had to do that day and Ginny said she was going to start canning the string beans. Andi felt like she was already miles away, because she was no longer going to be a part of this ranch, its work, or the lives of these people she'd come to love.

Luke hadn't come for breakfast and Andi hadn't expected him to. Part of her wanted to say goodbye to him, but the other part knew she couldn't face him. Maybe it was for the best that he wasn't here. Seeing him would make leaving next to impossible.

After everyone had finished eating, Andi could no longer delay the goodbyes. Randy gave her a hug, telling her that she was going to be missed. Andi was surprised when she pulled away that his eyes looked sad. She liked this quiet cowboy, but they hadn't spent much time together. She wondered what he was thinking. Randy was Luke's best friend. Maybe he knew how Luke felt about her. Or maybe he'd seen something between them that no one else had seen. Andi didn't know. She just gave him a kiss on the cheek and whispered softly to him, "Take care of him for me, okay?"

Randy nodded. Then he headed out the back door.

"I'll carry your bag out," Colt offered. He grabbed it from the foot of the stairs and walked swiftly outside with Bree at his heels.

Ginny reached out to Andi and pulled her into a side hug, then the two women walked outdoors, side by side.

The day was starting out to be a nice one. The storm had chased the humidity away, leaving in its wake a warm day with a cool breeze. Andi took a deep breath. The dampness of the pines caused the trees to emit an even stronger scent. No matter where she ended up, Andi would remember this scent for the rest of her life.

Colt opened the back door and set Andi's bag in the back seat. He then came around the front of the car where Andi and Ginny stood. "I'm really going to miss you, Andi," he said, suddenly shy.

Andi reached out and hugged him. "I'm going to miss you, too, Colt." She pulled away. "Keep in touch with me, okay? I want to hear everything that goes on in your life as well as at the ranch. Send me pictures, too. Of everyone. And Abby, and Bree, too."

Colt grinned and nodded. "I will. I've been emailing back and forth with Carly, too. Maybe we'll all see each other again, soon."

Andi smiled and kissed him on the cheek like she had Randy. "I love you, Colt. Take care of yourself."

Colt turned a soft shade of pink, but he smiled wide. "Well, got to get to work," he said. "Bye, Andi. Be safe. Don't break down again, okay?"

Andi laughed. "I'll try not to." She watched as Colt ambled away toward the barn.

Andi stood there, her gaze turning to search the pasture beside the barn. Abby was there, so she knew Luke had brought her back. But Chance was nowhere to be seen. She sighed.

"He isn't coming, hon," Ginny said softly. "Luke has never been one for goodbyes."

Andi turned toward the woman who took her in and treated her like family for three weeks. She loved Ginny like a mother. It was amazing, but it was true.

"Ginny, do you believe it's possible for a person to fall in love in only three weeks?"

Ginny gave her a slow smile. "Sweetie, you're asking the wrong person. I believe in love at first sight. It happens all the time."

Andi's heart swelled. She held back tears as she said her

final goodbyes to Ginny. Then she climbed behind the wheel of her car and slowly drove down the driveway as Ginny waved.

Andi drove her car to Luke's cabin and stopped. She had one more thing to do before she left. She knew he wouldn't be home. He was more than likely out riding Chance, trying hard to forget her.

Opening the back of her car, Andi carefully pulled the painting of the Lone Cypress out and carried it to Luke's door. She turned the handle, and the door opened easily. Stepping inside, she hesitated a moment as all the feelings of earlier this morning rushed toward her. Strengthening her resolve, she walked to the fireplace and set the painting on the floor so she could unwrap it. Then, carefully, she lifted the painting up and placed it on the mantel, making sure it was centered. Andi stood back and stared at the painting. It looked perfect there. As if it was always meant to be there. Andi loved that painting more than any of her other paintings and she wanted Luke to have it. It was a gift from the heart, and she hoped he'd understand that when he saw it.

After one last look, Andi walked out the door of the cabin for the last time. With tears in her eyes, she slid into her car and drove down the driveway to the highway without looking back.

Chapter Twenty-Seven

Luke led Chance into the pasture behind his cabin later that evening and went through the motions of unsaddling the tired horse, brushing him down, and feeding him. He patted Chance one last time before walking slowly through the pasture toward home. Luke stopped a moment at the fence, remembering how just last night he'd helped Andi over it as the rain poured down on them. Brushing the memory away, he climbed over, walked to the house, started up the generator, and entered through the side door.

Luke was tired. He was dirty, hungry, thirsty, and downright worn out. No sooner had Andi walked out the front door this morning, and he was dressed and saddling Chance. He'd ridden Chance up to the barn by the house, leading Abby behind him, and let her loose in the corral. Then he'd taken off up the trail for the back pasture at a gallop. He'd wanted to get as far away from the ranch house as possible. He didn't want to endure the pain of watching Andi leave and of saying goodbye forever. It was more than he could bear.

Luke had spent the entire day far away from home, riding fences, checking cattle, and doing everything he could to keep his mind off of Andi. It wasn't easy. Her scent was still fresh in his memory, and it would be for days, weeks, even years to come. He had played his hand, and he had lost. It was fair and square. Yet, it still hurt so damned much.

Luke sighed as he stripped off his dirty T-shirt and jeans and set them on the washing machine in the hallway. He went back to the bedroom to get clean clothes and showered quickly, washing the day's grime away. Once he'd slipped on a clean pair of jeans and a shirt, he headed outside to shut off the generator for the night. He preferred the light of the oil lamp tonight, just as he had every night before Andi had come into his life.

He hadn't eaten anything all day, and he wasn't really very hungry now. Opening the refrigerator, he pulled out a beer and saw a covered dish. He picked it up and inspected it. His mother had brought him leftovers from supper. There was fried chicken, mashed potatoes, and string beans on the plate, waiting to be heated up. Deciding he wasn't hungry enough to bother, he replaced it in the refrigerator, and walked out to the living room.

The sun was beginning to make its way below the distant hills, so the room was growing dark, fast. Luke set his beer down, struck a match, and lit an oil lamp by the sofa. When he looked up, his eyes grew wide. There, on the mantel above the fireplace, was the painting of the Lone Cypress.

Not believing his eyes, Luke walked over and ran his hand over the oak frame. It was really there. Andi had left him her most prized painting. He closed his eyes and bit his lip hard, trying to force back the emotions that were threatening to rise inside him. He'd pushed his feelings down all day, unable to bear them, but now, his chest tightened and his eyes stung. Andi had left him the one painting above all others that she loved the most. It nearly broke his heart all over again.

Luke took a deep breath and tried to calm his emotions. He opened his eyes once more, staring up at the beautiful painting of the lonely tree on the cliff. He knew how that tree felt. He was that tree. Andi had said that she didn't believe the tree to be lonely at all, because it had the beauty of the cliff, the other foliage, and the deep blue ocean surrounding it. But all Luke saw was a tree standing alone, waiting, being admired, but not touched by the world around it.

With a sigh, Luke picked up the book that he hadn't touched since the night Andi first knocked on his door. He lay down on the sofa and stretched out. He'd read a little, drink his beer, and go to bed. And tomorrow would be another day, then another, then another.

* * *

Luke was slowly pulled from his sleep by a loud, banging sound. He opened his eyes and looked around. It was dark, except for the glow of the oil lamp, its flame flickering shadows on the ceiling above.

The knock came again. Luke frowned. Someone was knocking on his door. *Who the hell is here so late?* He pulled himself up to a sitting position as the person pounded again on the door. Annoyed now, Luke stood and strode to the door, opening it swiftly. A set of big, green eyes stared back at him.

"Andi?" he said in disbelief. Luke closed his eyes and shook his head to make himself wake up. Surely, this was a dream. When he opened his eyes again, Andi was still standing there, looking up at him.

"Andi? Why are you here? I thought you'd left," Luke said, completely confused.

"I did leave," Andi said. "I got as far as the end of the driveway and I couldn't go any farther. I turned around and came back."

Luke stared at her. He was still unable to believe she was standing on his front porch. "You didn't leave? You mean, you've been here the whole time?"

Andi took a step closer to Luke. "Yes. I've been at the main house all day, waiting for you. And if you hadn't been out riding fences and brooding all day, Desperado, you'd have known I was still here." She grinned up at him.

Luke saw a glint of mischief in her eyes. He couldn't believe what he was hearing.

"Just answer one question for me," she said softly.

"Okay," Luke replied, confused.

Andi looked into his eyes. "Did you mean what you said earlier?"

Luke thought a moment, still trying to clear his head. "You mean about the electricity and adding on an art room?"

"Yes…I mean, no. Did you mean it when you said you would love me every day of your life, until the day you took your very last breath?"

Luke looked down at Andi as his heart swelled with love for her. "Yes, Andi. I meant every word of it. I love you."

Andi's eyes filled with tears, but she was smiling. "I love you, too, Luke Brennan."

Luke reached out and drew her to him. He bent down and kissed her, and she reached up around his neck, pulling him even closer. Luke couldn't believe he was holding Andi in his arms once more. He'd found the one woman in this world who knew exactly who he was and loved him anyway. He'd finally found his happily ever after.

When they finally pulled away, Andi gave him that

teasing grin again. "Of course, I do want those other things, too. Especially electricity. I really need that."

Luke smiled down at her. "Anything you want, Andi. You can have it all. Just as long as I can hold you every night for the rest of our lives."

"That sounds perfect to me," Andi said.

Luke's expression turned serious. "What about Derek?"

"He'll be fine," Andi said. "I don't think he and I were ever meant to share our lives together. He wanted things I didn't. It took you, and this ranch, and everyone on it to show me what I really wanted out of life."

"Is that what changed your mind about staying?" Luke asked.

Andi looked up at him, her eyes sparkling. "That," she said, pulling Luke close and whispering into his ear, "and the fact that I kissed a cowboy, and I liked it."

Luke laughed out loud. In one swift motion, he lifted Andi up into his arms and kicked the door shut. He turned and headed toward the bedroom.

"Where do you think you're going, Cowboy?" Andi asked, her arms tight around Luke's neck.

"I'm going to get started on my promise to you," he said, grinning. "I'm never leaving your side from this day forward. Think you can handle that, City Girl?"

"You bet your sweet ass I can, Hot Cowboy," Andi said.

Luke stopped just as he crossed the threshold to the bedroom. He nuzzled Andi's neck. "I love you, Andi Stevens."

"I love you, Luke Brennan," she said softly.

Luke laid Andi gently on the bed so they could start keeping their promises of forever.

-End-

Did you fall in love with the Brennan family?

Be sure to read more about them in book two of the Kiss a Cowboy Series. It's Colt's turn to fall in love.
A KISS FOR COLT (Kiss a Cowboy Series Book Two).

About the Author

Deanna Lynn Sletten is the author of MAGGIE'S TURN, FINDING LIBBIE, ONE WRONG TURN, MISS ETTA, and several other titles. She writes heartwarming women's fiction and romance novels with unforgettable characters. She has also written one middle-grade novel that takes you on the adventure of a lifetime. Deanna believes in fate, destiny, love at first sight, soul mates, second chances, and happily ever afters, and her novels reflect that.

Deanna is married and has two grown children. When not writing, she enjoys walking the wooded trails around her home with her beautiful Australian Shepherd, traveling, and relaxing on the lake.

Deanna loves hearing from her readers. Connect with her at:

Website: www.deannalsletten.com
Blog: www.deannalynnsletten.com
Facebook: www.facebook.com/deannalynnsletten
Twitter: www.twitter.com/deannalsletten

Printed in Great Britain
by Amazon